I0760673

VANDAL

RACHEL LEIGH

"There are no secrets
that time does not reveal."
—Jean Racine

Vandal that contains explicit sexual content, graphic language, and situations that some readers may find uncomfortable.

Cover design by Ya'll. That Graphic.

Cover Model: Kaz Vanderwaard

Photographer: Wander Aguiar

Editing by Fairest Reviews Editing Service

PROLOGUE

TOMMY

I've heard you can tell how dangerous a person is by how well they hold in their anger. For the past few weeks, I've held a raging storm inside of me and my friends are none the wiser. They've been elbows deep in their own shit that they haven't even noticed I'm dealing with problems of my own. I've been pulled in every which direction to help their asses. All the while, I'm holding an endless supply of fury because life, as I know it, is over. It's gone and it's not fucking coming back.

Pulling out a flask from the inside pocket of my Ari Soho jacket, I twist the top off and take a swig. Talon shoots daggers in my direction. He's noticed that I've been drinking a bit more than usual. Hell, I'm not denying it. If he was as royally fucked up from the inside out as I am, he'd be drowning in the bottle, too. Not to mention, this party is a drag. Sure, I love Marni and all, but slumming on the couch while her dad and his stuck-up friends snub us isn't exactly thrilling.

Lars and Willa walk in an hour late and Lars plops down next to me. Willa takes a seat on his lap. "What are you guys talking about?" he asks.

Talon looks around at the older group across the room then

he leans forward, bringing his voice down a few octaves. "I was just saying that someone out there has to be wondering how the fuck Josh's car went into Lake Ruin and how his body ended up in the pastor's basement. I mean, they've gotta be shitting bricks right now."

Lars comes forward with Willa still on his lap and whispers, "No kidding. I was thinking the same thing. We're in the clear for now, but someone out there knows something."

"Is it possible that Rick really is the one that hit him?" Willa shrugs her shoulders and looks back and forth at all of us.

"Nah, too obvious." Talon shakes his head in small, rapid movements. "And it certainly wasn't an accident. When we found Josh, it looked like he had been mauled to death. Like someone ran him over and backed up a few times to finish him off. Then, of course, Marni's dad came flying down the road and smooshed his ass even more."

Willa cringes. "Ugh, that's disgusting."

I chime in, "You should have seen his face, it was—"

"No."Lars shakes his head. "Don't go there."

Willa nudges Lars. "Ask about the camera."

"What camera?" Marni asks.

"There's a camera about halfway down your driveway, facing the road. I'm sure your dad already checked it, but it could have caught something."

Marni taps her finger to her chin. "Hmm, I don't remember a camera in the driveway. Hey, Dad?" she hollers across the room, "come here."

Anderson makes his way over to us with a glass in his hand. The ice clinks, sloshing the caramel-colored liquor. "Is there a camera in the driveway?"

He raises a brow and thinks on it. "Tiny white camera?"

Marni looks at Willa for confirmation. "Yeah, it was white."

"Oh yeah. It's from the old system. That cheap piece of shit wouldn't pick up a pack of wolves coming down the driveway."

"Is it armed?" Talon asks.

"Nah, I don't think so. That system was set up through a third party. I'm pretty sure we dropped them when we switched to a private system."

"What's the name of the company?" Lars pulls out his phone.

"Umm, Whitlock Security."

"We're gonna look into it," Marni tells him. "I'll let you know if we need anything to log in."

With his eyes on his phone, Lars grabs our attention. "It looks like they have an online system where you can see all saved footage from the start of service. Doesn't hurt to try. Go ask your dad what his login info is," he tells Marni.

Marni jumps right up and goes to talk to him.

Fifteen minutes later, she returns with a piece of paper. "Holy fuck, what did you have to do, track down the software developer?" I tease.

"Sorry. My dad doesn't keep track of this shit. I had to search his office. Then call his former assistant. Anyways, I got it." She hands Lars the paper and he begins typing the info into his phone.

"Bingo. We're in." There's a brief pause while we all watch Lars intently. "Fucking-A dude, we got it!"

"No way!" Everyone gets up and hovers around him. "There's one segment clocked in five minutes before Tommy and Talon would have gotten there. This has to be it. The other ones are all after we arrived. This is some incriminating shit; we need to delete this when we're done."

"What are you waiting for? Play it." I bump him from behind the couch.

We all watch as Lars taps play on the forty-two second long clip. The footage is choppy but we can see enough. A car flies by, but it goes as fast as it came. No brake lights, no hesitation.

"Wait, go back," Marni says, after another car is shown on the screen.

Lars drags his finger back. "There it is again. Anyone recognize that car? It's blurry, but it's something." He pauses the video on a black shiny little car that tapped his brakes right around where Josh would have been lying.

Marni slaps a hand over her mouth and takes a few steps back. "What's up, girl? You look like you've seen a ghost."

She shakes a finger at the phone. "Zoom in on those tires."

Lars pinches his fingers together on the screen then drags them to zoom in.

"Shit!" Marni huffs. "I know who that is."

"Who? Who the fuck has neon pink hub caps?" *Holy shit! Of course!*

"Wyatt McCoy." I snap my fingers. "I'm gonna fucking kick his ass."

"Like hell you are. Wyatt's my best friend!" Marni snaps back. "You better not lay a finger on him."

Something tickles my insides. I smirk as I unscrew the flask and tip it back, letting the liquid slide down nice and smooth. Relishing the burn—craving the satisfying twinge of pain it leaves behind. Yeah, life as I know it may be over, but I'm dragging that son of a bitch down with me and there isn't a soul in existence that can fucking stop me.

CHAPTER ONE

TOMMY

Pressing my finger to the valve of the aerosol can, I sweep my hand up, forming the base of the skull. Rapid spritzes release around the o-shaped eyes to mimic that of blood. Dripping freely down the raised cheekbones and falling into an invisible bath of gore. It's not meant to represent death—no, death is a mere possibility. My display of art is simply a warning. If he opens his mouth to speak, his future will be nothing short of painfully slow misery.

When the can rattles and all that's left inside is a metal bead, I drop it to the floor. It falls with a thud against the hardwood. I look down at my black fingertips. It'll take a few days to wear off, but it doesn't matter. My fingertips are always unusual colors from my desire to paint the town. It's what I love—art, graffiti, creativity. Finding treasures in the most insignificant things. Whether it be an old crumpled up newspaper that I transform into a bouquet of roses, or a brick wall that needs a speckle of color.

It's no doubt that this bedroom needed a little splash of decoration. My friends might say otherwise. They'd tell me I'm going in too strong and need to ease into things. Right now, they don't even know that Wyatt is the target of my revenge. As far as they're concerned, my issues only go as far as the fact that he's keeping a secret from us. But they don't know the hatred that has festered inside of me.

Marni would have my head if she knew I was even in this house right now. It's no secret that Wyatt is her best friend. She's like this overprotective mama bear to the boy and it's sickening. Wyatt taught us how to treat him with his submissive behavior. He doesn't fight back. Doesn't even bat an eye at the insults thrown at him. He made himself an easy target, and the bullseye was planted on his back when he decided to go for a joy ride on the night Josh was killed.

We're still not sure if it was him that hit Josh, but he was there, nonetheless. Cameras don't lie. I should know. I've been on the receiving end and I'd rather be six-feet under than have that footage released. Which is exactly why I'm here. Because Wyatt can turn the tables and expose me at any moment. Only, no one knows but Wyatt and me. And I'll do everything in my power to keep it that way, even if it means taking care of things myself and letting Wyatt take the fall for what happened to Josh.

My phone buzzes in my back pocket as I casually make my way down the winding staircase, but I ignore it. I know it's Lars and he can wait. My fingers trail featherlike against the wrought-iron banister as I whistle the tune of *Jeepers Creepers*.

When I hear the sound of the side door to the garage open, I immediately freeze. *Fuck.* I thought for sure he was tutoring someone after class today. It's a good thing I walked. Considering I live two houses down, it wasn't a lengthy hike.

Voices, followed by laughter, carry up the staircase, letting me know that Wyatt isn't alone. I listen intently as I try to figure out who his company is.

"When will your parents be home?" A masculine voice says. He continues on, but his words become muffled and unrecognizable. More laughter follows and I know immediately who it is.

Shane Velmont.

"Not until tomorrow night. Come on," Wyatt responds.

Footsteps come closer and my eyes widen. Shit. I've gotta get the hell out of here.

When I hear them draw near, I have no choice but to haul ass back up the stairs I just came down.

As soon as they step foot in Wyatt's bedroom, they'll know I was here, anyways. But I prefer to avoid that confrontation all together, if possible.

Once I hit the top of the stairs, I press my back to the wall. Instead of coming up, they walk right past the staircase and into the living room.

"You won't be needing these." Shane grumbles while Wyatt releases a heady breath.

Wyatt and Shane have developed some sort of relationship over the past couple of months. Everyone thinks it's the cutest thing ever, but it makes me sick.

"I've missed this. I've missed you." Shane's words come out in a low-croak.

I should book it down the hall to the walk-out French doors. There's a staircase back there that will lead me to the back yard. But I don't.

Instead, my feet stay planted while my heart hammers in my chest at lightning speed.

"Mmm. You like that, baby?" Shane says.

Wyatt doesn't respond. But there is no doubt in my mind that he's enjoying whatever is being given to him.

"On your knees," Shane demands. I hear the squirting of liquid and I assume it's lube. I imagine him lathering up his cock. Stroking it up and down to get it nice and slippery for Wyatt.

There's some static noise as they shuffle about, right before Wyatt lets out an airy moan. "Fuck," he bellows. "Oh, God. Yes."

The sound of skin pounding skin reverberates through my ears. It's all I can focus on. Pound. Slap. Smack. I can feel my cock threaten to break through the fabric of my grey joggers and I hate myself for it. I hate my body. I hate that I'm unable to move because I enjoy listening to them. Most of all, I fucking hate Wyatt for what he did to me. He fucked me up. He broke me.

"Get up," Shane barks. "Lie on your back."

There's this magnetic pull that begs for me to look. An agonizing ache inside of me to catch just one glimpse.

What the fuck is wrong with me? I wanna dismantle the part of my brain that's telling me to step down those stairs and watch them.

Sweat slides down my back as I adjust my dick in my pants. I need to get the fuck out of here.

Peeling myself off the wall, I move down the hall. I've gotta get the hell out of here. I tear open the door to the upstairs sitting room and make a b-line for the French doors. Pulling them open, I step out onto the deck and fill my lungs with air. "Fuck," I mutter under my breath, before jogging down the stairs of the deck and getting as far away from this house as possible.

My feet finally hit the cement slab of the ground-level patio in the back yard, and with the sounds of those two going at it solidly etched in my mind, I don't stop until I'm pushing through the front gate. I just need to erase the memory of this day and move on with my life. Too bad it's not that easy.

CHAPTER TWO

TOMMY

Without even reading the chain of text messages from Lars, I give him a call.

"Hey," I say when he picks up on the second ring.

"Where the hell have you been?"

"Busy. What's up?" There is no need to divulge any other information than that. These are my boys and all, but I'm beyond fed up with them constantly needing to know where I am. Chances are, they just need me to do something for them. I've been at their beck and call for months and it's time they step up and do what I want now.

"We need you to hold off for a little bit with Wyatt. Before we can confront him about what we saw, we need something from him. Therefore, we need to get in his good graces."

"Hell no," I spit out. No second-guessing behind it. No and no.

"His dad's company makes—"

"I said no. As a matter of fact, I plan to do everything *but* get in Wyatt McCoy's good graces. It's my turn for revenge. No questions asked. You bastards get to help me for once. We're taking that fucker down."

"Would you calm down and listen to me? The video showed that he was in front of Marni's house when Josh was hit. We need him on our side. Whether he hit Josh or not, Wyatt knows he was out there and then suddenly the body showed up in the pastor's basement."

Holding the phone between my shoulder and my cheek, I put on a pair of gym shorts. "He doesn't know it was us. And if he did, that's all the more reason to silence him. It's my call. Are you in?"

There's a beat of silence while I take the phone away from my ear and pull my t-shirt over my head.

"Looks like we don't have much of a choice. Come over after school tomorrow. We'll talk."

"I'll be there."

I'm about to end the call, but he keeps on talking. "Hey, I still wanna know who left that video. Magna Tech has the software to trace that number and the location it was sent from. We need to make that happen. So whatever your plan is, think about postponing it temporarily until we get what we need. This isn't just for Willa, it's for all of us." He ends the call before I can even respond, which pisses me the fuck off.

I shove my phone in my back pocket, fully prepared to say what needs to be said when I see them. I'm not surprised they need me to do more of their dirty work. We're all supposed to be in this together, and it's my turn. They should be taking care of what I need from them. Instead, they want me to play nice with the fucker who torments my mind.

Wyatt's dad is the founder of a company that manufactures software and devices used to hack into phones and computers for law enforcement. There is no doubt that we'd be able to uncover where the message to Willa came from. But there's also a good chance that it was sent from a burner phone. If someone was watching her and wanted to make good on their threat, they would surely cover their tracks. Especially if they're in cahoots with Wyatt. Everyone knows about his father's business ventures.

Really don't wanna pretend with Wyatt. I can barely stand being in the same school as him anymore. Besides, he's Marni's bff. If they want something from him, she can get it.

Snatching up my gym bag, I decide to go lift a bit before bed. It always helps to clear my head and regain my focus.

My footsteps echo down the empty hall. My parents are gone—again. Dad is staying in Los Angeles for a few more days on a business trip. Mom accompanied him. My parents are gone a lot, but out of all my friends, I have the most normalcy. My parents are still married after twenty-seven years. They're in love and we were raised in a loving home. I'm also fortunate to have two older brothers who I've remained pretty close with over the years. Micah and Byron are twins and both in their sophomore year at ASU. Separate majors, but always together. Aside from the past couple of months, we've always told each other everything. I know if I ever needed anything, I could count on them. I've had it pretty good compared to my friends.

So, my life may be unraveling in the present, but I don't have the scars from my past that Zed, Talon, and Lars have, aside from a tragic memory as a child. Fortunately, in the end, we all have each other. No matter how pissed I get at them, we ride or die.

"Leaving for the evening?" Madeline, our housekeeper, comes out of nowhere and my feet practically leave the ground.

"Holy shit, Madeline. I didn't know you were here." I snatch my keys off the center island in the kitchen.

Her fragile hands wrap around my arm and squeeze. "You look like you're losing weight. Have you eaten dinner?"

I chuckle. "If I look like I'm losing weight then that's all the more reason for me to haul ass to the gym. Yes, I've eaten." If anyone needs to eat more, it's her. She's ninety pounds of delicate skin and bones. Short, frosted hair, and the softest voice that's ever spoken. At the age of seventy-two, you'd think she'd be ready to quit and enjoy life, but she says we give her purpose. Madeline never married, had kids, or grandkids. In fact, she's been with my family since my brothers were born, twenty years ago.

She tsks. "Don't lie to me, boy."

"Wouldn't dare." I smirk as I walk through the kitchen to the mudroom where my shoes are.

I should also add that she's like a second mom. Always making sure we're fed and bathed. Well, not so much bathed anymore. That would just be weird. Though, she did make a comment last week about me smelling like a footlocker.

Now that we're all practically grown, she's not full-time anymore, but she's here a couple days out of the week just to clean up after my ass. She does a damn good job making my bed, too. While my parents have always been conservative and value our reputation in the community, Madeline would whisper in my ear, *never be afraid to take chances, but always stay true to yourself.*

Countless times, she's bailed me out of situations that could have been dire had my parents found out. Like the time when I was thirteen and I stole Dad's prized, sixty-nine Chevelle and took it for a joy ride around the block. I drove right into our mailbox and left a pea-sized chip in the paint. Madeline drove straight to the hardware store and bought a new mailbox and some matching paint. Of course, she made me do the work while she stood behind me with her arms crossed and a disapproving scowl on her face, but she never told a soul. She's good people and I dread the day that she does leave us for good.

"Don't stay out too late. You have school tomorrow." I hear her yell as I slide my shoes on.

"I won't." I drag the words out before opening the door and stepping into the garage.

I slide into the driver's side of my truck and start the engine.

"Dying to Live" by Sevendust continues to play from my drive home earlier. I turn the volume up to drown out any thoughts that might attempt to slither their way into my mind.

Little good it does. That's the thing with noise, it doesn't give you silence even in your own head. Only, it's not the lyrics or the tempo that's rattling my brain, it's him. Digging his fucking claws inside of me and threatening to shred every bit of morale I have left.

Just when I thought things couldn't get any worse, I had to give into one selfish desire. Consequences be damned. Now, I'm left with a mountain of regret, a suffocating heart, and unwanted thoughts that scour my mind at the most inopportune times.

Pulling up to the backside of the high school, where the doors lead to the weight room, I'm relieved to see the parking lot is empty, aside from a vehicle parked in the distance. Don't think it's Coach, though it's hard to tell. It's only January, but I'm pretty sure he's already started laying the smack down on the upcoming varsity football players. If I'm going to miss anything about high school, it'll be football. There's nothing quite like those Friday night lights and a crowd full of screaming fans all there to watch you win.

Coach lets us use the weight room and gym in the evenings when there are no home games. Usually the janitor locks the doors when he leaves around eleven o'clock, so I've got a good hour and a half of lifting time. Technically, we're not supposed to lift without an extra person here, but no one really follows that rule. When I open the door, my eyes immediately roll. "Fucking serious?" I mutter under my breath. But, it's not quiet enough because it grabs Shane's attention.

"Good to see you, too, Tommy," Shane says as he drops the ankle weight that his legs are wrapped under. It slams against the metal footing of the machine and he stands up, taking slow strides toward me. "You've got some fucking nerve showing your face after what you did to Wyatt's bedroom wall."

I snicker. "Is that what you'd call it? Nerve? I call it *I don't really give a fuck.*" I walk past him, nudging his shoulder with mine. I won't even attempt to deny what I did. The whole town is well aware that ninety-nine percent of the graffiti or art displays on the most unlikely objects usually come from me. Most like to paint on canvas; I prefer to take a riskier approach to show my skills.

He trails behind me, huffing and puffing, and I just throw my head back and laugh. "Dude. Get lost." I sweep the air with my hand.

"What's Wyatt ever done to you?" I can feel his breath hit my back and the warmth of it only adds to my fury.

My bag drops beside the weight bench and I swing around, planting two hands on his sweat-drenched wife beater, giving him a gentle shove back. "Drop it, man. I'm warning you right now. You don't wanna go there." My voice is calm but laced with anger. If he pushes me one step further, I won't be able to refrain from laying his ass out.

He lets the threat pass through one ear and out the other. "Stay the hell away from him."

"Or what? Huh? What are you gonna do about it?" I step up to him, nose to nose.

"Whatever I have to do."

I grimace. "Oh, how cute. Two little faggots sitting in a tree." My blood begins to boil rapidly through my veins. Balled fists gather on either side of me as my jaw ticks with fury.

"You can save your homophobic cruelty because it doesn't touch me. You're nothing but a bully who screams for attention. Well, congrats, asshole. We see you. We hear you. And we don't fucking like you."

Unraveling my fists, one finger at a time, I draw in a deep breath in an attempt to calm myself. My neck stretches as my head rolls on my shoulders the snap of each crack, loud and noticeable. "Walk away from me right fucking now." I grit through my clenched teeth. When he continues to stand there with a devious smirk on his face, I bump my chest to his. "You've got thirty seconds to get the hell out of this room and if you so much as look at me the wrong way, I'll tear you to fucking shreds. How do you think Wyatt will feel when he finds out that you've been flashing your dick for money on the WatchMeNow app?"

During our research of Talon's Dad, we found that there was one other local on the site, Josh. As time went on and the app grew, so did the subscriber count. And so did the local members. As of right now, it looks like there are four people in Redwood who currently use it. We were able to hack Josh's account and delete all of his info since there were a lot of exchanges between him and Talon and him and Marni.

Marni also deleted her account, but we keep Talon's active just to scope things out. We know that Shane is a user. There's also some junior chick who just likes to show her tits, and one other person whose identity we haven't been able to pinpoint. The guys have given up trying. They say it doesn't matter, but I'm still looking into it.

Amongst other puzzle pieces I'm still trying to put together. Such as, who sent me that SD card? Who knows what I did? I side-eye Shane, thinking it could have been him. It's a possibility.

His expression goes bleak as his complexion mimics the whites of his eyes. "How do you know that?"

"Twenty-three watchers the other day. Impressive. All just to watch you jerk off and lick your own jizz off your hand. You get many private calls on there? I've heard they pay a pretty penny for that shit. You know, if you need money, I'm sure Wyatt can front you."

It's true. Wyatt is worth a fortune. His dad started up his

own business with the millions he was given from his father when he passed away. Rumor has it, Wyatt was left just as much as his dad. He'll never want for anything. Except for his sanity, when I'm through with him.

Taking a few steps back, Shane turns and walks away. Giving me a second look over his shoulder. He knows I wouldn't hesitate to blast him. The reputation of the rebels precedes us. While I may have a few more emotions than the others, there is one that I feel very deeply and tends to mask all the others —hate.

CHAPTER THREE

WYATT

Tommy thinks he's invincible. Hell, they all do—Tommy, Lars, Talon, and Zed. Everything was fine when I was invisible to them, but once they took notice of me freshman year, they made sure that everyone else noticed me, too. And, I don't mean they polished me up and made me shine.

No. They made a mockery of me, day in and day out. From knocking books out of my hands and filling my locker with balloons to going as far as taking all of my clothes from the locker room when I was showering after gym. I ended up having to borrow a pair of sweatpants and a hoodie—three times my size— from Mr. Rice. One might assume it's because I'm gay, but that's not the case. I didn't come out until last year and their bullying started long before then.

The thing that really gets me is that Tommy was always the most decent of the bunch. He was quiet and sort of just blended in behind the crowd—sometimes even defending me. He played along with their antics, but never really took a lead role in my humiliation. It wasn't until a couple months ago that everything changed.

I've noticed the way he looks at me. It isn't with domineering eyes; it is sheer curiosity and need I say, attraction. I've caught him checking me out a few different times, but he'll never admit it. Not to me, not to his friends, and never to himself.

Dragging the roller on the paint tray, I slop it up and lift it to the wall. One more coat and this morbid display of art will be masked by the thick layers of paint. But, I'll always know it's there. Just because it's hidden, doesn't mean it never existed. I can say the same about Tommy's secrets. He can deny it all he wants, but I've seen the look in his eyes. I know what he felt once.

Regardless of that brief moment of chemistry between us, I can't deny the hate that seeps from his pores. I'll never be able to call Tommy a friend, let alone anything more than that.

If I could take that day back, I would.

Now, when Tommy looks at me, all he sees is red. Like I'm the one outing him. Like it is my fault. Just once, I'd like to glance over at his table in the cafeteria and see the corner of his lip tug up as he slides his gaze back down at his tray of food. All the while, knowing that a thousand butterflies just fluttered through his stomach when our eyes met. I know he felt it, because I did, too.

Every time I looked at him I felt it. Still do.

The palm of my right hand begins to burn as the handle of the roller presses firmly against it. My fingers tangle around it as I stroke up and down, back and forth. I know that I could have easily hired someone take care of this for me, but then I'd have to explain and that's not something I'm willing to do.

It's no secret that Tommy and his buddies can't stand my existence, but this isn't just some misfits pulling a prank. This is Tommy trying to get me to emotionally detach so that I lose all control. I'm not willing to do that. I'll just sit back and take what's given to me for the time being. Someone out there knows what happened between us, so I'll let that person be Tommy's downfall while I keep my hands clean.

Personally, I don't even care. It's not like I have anything to lose. My sexuality isn't a secret. Tommy, however, would likely die before he'd let the world know what we did.

I drop the roller onto the tray and take a step back. My fingertips are coated with a thin white layer of paint. I rub them together violently as I stare at the white wall with a transparent skull looking back at me.

Brushing the air with my hand, I call it good for now. I'll do another coat tomorrow.

Not even bothering to scrub the residue off my fingers, I grab my backpack off the floor and pull out my European History book, tossing it on the bed before dropping down next to it. We've got a big test tomorrow and I need to study my ass off. I'm excelling in all my classes, but for some reason, I get distracted in History class. Actually, it's not just *some reason*. It's Tommy. He sits directly behind me and I swear most days I can feel his eyes burn into my skull. Not to mention, the constant paper wads that are tossed into the tunnel of fire, a.k.a. the burning hole in the back of my head.

My eyes skim over the pages, but my mind doesn't take in anything that I'm looking at. This class is an enigma. Is it even necessary to know what happened during the Industrial Revolution? I slam the book shut and give up before even giving it a chance. Doesn't matter, anyways. I've already been accepted to Arizona State. I already know that I'll get a Business degree with a minor in computer technology, and I'll work for Dad at Magna Tech—eventually stepping in next to my uncle as CEO. Nowhere in that plan does it require me to have knowledge of the Textile Industry.

Or, it's just my way of making excuses when what's really weighing heavy on my mind is my relationship with Shane. I pined over him all of junior year. Practically begging for his attention. When he finally gave it to me, Tommy stole the show. I was no longer attending school for an education. I was waking up each day just to steal a glance at Tommy or catch him stealing a glance at me. I was infatuated with the bad boy. He wasn't cruel at the time—at least not to me—so it was a healthy crush. Until it wasn't.

It was three weeks after Halloween. I was trying to come to terms with the whole Josh fiasco, and Tommy seemed like he was in a bad place. I really did just want to talk to him and make sure everything was ok. Gym class had just let out and he was sticking around to lift weights like he often does. I had just finished showering and sat down on the bench by the door to the weight room when I heard a locker slam shut. Followed by the sound of bone meeting metal.

"Fuck!" Tommy growls from about six feet away. He can't see me, but I know that he just punched the locker in a fit of rage. Where that rage was coming from, I haven't a clue.

The sound of his sneakers squeaking against the locker room floor ring closer, so I spring to my feet. "Hey, Tommy. Got a minute?" I say nervously. It's not that Tommy intimidates me in the same way as the other guys, but he makes me feel this excitement that ripples through my stomach and kicks my heart into hyper drive.

"No," he says, without even making eye contact. His gaze holds tight to the door beside me, but I throw my arm out to stop him from exiting. "What the fuck is your problem, dude?"

"I could ask you the same thing? What'd that locker ever do to you?" I bite back a smile, but I'm immediately regretful of my words, because now is not the time to try and crack jokes with a fuming guy who is packing more muscle in his forearm than I have in my entire body.

His eyes shimmy down to my arm that's still braced between the door frames. I jerk it away quickly, but they follow where it drapes at my side and hold tightly as he speaks. "You've got three seconds to say what you wanna say then get the hell out of my way, Wyatt."

"I just wanted to make sure everything is ok. You've been off your game in gym class. Missing school. It's not like you."

With a scowl, he looks me dead in the eye. "Since when do you take notes on what the fuck I'm doing?"

"I don't take notes, per se." I shrug a shoulder. "I just...notice."

He takes a step closer, invading my space, and clenches his jaw. "Well, take notice of this. What I do is none of your damn business."

My heart beats like a jackhammer in my chest, but it's not out of fear or worry that Tommy is about to crush me. No. He doesn't want to hurt me. My racing pulse is attributed to the way his eyes keep dancing from mine down to my lips.

Anger drips from his gaze as his fingers compress around my throat. My Adam's apple bobs violently against his palm. Though, my focus is solely on his erection pressed against my hip bone. The back of my head mounts firmly to the locker as my eyes look downward. Even though I don't say anything, it's my way of acknowledging the facts. His eyes slide down to the sliver of space between us then abruptly back up to mine. His face flushed, his eyes wide with humiliation.

In an instant, his fingers release and my shoulders drop. "Tommy, wait," I say when he pulls open the door to the weight room. I follow him, and it's empty inside. Just him and me, alone.

"Get the fuck out of here." He keeps on his path over to the weight bench. He can't even look at me. Dare I say, Tommy Chambers is embarrassed? It's a new look for him, but one that squeezes my heart.

"It's nothing to be ashamed of. You do the same thing—" My words trail off when he storms back over in my direction. Taking a few steps backward, my back hits the closed door of the weight room.

Suddenly, he's no longer shying away, he's furious. His fists balled at his sides and his forehead creased while his eyes zero in on me. "I what, Wyatt? Turn you on?" He gives me a shove, but I don't move because I'm braced against the door. "That's because you're fucking gay."

I grab the handle of the door behind me and walk toward him as it opens. I slither back into the locker room, but he follows. "I didn't mean—"

"What?" He seems taken aback, but it's all sarcasm and show. "You didn't mean to insinuate that I'm gay, too? Because I'm not." We're nose to nose and I immediately realize I should have just left when he told me to fuck off the first time. He shoves me again and this time, my back slams into a row of lockers.

"Ok. I get it. Calm down." It's a lie. I don't believe a word he's saying. Call it intuition, or call it learning his behaviors over the years —but, this act is nothing but a facade. I could be wrong, but I highly doubt it.

"Do you? Because I'm not so sure."

He's talking in circles and I know it's because not only is he still rock hard, but he's also now purposely forcing his cock into me. His hands brace either side of my head with his palms pressed to the locker.

The array of artwork on his toned arms catches my eye, but my mind doesn't register what I see. All black and gray with different designs and pictures that likely tell some kind of story. I should know the details of every tattoo he has with how much time I've watched him, but I don't. Usually when I'm watching, I take note of his expressions—trying to read his thoughts.

My eyes squint and I give him a look of confusion while he stares back at me. Is he screwing with me right now? Or does he want me to make a move? Shit, he is a hard one to read. "Back up and let me go and I'll leave you alone." But, he doesn't move. Instead, he stands there, observing me while I do the same.

Fuck it.

I grab him by the face and pull his mouth to mine.

Wrong move.

With an open palm, he slaps me across the face. My body jumps about two inches off the ground when he grips my chin between his thumb and forefinger. But he doesn't pull me back to him. He pushes my face down until I'm on my knees in front of him.

With one hand, he slides his shorts and boxers down and they pool at his ankles. "You like dick? Then suck it, you little bitch."

I look at him to see if he's serious, but he tips his head back and pushes mine back down. My hand trembles as I take his cock in my hand. I begin stroking it slowly, waiting for him to kick me down and stomp on my face—but he doesn't. He lets out a subtle moan and begins rocking his hips with the movement as I pick up my pace.

My thumb grazes over the head, sweeping up a bead of precum then rubbing it down as I stroke all six to seven inches of his length. Darting my tongue out, I flick it underneath his silky head then take it into my mouth.

Stroking and sucking while he continues to grind against my face. My free hand cups his balls and I give them a gentle squeeze. Then reality hits me that I'm actually giving Tommy head in the locker room. A guy that I've watched in secret. One that has watched me, too. He might be attracted to girls, but he likes guys, too. And for whatever reason, he wants me. The guy that his friends have picked on day in and day out in the halls of this school. The smart kid that wears suits and blazers and enjoys playing chess and tutoring his classmates. This rebel chose me to be his first.

Something in him snaps and he begins picking up his pace, so I do the same. But it's hard to keep up when he starts ramming his cock so far in my mouth that I can feel it hit the back of my throat.

"You like sucking cock? Then fucking suck it, don't play with it." His fingers wrap around my hair tightly as he violently thrusts himself against me. I try to ease a couple inches out, but he doesn't budge, he just rocks harder. I don't gag, though. I take it all.

"Fuck," he mutters under his breath. "Close your eyes. Don't fucking look at me." I can feel his head swell inside my mouth, almost hitting my tonsils. His body tenses up momentarily and without any notice, he releases. Shooting down the back of my throat. One final thrust and he pulls out. I swallow hard, then wipe the back of my hand across my mouth. Smiling on the inside, I don't dare show it. I don't even dare look at him.

Grabbing both sides of his shorts, he pulls them up swiftly. "You tell anyone about this, I'll fucking kill you." His voice is stern and laced with intention. He goes to walk away while I'm still knelt on the floor with my head hung low, but he stops. "Oh, and for the record, I'm not fucking gay." Then he pulls the door open and walks away.

"Keep telling yourself that," I mumble as the door latches closed.

Ever since that day, I've lived with a mountain of regret. If only I could go back and change what happened. Tommy wouldn't hate me to the depth of no return. He wouldn't blame me for the video that was sent to us of what went down between us in the locker room.

I wish I could say that is my biggest regret. Unfortunately, bigger things have been eating at my insides. Secrets that could destroy my friendships—my life.

I slap the notebook off the bed and drop onto my back when my phone rings from the nightstand. Stretching my arm over my head, I slap around until I've got it in my hand.

Marni.

"Hey, girl. Sorry I never called you back after Shane left. I sort of had some shit to deal with."

"Does this shit have anything to do with Tommy?"

Shooting up, I turn and look at the silhouette of the skull on the wall. "Why would you ask that?" There's no way she could know. Sure, everyone knows that Tommy has a vendetta against me. But I've never divulged any information into the depths of his disgrace.

"Just a hunch. Listen, I can't say much. But, stay away from him, Wyatt. I think Tommy's up to something."

Nodding my head, I agree. "Yeah, no kidding," I grumble. "What's up with the warning, though? Did he say something?"

"Like I said, I can't say much. I just don't want to see you get hurt."

"Right?" I drag out the word. "The pact with your new posse. I get it. Forget about your best friend and your loyalties to him.

The four rebels of Redwood take precedence. Ya know, you owe me one if I remember correctly."

"You know I love you, Wyatt. But—"

"Ah, there it is. The infamous *but*. Don't worry about me, Marni. I might look weak and breakable, but I'm stronger than you think. As long as it doesn't involve demons and a bloodbath, I'll be fine."

She doesn't say anything else and I take it as her way of saying that it does, in fact, involve demons, or at the very least, a bloodbath.

When she finally breaks the silence, she changes the subject. "How are things with Shane?"

"Really good. Moving in the right direction." I lie. The world sees a cute couple who are finding happiness with no shame. But, the truth is, Shane has been more of an asshole than usual. He's fucking hot as hell, but I need more than looks. He's bossy, demanding, and has these outbursts that can get pretty scary.

I need someone who is going to pull me up when I'm down and hold on tight. Someone that I can share my secrets with and trust that I've put them in a safe place. I'm pretty sure that Shane looks at me as his toy. Someone he can boss around and do what he wants with. I can feel the end drawing near, and I just hope that he doesn't lose his shit when it comes.

"I'm glad you're happy, Wyatt. Let's keep it that way. See you at school tomorrow?"

"You know it." I end the call and let my phone fall to my side.

Tomorrow. I have no idea what tomorrow will bring, but right now, I could settle for being the loser that no one notices. It seems I'm on the radar of a couple people lately, and they keep popping up out of nowhere. If I was actually as weak as they think I am, I'd hide. But I'm ready to fight back and I think it's time to start.

CHAPTER FOUR

TOMMY

"Hey, I'm ditching last period and we need to have a meeting," I tell Talon over the phone as I weave through the cars in the parking lot. "It's time for me to start calling some shots here and I have some shit that needs to be said."

"Hey, Tommy." Shay bats her lashes and gives a flirtatious wave while she stands at her car with her groupies. I acknowledge her with a nod and keep on walking.

"Alright, Marni and I are taking a road trip to LA to see her brother tonight, so we'll have to make it quick."

"Listen," I shout, then look around and make sure no one heard my little outburst. "I played your game. You're playing mine. I don't give a shit where you have to go. After everything I did for you guys, you should be begging to help me."

"Chill, man. We'll talk. What the hell is your problem lately?"

"Life, Talon. Life is my fucking problem." I draw in a breath and shake off the anger that's beginning to rise inside of me. "Call Lars and let him know. I'll see you guys this afternoon."

"We'll be here."

"Oh, and Marni needs to be present. She needs to hear this, too."

Talon hangs up the call and I know he's already pissed. He knows what's coming. Marni and Wyatt have been close since grade school. She's not going to like this, therefore Talon isn't gonna like it either. The fact is, there is a chance that Wyatt is the one who hit Josh. Hell, he could even be the one who was stalking Willa. It's not likely, because Wyatt is afraid of his own shadow, but it's the quiet ones that the world needs to watch out for. They usually harbor the most secrets.

Regardless, I have to approach this carefully because one wrong move and my secrets could come spilling out right along with Wyatt's.

Alan is holding the door open for everyone coming up to the main doors like he does every day. "Thanks, man."

We've got a lot of pricks at this school, but I've always made an attempt not to be one of them. Some people make it really hard and I fail at that attempt from time to time, but I'm not as deranged as my friends. I don't treat people like I'm any better than them, because the truth is, most of them are all better than me. I like to think that in a way, I make my friends want to be better. I know that they have pasts that they'd all like to forget about, but they've been molded by the events they've faced and I don't blame them for having a little hate in their hearts.

Biting my tongue, I walk right past Wyatt, who is at his locker. He's slouched down pulling books out of his bag. His sandy blond hair parts to the side and tiny wisps with naturally highlighted ends hang down over his eyes. He's wearing his typical designer cardigan—maroon today—and a pair of black twill pants with Converse shoes. I get a whiff of his cedarwood cologne as I pass by him and he doesn't even see me.

My heart begins to race when memories of the sounds I heard yesterday slip into my head. Wyatt and Shane went at it like wild animals in the living room while I stood at the top of the staircase and listened. It was an enlightening experience. I learned that Shane definitely wears the pants in their relationship.

Shane is a lot more outspoken than Wyatt. He's the quarterback of the football team—one of the jocks. I play ball, but I don't run with the crowd he does. People look up to him, even though he's a douche to the entire student body. Not in the same way that me and the guys are. We're more reckless and carefree. We have each other's back no matter what and we only give shit to those who deserve it. Shane and his boys are just plain assholes for no reason at all. Something that I don't put up with.

Which is exactly why I find myself picking up my pace when I see Shane trip Alan as he walks down the hall. After holding the door open for his ass and every other fucker in this school, this is how they treat him. "What the fuck is your problem, dude?" My palms plant firmly into Shane's chest as I give him a push backward.

Alan scrambles on the floor to get up and I extend my hand out to him and give him a pull to his feet before he scurries off.

Returning my attention to Shane, I shove him again. "You give me a lesson on bullying last night and then you come into this place and push around innocent people? Now who thinks they're big and bad?"

He just laughs in my face, which only riles me up more. I push him again and again until his back hits the locker. Nose to nose, I grit through my teeth. "You better watch yourself, Velmont. People are always watching." I pat his cheek like a child and walk away. I don't need to press further; he knows what I'm talking about. He doesn't dare let the news of his new venture to make money see the light of day. He could lie and say that it's because he likes the attention, which is just as bad, but we know it's for the money.

Shane's family lost everything last year when his dad was

convicted of embezzlement at the company he worked for. I'd feel sorry for Shane if he weren't such a jerk, but he's still the same spoiled brat he's always been.

So much for avoiding any confrontation with Wyatt as he comes stalking toward me. Mentally preparing for another scene, I draw in a breath and steel my back. But, he doesn't stop. With his eyes laser focused on mine and fire behind those baby blue orbs, he walks right past me. Of course. He has to go check on his boyfriend and make sure I didn't bruise his ego.

Tearing open my locker that has a black bat with a crown on its head covering the entire door, I grab my European History textbook and a notebook with a pencil stuffed down into the spiral binding then slam the door shut.

During one of the dances after a football game last year, I got shitfaced on some spiked punch and wandered down the hall with a Sharpie and got a little carried away. Principal Scott wasn't pleased. I scrubbed for an hour while she stood over me with her arms crossed and a heavy scowl. The damn bat wouldn't come off and now he's there for life.

I slide into my seat in the back row with a minute to spare. I shouldn't notice that Wyatt isn't here yet. But, he's not. It's not like him. Wyatt's pretty punctual. Which can only mean one thing, he's with Shane. Likely cleaning his pride up or sucking his cock in the locker room. Seems to be Wyatt's commonplace for handing out favors. At least, it was in my experience.

Watching the clock on the wall tick, I tap my pencil on the table while my foot taps in rhythm. The bell rings, and he's still not here. *Where the fuck is he?* Better yet, why the hell do I care? Maybe he really is tending to Shane. Something sinister slithers through my chest. After what he did to me, he doesn't deserve the happiness that he's found with Shane. It irks me that he's got so much good going for him, and here I am, slowly dying inside.

My seat slides back with no hesitation. The metal scraping

so loudly against the linoleum floor that I grab the attention of everyone in the room. Ignoring them all, including Mr. Bing, I snatch up my books and dip out the cracked open door.

My feet echo as I walk down the empty hall. There's some distant chatter coming from another classroom, but there's no sign of Wyatt or Shane. Turning around, I walk swiftly toward the main doors to see if Wyatt's car is still parked in its usual spot, but I stop my movements when I hear voices arguing in the guys' bathroom.

I walk in the maze-like entrance, but stop before rounding the corner. With my back pressed against the cold brick wall, I listen—feeling like this is all too familiar. This time is different, though. There is nothing pleasurable coming from this encounter.

"Why are you still talking? Just shut the fuck up." Shane growls with authority.

"I'm just simply stating that you don't need to push Alan around like you do. Or anyone else for that matter."

There's a thud. Not loud, but I swear I felt it reverberate through my body. "Are you taking his side?"

"No." Wyatt retorts. "I'd never—"

"You better not. Tommy is the enemy. It'll do you good to remember that. He fucking hates you, Wyatt. He'll never be your friend and you're delusional if you think he'd ever be interested in you."

What the fuck?

Why the hell are they talking about me like I'm even the least bit significant in their lives? We aren't friends. Hell, until recently, we weren't even enemies. They have no business even saying my name. Unless Wyatt told Shane. Heat rises to my face, and I can feel my cheeks flush blood red. I snarl with clenched fists as I round the corner. "Does someone have something to say to me? Because I'm right fucking here." I throw both hands on my chest. "Fucking say it." My words spill out before I can even comprehend that Shane has Wyatt pinned to the wall with his fingers clenching his jawline. There's a flash of panic in Wyatt's eyes and it's oddly unsatisfying.

They both just stare back at me, stunned and speechless. Shane finally lets go of Wyatt then brushes himself off like his hands are dirty. Which they are. I just caught him physically assaulting someone he claims to care about. Regardless, that's not my concern. I wanna know what they were talking about.

"Get the hell out of here," Shane says as he makes his way over to the sink. He squirts a few drops of soap in his hands and turns to face us as he lathers them up. "This is between me and Wyatt. Mind your own damn business."

"Well, it seems that it is my business because I just heard you talking about me. Now tell me why." I drop my books to the floor and stuff my hands in the front pockets of my black pants, taking a stance. I'm not leaving until I have answers. I look at Wyatt. "What were you two talking about?"

Wyatt no longer looks scared, he looks fucking terrified. "I've gotta get to class." He slides between me and the wall and goes to walk away, but I grab a hold of his arm. "We need to have a little talk," I whisper in his ear.

His eyes shoot back to Shane, who is drying his hands with some brown paper towel while watching us intently.

Wyatt jerks his arm away. "I have to go."

"You can run. But you can't hide." I smirk. I'll catch him soon, and when I do, he's gonna come clean about what he did and who the fuck he told. Someone knows about our encounter in the locker room, and I guarantee Wyatt was behind it.

Once he's gone, I don't leave. Slow strides bring me face to face with Shane, and this time, I don't hold back. I grab him by the throat, my fingers linked around the delicate skin of his neck, and I slam his head into the wall. "How do you like that? Does it feel good to be restrained against a fucking wall?"

"Get the fuck off me." He swings an arm around and his hand slaps the back of my head.

Unfazed, I glare at him, making my point loud and clear as I squeeze harder. "If I see you lay your hands on Wyatt, or any other kid in this school again, I'll snap your fucking neck. You had me pegged all wrong. I'm not a bully. I'm a god damn tormentor and I'll pick at every fucking scar you have if you fuck with me. Are we clear?"

"You don't have shit on me. So what if I used some stupid app."

"It's not about what I know, it's about what I can make people believe." One final squeeze and my body jerks as I fight against it. Wanting to just strangle the fucking life out of this kid, I resist and push myself away from him, hurrying out of the bathroom before I do something I regret.

Problem is, I'm not sure who I was just defending there, Wyatt or myself. Knowing that he put his hands on Wyatt like that ticked something off inside of me. If anyone is going to make Wyatt miserable, it's gonna be me.

STICKING TO THE PLAN, I leave school early. Last period is just a free hour in the computer lab, so it's not like it's necessary to be there. I'm pretty sure I've ditched more days than I've attended this year.

When I pull up to Talon's house, I'm happy to see that he called everyone like I asked. The gangs all here, aside from Zed. We have no idea where he is. We haven't tried to reach him, and he hasn't tried to reach us. All I know for sure is that he's not in Redwood anymore. There are times that I miss him, but I think it's the memories of who he used to be that I miss the most. Zed changed after his mom died and I don't think we'll ever get him back.

I'm surprised to see that Willa is even here. She and Lars must have ditched last period, too.

Slamming my truck door closed, I make my way up the driveway, feeling like eyes are on me from every direction. Talon has armed the outside and inside of his home with more cameras than the fucking White House. With everything we've had going on, it's necessary.

Without even knocking, I walk right in the front door. Talon's house is home to all of us. If we ever need somewhere to go, crash, or just chill out, this is the place. We're all family here and all the shit we've been through just brings us closer, even if we don't always make it apparent. These boys are my lifeline. My go-to crew. We're bonded for life and no matter what happens, we've got each other's backs.

Everyone is gathered in the sitting room when I walk in. Lars stops talking mid-sentence and all attention jumps to me. "Hey." I side-eye the group. "What's going on?" Everyone is looking at me like they were just sitting here planning my funeral.

"Have a seat." Talon slides down on the couch and pats an empty space between him and Lars. Marni is standing in front of the fireplace with her arms crossed over her chest and an unpleasant look on her face. Willa is cross-legged on the floor wearing a smile, naturally. She always looks way too happy. Even if she's not, we'd never know it.

"Okayyyy." I drag out while I glance from person to person. "Something tells me I'm not gonna like this. Let's keep in mind that I'm the one who called this meeting."

Lars claps his hands together abruptly. "I'm just gonna lay it out without beating around the bush. You can't go after Wyatt yet."

My eyes close and my head drops back on the couch while I fight the urge to completely lose my shit. "What do you mean I can't go after Wyatt *yet*? We saw him on the video, there's a 50/50 chance that he hit Josh and if he did, he needs to pay for his sins." I lift my head and look Marni dead in the eye. "This is about her, isn't it?" Marni is my friend. I actually do like the girl and I'm glad that her and Talon found each other, but if she thinks she's going to get in my way, she's sadly mistaken.

Marni storms out of the room. Fuming, she stomps her feet with forceful steps.

Talon leans forward and presses his elbows to his knees while his fingers tap together. He looks at me like I just pissed in his Cheerios. "You know damn well how close Marni and Wyatt are. If something is going on with him, we need to let her deal with it."

I lift my head and let it all out. "What the fuck ever happened to *no questions asked*? From start to finish? Everything in between? Huh? Did you all forget about what I did for you? Scraping a dead body off the street like it was roadkill. Throwing together last minute alibi parties. Breaking up countless fights between you assholes. And let's not forget, pushing a fucking car off a cliff. All so you could get your girls and get your revenge. Now you all expect me to just sit on my revenge for a while because it'll piss off Marni? No. Fuck no!" I jump to my feet and begin pacing back and forth. Something I do often when I'm trying to refrain from breaking shit.

"No one forgot what you did," Lars says. "We're all grateful for your help. But, we need to tread lightly."

"You keep saying that. You all keep acting like Wyatt holds our future in *his* hands. If he killed Josh, we have the power. We call the shots."

Marni comes back into the room with something to say. "Tell me this, Tommy," she shouts, "is your revenge on Wyatt really because he may or may not have hit Josh? Huh? Because the way I see it, you've had a problem with him for a while. We just watched that video last week. So, tell us the truth, what do you really want from him? Better yet, what did he get from you?"

I walk over to the window and tip one of the blinds, looking outside so I don't have to look at them. "No questions asked," I say point-blankly. I don't have to tell them a damn thing and she shouldn't even be asking.

"Wyatt has two things that we need. His dad's hacking device and knowledge about that night that we don't have," Lars chimes in. The more they talk, the angrier I get. "We can't do anything without a plan. If we go in blind, we could screw ourselves."

I spin around so fast that my entire body feels dizzy. "He has more than that, ok. He fucking has something on me. Is that what you all wanna hear?" My voice rises, louder and louder with each word. "Last weekend at the fire, I threw something in it that was supposed to ease some of the stress in my life, but that wasn't the only copy. There's another one and I'm ninety-nine percent sure that Wyatt is behind all this. Hell, it's possible that Wyatt was even the one who was watching Willa and left those messages. Just because he's Marni's friend doesn't mean he's innocent. So you wanna tread lightly, go for it. But I'm going in balls deep and I'm taking that fucker down."

Everyone goes silent when I finally shut up. I swallow hard, wishing I would have ate my words because I just said way too much. Now, Marni will likely run to her little bestie and ask what I'm talking about. But if she does, she knows she's out. Talon knows it. We all know it. Our loyalties lie in this group and if she turns on one of us, she's done for. I don't wanna see it happen, but she's the one who needs to watch her step. I know for a fact that I'll be keeping an extra eye on her.

"He's right." Willa speaks for the first time since I got here. "You guys made a deal and Tommy deserves the same security and trust that he offered you all."

I point at her. "I always knew I liked you. Thank you." My

focus shifts to Marni. "I'm willing to meet you halfway on this, because I also value your friendship. Tell ya what, I won't kill him." Her mouth drops open. I didn't really plan to kill him anyways. "I won't kill him and instead, I'll use the knowledge of him being in the vicinity when Josh was killed as my bargaining chip to get into Magna Tech and track the call on Willa's phone. Once those two little bolts are tightened, I get to play my game." This is the tricky part and where I might actually need some guidance. I look at Lars. "The only thing is, telling him that we know he was out there that night is a big risk because it also means that he will know we saw Josh, too. He could assume we killed him and panicked."

Talon stands up and walks over to Marni then looks back in my direction. "If Wyatt saw Josh in the road, which I'm almost certain he did with the rolling stop he made on that footage, then he's also got to be curious as hell who moved that body. Josh sure didn't peel himself off the road and lay down in Pastor Jeffries' basement. He knows someone moved him. Whether he hit him or not, he has to be wondering what the fuck happened."

"Regardless of what we need from Wyatt, I'm out. I'll keep my mouth shut because I made a deal with you all. But I want no part in any of this. I don't wanna hear about it or see any of it." Marni makes her point clear before walking out of the room again.

"So, Wyatt's your one shot? You sure you wanna waste it on someone so insignificant? I mean, what could he possibly have on you?"

My heart rate excels when I think about what it would do to me if my secret is exposed. "Nothing you need to worry about, because what he has will never see the light of day. Which is exactly why I have to do this."

"Alright then, tell us what we need to do."

I smirk. "Gimme a week and then get ready to plan the biggest fucking party this town has ever seen."

"Aww hell. Shits about to go down." Lars slaps his hands to his legs. "Should we plan on a body?"

Willa's eyes widen in shock, but she doesn't say anything.

The corner of my lip tugs up and I give Willa a wink. "That's to be determined." I'm joking, but it's still fun to toy with the wallflower. I don't have any intention of killing Wyatt. Not yet, anyways. But if I find out that he was behind the recording in the locker room, just to try and make a mockery of me, I'll sure as hell drag his ass down with me. If it was Shane, there will be a body to dispose of.

Lars tosses a controller at me. "Alright then. Now that all that shit is settled. Let's play some COD."

"Don't trash the place. We'll be back Friday night," Talon says as he takes an armful of bags from Marni who rejoined us.

"Two days and ya'll need all those bags?" I tease. "Looks like you're leaving for two months."

Marni rolls her eyes at me and I can tell she's still pissed. "If I had my way, we would be." She walks toward the door without even saying goodbye. She's definitely ticked, but she'll get over it.

"Bye, Marni." I look at her and holler with a smile. She just snarls at me and leaves. It's actually funny seeing her riled up. It's been a while since we've got to see Marni mad.

Talon follows behind her with slouched shoulders. Probably wishing we would have had this conversation after he took a three-hour drive with her. "Thanks a lot, guys. I'll catch ya later."

Once the door closes, Lars tosses his controller to the side. "What the hell?" I bellow, "I thought we were gonna play."

He looks at Willa who is eyeballs deep in her phone then turns toward me on the couch but makes no attempt to quiet his voice. "Alright, she's gone. Now, be real with me. How bad is this gonna be?"

Willa raises her eyes. Listening but not wanting to engage in the conversation.

"Honestly, I'm not sure just yet. But I will tell you that I'm getting the answers I need after you all get yours. Come hell or high water, Wyatt McCoy will talk."

CHAPTER FIVE

WYATT

Things got a little out of hand with Shane today, but he apologized and eventually, I forgave him. Even though he gets angry sometimes, I know he only does it because he cares about me. He's well aware of how Tommy treats me and he doesn't want me around him. He doesn't even want me to talk about him. Or look in his direction. So today when I simply stated that Tommy was right and he shouldn't have tripped Alan, he made his feelings more than apparent.

He doesn't have anything to worry about, because I have every intention of staying as far away from Tommy Chambers as I possibly can. I just wish my heart would work with my brain on this matter. I know that he hates me with a passion, but I can't help it that every time I see him, my heart jumps into my throat and my emotions take over any logical thinking.

Maybe it's his confidence. The way he carries himself with his head held high and his secrets buried underneath the sleeve of his shirt, directly next to his heart because he sure as hell doesn't wear that on his sleeve.

If I could have his confidence and the ability to make everyone around me smile and cry at the same time, maybe I wouldn't feel the need to hide behind guys like Shane. I could stand tall, be proud of who I am as an individual. It's just that, next to Shane, they don't judge me. I'm not the gay nerd; I'm the quarterback's arm candy. Even if their QB is somewhat of a jerk to all of them.

I never meant to fall for Shane, and I'm not even sure that falling is what I'd call it. He took notice of me and I liked the attention he offered. Redwood is a small town and when you stick out like a sore thumb because of your sexual preference; it's nice to have someone by your side who knows that feeling. Shane has been that person for me. It wasn't always like this.

Shane wasn't always this much of a jerk. Lately, though, he just seems to be getting worse. I'm not sure if there is something eating at him, or if he was just putting on a show in the beginning to draw me in.

Tommy might be hardcore to those who he dislikes, but he's loyal as fuck to those he does. I'd rather stand in his corner of rebellion than next to a guy who pushes people around for kicks.

But, Tommy will never have me—not even as a friend.

Which is exactly why I've been staring at this damn wall for twenty-minutes with the roller in my hand. Drilling it into my head and my heart that he despises me. If a bleeding skull plastered on my wall wasn't enough clarity, the note I found on my car after school should be.

Trouble awaits if you don't change your path. Do it again and you'll feel their wrath.

What the hell does that even mean? It's not like I forced his pants down and shoved his cock into my mouth. He wanted it. *And change my path?* My path to business school? Working for my dad? I have no fucking clue what that means.

It seems that everyone prefers that I stay away from Tommy. First Shane, and now Marni. And they're right. I just need to get him out of my head.

I swipe the roller up and down. Then back and forth in swift movements. Watching as his artwork—terrifying, but beautiful —slowly fades away for good. Hoping like hell that it takes my feelings for him along for the ride. Burying them deep underneath the surface, never to be felt again.

Twenty-minutes later, it's covered. A sense of relief washes over me. I'm glad that I decided to do this myself and not let the help do it. I needed this reminder. As painful as it is, I desperately needed it.

As far as cleaning up the mess, I'll let the groundskeeper do that.

I'm washing up in my bathroom when I hear my phone buzz on my desk. Grabbing a hold of the hand towel, I dab my hands dry and toss it in the sink then hurry to my phone before I miss the call. I make it just in time, but hit ignore.

That ship sailed three months ago. I'll die before I ever talk to that son of a bitch again. Every time that I think Shane mistreats me, I remember who I was with before him. Someone who didn't carry an ounce of respect for me or a sliver of affection toward me. I was a doormat. A dirty secret. Pleasure behind closed doors only to crush my soul in the process. It's happened twice. I'm not sure I can handle that kind of pain again. I'm still reeling from the blow of Tommy (no pun intended).

I plug my phone into the charger on my desk and fall into bed in just a pair of boxer briefs. My phone sounds again, but this time, I don't even bother looking at it. He's probably drunk again. Lately, he's always drunk.

***

I wake up to the sound of footsteps coming down the hall. My eyes blink a few times before I slap my hand around on the nightstand and grab my phone: *12:32 a.m.* Mom and Dad are still out of town, and Elsa was off today.

Tossing my blanket off of me, I throw my legs over the side of the bed and adjust my boxers. Soft steps lead me over to the door and just as I go to press my ear to it, the handle turns from the other side. My back plants firmly against the wall as I wait for it to open. Using the element of surprise, I stand still, holding my breath.

Once it cracks open and a beam of light from the hallway shines through, I jump out and grab the stranger by the arms. My heart races as I take in the man in front of me. Dressed in all black, with a black ski mask over his face.

My strength is no match when he grabs me by my upper arms and practically lifts me off the floor and carries me over to the bed. "Whatever you want, take it. I don't want any trouble." I choke the words out before he slaps a hand over my mouth. The alarm system was set; it should have sounded when he broke in. Whoever this is must know the passcode, or somehow disarmed the system. "How did you get in here?"

He doesn't speak; he just lingers over me as if he's expecting something from me. It's too dark to get a good look at this guy, but a sliver of light shines in and reflects off those eyes. Those intoxicating, steel blue eyes. They're so familiar. Wide, but lost —in search of something to help him find his way. I whisper, "Tommy?"

Still nothing.

His hand twists behind him and he reaches into his back pocket and pulls out a can. *Spray paint.*

"I know it's you, Tommy."

With his forearm pressed to my chest as he braces me against the mattress, he gives the can a shake. When he holds it only inches from my face, I pinch my eyes shut tightly. "What the hell are you doing?"

I'm not surprised when he doesn't say a word. Instead, I

listen as the sound of paint spraying from the can rings around my head. Vapor hits my face as I squirm beneath his hold. My eyes open. "Get off me!" I shout. My legs wail in the air, but my movement only forces him to press his forearm harder into my chest.

When he stops spraying, my body freezes. His face hovers over mine. Heavy breaths cause the mouth of the mask to suck in with each inhale. The fire in his eyes burns into mine, and though I should be afraid, I'm not. "Why are you doing this?" I ask him, knowing full well that I won't get a response.

I can feel his body tense up on top of me and it's like something snapped inside of him because he pulls away abruptly.

Lying there, still and silent, I watch as he continues to spray around the outline of my body—blood red paint. I don't try to stop him, there's no point. I won't win.

Once he finishes, he stuffs the can into his back pocket and finally speaks. "Get up."

When I don't move, he grabs me by the arm and pulls me off the bed. My entire body goes numb when he pulls a switchblade out of the inside pocket of his black jacket. I take a step back, bumping the back of my legs into my nightstand. "Tommy….." I hold my hands up in surrender. He comes toward me and flips the blade open, his eyes locked tightly on mine.

The cold metal tip of the knife hits my chin and I hold my body completely still. One wrong move and that blade goes right inside of me. My heart beats so fast that I'm afraid the vibration alone is going to drive it under my flesh. I can hear his jaw lock as he grits through his teeth. "You toyed with the wrong guy."

In one swift motion, Tommy steps back and lifts his arm stabbing the knife into the mattress of my bed. I don't blink. I don't move. I don't breathe. I just stand there, stunned.

I'm not even sure at what point he walked out, but when the door slams shut, I release all the pent-up air in my lungs.

Bending over and grabbing my knees, I draw in a hefty breath with my hand on my racing heart.

Once I'm sure I won't pass out, I walk over to the wall and flip on the light. Exactly as I expected, the outline of my body is sprayed in red and the knife is stuck right into the mattress where my heart would have been.

CHAPTER SIX

WYATT

It's been two days since I got the note and was given the most descriptive threat imaginable. I'm not really sure how I feel about it all. Even though Tommy broke into my house, I still don't think he'd hurt me. He's trying to prove a point, one that I've said many times has been proven. I got it. Don't tell anyone. Consider it done.

Just as much as he doesn't want anyone to know, I don't either. I'm not proud of what happened. There are times I want it to happen again, but not at the cost I've been paying.

Thursday and Friday at school were fairly uneventful and I'm not complaining, but it was like this dark cloud descended over Redwood. I can't help but feel like danger is lurking around the corner.

I've been on edge and remained cautious like Marni advised—steering clear of Tommy and just carrying on with my life. But it's Friday night and there's a party at the power lines that Shane wants me to go with him to, and I also promised Shay I'd be there.

I'm brushing my teeth when I hear a voice outside my open

bedroom door. Dropping the toothbrush down, I dip into my room. Standing still and silent, I listen.

It's Dad, and he sounds pissed. "I told you not to call this phone again. This will be the last time I say it."

Walking abruptly to the door, I dip my head out of the room and see Dad standing there. "Hey, Son. I was just coming to talk to you."

"About?" It's extremely uncommon for Dad to come to my bedroom, let alone in a pair of jeans and a t-shirt. Dad's all business. Suits, ties, and shiny shoes.

He nods toward my room. "Let's go inside."

My brows dip and everything about this feels awkward. I don't think Dad has ever even been inside my bedroom. "Ok. Sure."

I look around at the mess, expecting him to shout for Elsa to come clean it up. Dad despises clutter and, *fuck,* I never took care of the paint tray.

"What the hell is this?" He points to the roller laying in a tray of dried paint that's been there since Wednesday.

"I uh, had an art project and accidentally got some black paint on the wall. Had to cover it up." It's ridiculous and unbelievable. I'm not even taking an art class, but he doesn't know that. I could have dropped out of high school and the old man wouldn't even notice.

"And you cleaned it up yourself? Why didn't you ask Leo or Sam to handle this?" Leo and Sam are the groundskeepers. They fix whatever is broken and keep the yard in tip-top shape. If only they could fix my broken family. "Never mind, forget that. The reason I'm here is because we need to have a talk about the future—your future."

"My future?" I question. "I thought you had it planned out already. Four years at State and then I step in next to Uncle Mike as CEO of Magna Tech."

"That was the plan, but we're going to have to forgo your

schooling and take you in straight out of high school. I fired Michael this morning and he won't be returning." Uncle Mike has been my dad's best friend since they were kids. Dad even refers to him as my uncle, so just saying his name—Michael—like he's simply an employee is asinine.

"What do you mean you fired Uncle Mike? Why would you do that? He's your best friend."

Dad slaps a hand to my shoulder. His arm is stiff and I can see the discomfort in his expression. Human affection does not come easy for Royce McCoy. "Well, Son, when you walk into your wife's suite that she's been staying at for three weeks, just to surprise her, and you find her hanging from a swing in the middle of the room with your best friend's face in her pussy, you realize that it's time to reevaluate your plans."

My face drops in my hands and I let out a breathy groan. "Fuck." I turn to face him. "Uncle Mike?" His head bobs up and down slowly. That was a little too much information. He could have just said that Mom and Uncle Mike were having an affair. But he painted me a clear picture that will forever be etched in my head. Digging my fingertips into my eyeballs, I try to erase the image. It doesn't work, so I smack the side of my head a couple times. "What does this mean? Are you and Mom finally getting a divorce?" If you're wondering why I'm not surprised, it's because I'm not surprised, at all.

Sure, Uncle Mike was a bad move. But, Mom and Dad haven't been faithful to one another for years. They still share a home, a bed, and a legal binding contract that says they are married. But, as far as a marriage full of love—it never existed. Dad accidentally knocked Mom up when she was nineteen years old and his parents forced him to marry her. That accident was me, and there was never another.

My parents are younger than most of my classmates', and also more successful. Well, Dad is. He had a pipe dream and he ran with it. Of course, he had a helping hand from my grandfather, who passed away five years ago. He left Dad his millions, and his entire estate outside of Redwood was left to me.

"Nah, divorces are for quitters. We'll stay married and your mother will learn to control her sexual desires when it comes to my employees. As for Uncle Mike, he'll get nothing but a severance that will set him up for a couple years. Our partnership is done."

Typical *don't touch what's mine* sort of male behavior. Sure, Mom can sleep around, but it has to be a complete stranger who could potentially give her the gift of an STD. But if it's someone Dad knows and trusts, he loses his shit.

"Whatever. I don't even care about that. You and Mom's thing is just that, your thing. But, as for my future, I don't like change. I won't even know what I'm doing without schooling."

Dad rubs his hands down his jeans and stands up. "Well, embrace it because you're needed. Prior experience isn't necessary. In fact, it could hinder your knowledge. It's best to learn the way we work versus readapting to a new company after you've spent time interning elsewhere. It's better this way. You *will* work for Magna Tech and you will start after graduation." He smiles like he's about to offer me another option. "I'll tell you what, I'll even be generous and give you a week off. You'll start one week after graduation."

He pats a hand to my shoulder then walks away with his perfectly straight posture, leaving a trail of his strong designer cologne behind him while taking my future out the door with him.

"Gee, thanks." I grumble as the door latches closed behind him. How kind of him to give me a week to enjoy being a teenager before I start my career as CEO—straight out of high school, with no business knowledge. A 4.0 is great, but a little training would be convenient in this situation. I doubt Uncle Mike will be allowed to stick around and show me the ropes.

Nope. Chances are, I'll walk in blind and take my seat on the throne at this hellhole.

Long gone are the dreams of partying all night and going to class with a hangover. Frat parties, hot guys, and beer bongs. Being away from this town and giving myself the opportunity to become more than Royce McCoy's well-heeled son. I shouldn't be surprised that Dad just flushed it all down the toilet without even blinking. When you're born to a man like my father, your life is already mapped out and having a mind of your own is impossible.

Snatching my phone off my dresser, I tap Shane's name on my recent contacts. It rings a couple times and I expect the voicemail to pick up, but then he answers. "Hey."

"Where are you?"

"We're heading out to the power lines right now in Max Ruben's pickup truck. You coming?"

"Can you pick me up on the way? I'm drinking tonight."

"Bullshit." He laughs.

"No, for real. I wanna get drunk tonight."

After a beat of silence, he responds, "It's pretty full in here. Just drive out and we'll find you a way home." Laughter erupts in the background and it becomes hard to hear anything. Two seconds later, the line goes dead.

It shouldn't hurt, but it does.

I don't drink often. Or ever for that matter. It just doesn't appeal to me. But, if I only have three and a half months before I'm forced into adulthood, I need to live a little while I can.

I tap Shay's name and she picks up on the first ring. "Hey, are you going tonight?"

"Of course I am. Wanna ride with me? Apparently Marni is too tired from her trip. Ya know, she's practically married now."

I chuckle, knowing exactly what she means. Marni has been distant since she started this new life as one of *them*. "Yeah, pick me up. I plan on getting drunk, so I'm crashing at your place tonight. "

After a very long scream of excitement, she says, "Be there in ten."

I end the call and stuff my phone into the back pocket of my black, twill pants then zip up my grey Brunello sweater and adjust the collar on my polo shirt underneath—stealing a glance in the mirror before I head out. Not exactly bonfire party attire, but it's me.

When I get downstairs, I slide into a pair of Chucks and stand by the door until Shay flashes her lights outside. It's our thing. None of us ever want to deal with each other's families, so we just flash the lights or shoot a text.

Dad's in his office screaming at someone and I almost feel sorry for whoever is on the receiving end of that call. I slide out the front door without even saying goodbye. I always come and go as I please. Rules have never been a thing in this household.

Shay is parked in front in the circle drive. I jog down the plank stairs and open up the door of her rusted-out Volvo and climb inside. "Thanks for picking me up," I say as I close the door.

She peels out and lays on the gas as we whip down the quarter-mile driveway. I grab the *oh-shit handles*. "Woah, Nellie. We in a hurry or what?"

"When my friend, who once took a shot of whiskey and spit it out because it burned his tongue, tells me that he's drinking tonight, I take him to drink."

I convulse in hysterics, remembering that day. "That was freshman year. I was a kid."

"And you haven't drank since then."

"Point taken." Although, I did have a beer at a party Talon threw last year. I only drank it because I was trying to calm the nerves of being in his house in the first place.

"Alright. Who, what, and why?"

"Who? What? Why?"

"Who pissed you off? What did they do? And why the sudden desire to drink? It's not like you."

"My dad just decided to lay it on me that he needs me to come work for him right after graduation. I won't be going to State. Therefore, I need to get some youthfulness out of my system before I put on a suit and tie and live behind a desk at Magna Tech."

"And you told him to fuck off, right?"

I look over at her and she's dead serious, but she also doesn't know my dad all that well. Like I said, we avoid each other's screwed-up families. "Actually, the opposite. If I told my dad to fuck off, I wouldn't be in this car right now. He'd probably ship me off to a private school to finish out my senior year." My head shakes. "No. I'll do it. I've always known this was the plan."

"His plan, or your plan?"

Shay doesn't understand. She lives the most normal life out of everyone I know. She has two normal parents who work nine-to-five jobs, and lives in a cute little ranch home on half an acre. She's got sisters she's close with and plans to take out student loans to pay for her schooling at a community college. Most people in her shoes would want what I have, what a lot of the kids at Redwood have. Bright futures with no worry about finances. But, not me. I'd rather have normalcy and the ability to be who and what I want to be. So, yeah, it's his plan. But, I don't tell her that.

"It's our plan. Just drop it. What's done is done."

She salutes me with her hand to her forehead. "Aye, aye, captain. Consider it dropped. So, how are things with you and Shane going?"

Why the hell does everyone always ask me that? Are they expecting things to be any different than the last time they asked? We're not even in a solid relationship. Granted, we're the only gay couple at Redwood and everyone thinks we are just so damn cute, but we're just like any other high school couple. We argue, we makeup, we fight, we fuck—the end. I answer her regardless. "We're fine." Even though I'm not fine.

"And you? Any guys on your radar tonight?" Shay is fairly promiscuous. I wouldn't call her a slut, because that's just wrong. But, she does tend to find comfort in random guys.

Her brows waggle in the dim light of the dashboard. "We'll just have to see."

My head shakes with a smile. *I'm sure we will.*

Making our way down the uneven terrain, our bodies bounce up and down in the front seat. Shay grips tightly to the steering wheel while I brace myself with two hands on the dash. "Has anyone ever told you that you're a crazy driver?"

"Yeah, you. Every time you get in my car."

We finally come to a stop in the back row of about a dozen cars. There's another row with even more on the other side of the field. This kind of party is a cop's dream. About forty underaged students gathered around a big ass bonfire in the middle of a long strip of open space. Suddenly, I'm rethinking my plan to drink away my sorrows.

That is, until I see Tommy standing directly in front of the fire. He's got both hands in his front pockets and his bottom lip tucked under his top teeth while he engages in conversation with a couple girls. He cracks a smile and for some reason, I smile in response. Butterflies flutter through my chest and my breath hitches when I try to fill my lungs.

Then I remember that he painted the outline of my body on my bed and made it clear as day that he will shred my insides if I tell anyone what happened.

"Earth to Wyatt." Shay snaps her fingers in front of my face.

Coming out of my daze, I look up at Shay. "What'd you say?"

"I said let's party. Come on." I look over at her standing by the open passenger door, not even realizing she had already gotten out.

One foot at a time, I get out of the car. Drawing in another deep breath and bracing myself for what this night might bring. I catch Shane running down the field and jumping up to catch a football being thrown at him. Once he catches it, he slams it to the ground and does the little happy dance he does whenever a touchdown is scored during a game. He's in his element right now.

Making no attempt to hurry, I follow behind Shay as we walk over to the fire. My hope is to blend into the crowd and the scenery, avoiding a confrontation with Tommy or Lars. I see Willa standing next to Lars with his arm wrapped around her shoulders and, for the first time, I notice her little baby bump. It's hard to believe those two are going to be parents. And I thought that my life was over after graduation.

As hard as I try not to look at Tommy, my eyes always find their way to him. My heart drops when his stare catches mine. *Look away. Look away.* But, I can't, and he doesn't either. He continues to talk to whoever it is standing in front of him, but his eyes remain on mine. Swallowing hard, I feel my Adam's apple bob in my throat.

Tommy rakes his fingers through his disheveled hair. The tattoos that run down the length of his arm are visible with his sweatshirt sleeves pushed up to his elbows. Sweat runs down my back, dipping beneath the waistband of my pants. It's not credited to the intense heat that the fire puts off, it's something else, or should I say someone else, that has me all hot and bothered. At this moment, his eyes don't hold hatred. In fact, I see no emotion whatsoever behind them. His smile leads me to believe he's in a good mood. Though, it's clearly not because of me.

As quickly as I caught them, his eyes peel away from mine and back to the girls he's talking to. In a flirtatious manner, he grabs one of them by the waist and squeezes. She giggles in response and my heart climbs back into place. Whatever that moment was has passed.

"Here you go," Shay says, coming out of nowhere, even though I thought she was beside me this entire time. It hits me that I was standing here alone just staring back at Tommy. I look around to see if anyone noticed. That's when I see Shane. The hatred that I expected to spill from Tommy's gaze on me is in Shane's possessive gawk. Daggers dig deep inside of me. I can feel them pierce the back of my head and if he were any angrier, I'd be roasting in that fire right now.

Heavy steps bring him to my side and he grabs ahold of my arm, jerking me away from Shay while my cup of keg beer sloshes all over the arm of my sweater. "What's wrong?' I ask him in a mellow tone.

He continues to pull me away from the crowd before he responds. Music begins blasting through the speakers in the back of someone's pickup truck. "Last Resort" by Papa Roach carries down the trail that Shane is leading me. "How long have you been here?" He snaps at me as he shoves me out of his reach.

"Just got here like three minutes ago. Why?"

"So instead of coming to say hi, you just stand by the fire checking out the enemy?"

I'm a bit taken aback and not sure how to respond to the way he's acting right now. "Chill out. I was waiting for Shay to bring me a drink. I haven't said a word to Tommy."

His lips twitch with humor, only his laugh isn't one coming from happiness; it's sadistic and dare I say, frightening. "I told you to stay away from him. If you wanna mingle with a man that I can't stand and who wants to hurt you, then we're done."

My chin drops to my chest as I dig the toe of my Chucks into the dirty sand. "Really, Shane? This again?" I can't even look at him. Part of me wants to just shout in his face and tell him to screw off and we're done, but the other part knows that Shane will not let this end so easily. We will not be friends, and he will make that clear every single day. Staying away from Tommy isn't a problem. Is it?

"Yes, this again." His hand smacks the back of my head. "When will you get it through your thick skull that he'll never want you?"

I slap his hand away. "Whatever, I'm out of here." I don't feel like explaining myself, and I shouldn't have to.

"If you walk away from me, we're over." His voice drops down a few octaves and becomes solemn. "I mean it, Wyatt."

I stop walking. Frozen in place, knowing that he's not joking. If I keep going and end things between us, Shane will make my life hell. He will bully me to no end. His friends will turn on me and my life will become abysmal in the halls of that school. I'll get it worse than Alan, Isabel, or Niko—the three smartest, but least privileged kids at Redwood. I'll be his new target.

Screw it.

I take another step.

And another.

Closing that chapter and starting another.

The next few steps back to the fire feel invigorating. It's not often that I stand up for myself, but I just did. For the first time in a while, I got to make a decision for myself. Not for my dad, not for my mom, and not for Shane.

Tipping back the half-emptied cup in my hand, because the rest spilled all over me, I take down the contents in one swallow.

"Woohoo." Shay hoots and hollers. "McCoy is getting drunk. McCoy is getting drunk." She sings her own tune as her body sways back and forth.

I'm watching the flames of the fire when a familiar arm comes into sight. Wrapping around Shay's waist while she sways to the music playing. My eyes slide up the arm to the face of the guy attached to it. With menacing eyes, Tommy looks back at me as his body moves in rhythm behind Shay. Grinding against her ass, he stands there, watching me with a knowing smirk on his face.

Feeling the need for an out before I make a fool of myself and take his looks as something they're not, I go get another drink.

There's about a dozen people gathered around the keg when I grab a cup from the bag lying on the ground next to it. It's just my luck that Shane is the one holding the nozzle. I wait patiently as he fills the cups of everyone around him. Laughing, chatting, having a good time. More people come up and he continues on, filling them all while completely ignoring me.

A couple look from Shane to me, knowing that I was here before them, but he doesn't even acknowledge my existence. *And so it begins.*

As if the gods of humiliation are completely against me, Tommy and Shay walk up together while Tommy has his arm draped around Shay's shoulder. I see she found her guy for the night. Nausea churns in my stomach, but I try not to think too much about it.

With his cup hanging from his hand at his other side, Tommy grabs Shane's attention. "He was here first," he tells him with a nod in my direction. Once again, Shane ignores me and, this time, he ignores Tommy, too. I'm not really sure why Tommy is even coming to my defense. It's possible that his hatred for Shane runs deeper than his hatred for me.

"Shane!" Shay snaps. "What the fuck? Fill up Wyatt's cup." She looks over at me. "Is something going on with you two?" she whispers.

"I said he was fucking next!" Tommy shouts while Shane continues on with his business of filling cups. Like he wanted to be in charge of this damn keg just to purposely piss both Tommy and me off.

"My bad," Shane retorts. Aiming the nozzle at me, I know

what's coming before it even happens. As soon as the foaming beer begins squirting all over my sweater, Tommy lunges at Shane, taking him straight down to the ground.

"You asshole!" Shay hollers, then turns to me and begins rubbing her hands down my sweater. She thinks she's wiping it away, but she's only making it worse. The liquid seeps through both layers and I suck in my stomach in an attempt to ease the cold sensation.

"I'm fine. Don't worry about it."

Lars comes out of nowhere and pulls Tommy off Shane. I'm not even sure what happened on the other side of the keg because I couldn't see, but when someone pulls Shane up and blood drips from his lip, I know that Tommy got him.

"I'll fucking kill you, Chambers!" Shane points and shouts as he's dragged away by a couple guys from the football team.

Tommy casually grabs the keg nozzle, fills his cup and walks away. Shay and I exchange a *what the fuck just happened? look.*

Her shoulders shrug and she fills up both our cups. But, I don't leave. I slam my beer and fill it up again. And again, until my head begins to spin and someone snatches the nozzle from my hands. I laugh in response because, all of a sudden, I'm feeling really damn happy. Probably the happiest I've been in a very long time.

Swaying back and forth with a full cup in my hand, I make my way over to Shay by the fire. Of course, Tommy is with her. Only this time, he's standing in front of her with his arms around her waist while he whispers something in her ear that makes her giggle. He sure is laying it on thick tonight with the ladies. First, the group of girls he was with when I got here, and now one of my best friends. I doubt it's intentional, but it sure does feel that way. Then again, I'm drunk for the first time in my life and everything around me feels surreal.

When I stumble toward the fire, I begin laughing at myself. Quickly stopping when everyone looks in my direction. Shay pushes Tommy a couple inches away from her. "Hey, you ok?" she asks me.

I hold up my cup in cheers. "I'm fucking fantastic." I take another drink, making every attempt to ignore the fact that Tommy hasn't even turned around to look at me. He just stands there like a statue with one hand on Shay's waist. Why won't he look at me? He just came to my defense but now he's not the least bit curious what I'm doing with his back turned to me. I take another drink, a big one. Some of the beer dribbles down my chin and I swipe it away. "This party sucks."

"Ok," Shay says, as she steps around Tommy. "Let's go sit down. I'll take that." She snatches the cup from my hand.

"Hey, I was drinking that. I thought this is what you wanted? Isn't this what cool kids do on Friday nights? Drink and make an ass of themselves?"

"No. Idiots like me do that. You, do not. You're better than this."

"Am I? Because, I beg to differ." We keep walking until we stop at a large rock sitting away from the party. Shay guides me down on it and I grab my cup back and take another drink. "If I were better than this, I wouldn't be here with my ex-boyfriend who's killing me with his stare, or a guy who—" I stop myself. Thank God, I stopped myself. Ok, that's enough of that. I give the cup a toss, but it doesn't go far.

"What happened with you and Shane? This all came out of nowhere."

"He's just been weird lately. Doesn't matter, it's over. But the important question is, what the hell are you doing with Tommy Chambers?" As if he heard his name from thirty yards away, he begins walking in our direction.

A smile spreads across Shay's face and I immediately know that he's making her feel the same way that he makes me feel just being in the same room. I don't like it one bit. "Nothing. We're just having fun." My eyes look past her as Tommy draws closer. Shay swings around and sees him coming, then turns back to me. "You know it's nothing more. I don't do more than casual hookups when it comes to the boys at this school."

Shay longs for attention, and I think that's why she sleeps with so many guys. Even if it's just for a night, she holds onto that feeling until the next time.

"You ready to go?" Tommy asks as he nuzzles his face into the folds of her neck. Her head tilts instinctively and she nods.

Ugh, I feel sick. "Go where?"

"Back to my place. My parents are gone for the night. Come on." She reaches for my hand.

"No. I'll just catch a ride with Shane." My words slur, but in my head they sound legible. Is that a thing with sounds? Or is that just writing? Either way, I make my point.

"What? No, you're not. You just dumped that asshole. I'm not letting him take you home."

Tommy's head snaps in my direction and he raises a brow, as if he didn't hear Shay correctly. But he doesn't question it.

"I'll apologize and we'll make up. I'll be fine. Just go."

"She said let's go. So let's go," Tommy grumbles.

But I don't move. Like a stubborn child, I stay on the rock. Crossing one leg over the other, I ignore them. There is no way in hell I'm going back to Shay's house and listening to these two fuck like rabbits all night.

Strong fingers wrap around my forearm and I'm jerked off the rock. "You have a problem hearing, McCoy?"

"Hey, be nice to him." Shay swats at Tommy's arm, and I wish she'd just punch him for both of us.

Ripping my arm out of his reach, I stumble back a few steps, but Tommy reaches out and pulls me back by the arm. With liquid courage swirling in my veins, I say what needs to be said. "You have some nerve to try and bark orders at me after what you've done."

He's still holding onto me when he leans closer and whispers in my ear, "Don't you dare say something you'll regret." Jerking his hand away in an aggressive manner, he steps back. "Now, let's go."

"Fine. I'll go," I tell Shay. " But drop me off at home. I'm not staying at your house with this guy there."

Tommy's lip curls in a snarl and I roll my eyes at him. Much like everyone else, Shay is not aware of my history with Tommy. She knows that the guys have pushed me around a bit, but as far as she's concerned, Tommy is better than his friends.

Walking a few steps behind them, I keep my distance. The closer we get to the car, the angrier I become. This is unreal. She's gonna to take this guy home and sleep with him. A guy I have crushed on in secret for almost a year. One who has a firm grasp on my heart and keeps squeezing and squeezing, trying to drain it of life.

She has no idea the guy she's acting all giddy over vandalized my bedroom wall, left me a threatening note a couple days ago, and then broke into my house in the middle of the night. The real kicker, no one will ever know. I'll hold it in. Keep it bottled up, nice and tight, and the world will be none the wiser because I'll never share any of it.

CHAPTER SEVEN

TOMMY

"If he throws up back there, I'm dragging him out by his feet and we're leaving him on the side of the road," I tell Shay who's sitting in the passenger's seat of her car. I didn't drink tonight for a reason; I knew I'd be driving her home as soon as I saw her and Wyatt walk up to the party. Shay has a little crush on me, and I love nothing more than sticking it to Wyatt. This is the perfect opportunity to do just that, while also showing him that I like pussy.

She laughs like I'm joking, but I'm really not. "He's sleeping. He'll be fine."

"You know where he lives, right?"

Yeah, I know where Wyatt lives. He's on the same road as me. Has been my entire life. "I'll get him into your house. Probably best not to take him home like this and risk his parents being there."

"Thanks, Tommy." Shay places a hand on my arm. Her soft fingers move up and down slowly. "You're a good person."

If only that were true.

Everyone talks like I'm this hero inside with the shell of a misfit. Tattoos and piercings that do little to help my case, but somehow, everyone looks past them and sees only the good. It's true that I despise uncalled for bullying, but I'm no saint. I've got my demons and just like everyone else who carries the burden of a past, I'd like to lay them to rest and move on with my life.

When I say uncalled for bullying, I mean, bullying for no reason. What I'm doing to Wyatt may be considered ruthless to some, but it's only because they don't know what he did to me. They don't know the secrets we keep. The shame he's brought on me and the humiliation that video has caused. I know he's behind it—it has to be him and Shane. Not to mention, this whole situation with Josh. There are all these puzzle pieces that somehow fit together and I just have to find their place in the bigger picture.

I pull up the empty driveway at Shay's house and kill the engine.

Shay leans over the seat and begins shaking Wyatt's leg. "Wyatt. We're here. Wake up." Dropping back down, she sighs. "He's out cold."

"Go unlock the door and I'll get him inside."

We both get out and Shay heads toward the house while I round the car to the back door. I'm really stretching myself beyond my means here as I scoop up his limp body and toss him over my shoulder.

"Put me down," he grumbles.

"I'm telling you right now, McCoy, you throw up on me and I'll drop you on this cement, so you better hold your booze well."

His arms flail against my back as he tries to get a grip on my shirt, but he doesn't fight me to put him down. He seems to lack the strength and mobility. Either that, or he likes having his dick pressed against my chest. He smells like a brewery mixed with some damn good smelling cologne.

Looking down, I notice his sock is barely hanging on his foot. "Where the fuck did your other shoe go?"

I swing around to look behind me but don't see it on the ground. When I spin back around to go in the house, I feel his body jolt when his head ricochets off the side of the car. "Oh, shit." I shriek. "Totally didn't mean to do that, man."

"You punched me." His fist punches against my back, but it feels like he has the strength of a toddler.

"How the hell did I punch you when both of my hands are wrapped around your damn body?" I take a step up to the porch, then another.

"I felt your fist hit my head," he stumbles over his words, "you really are an asshole."

"It was the car. Now, just shut up unless you wanna sleep on the ground tonight."

"You broke into my house."

I stop walking and just stand there in the driveway with a drunk Wyatt tossed over my shoulder. I need to kill this conversation before we get in that house.

"For good reason. You needed a reminder that if you share that video, that will be your fate."

"Why would I share the video? You think I'm proud of what happened?"

"No. I don't think you're any prouder that I am, which is not at all, but I do think you have a plan to use it against me. And if you do, you won't live to regret it."

He doesn't respond, but when I hear him swallowing continuously like his mouth is watering, I know that I need to get him off of me before he spews down my back.

When I get to the door, I give it a loud kick and Shay opens it, standing with one arm bracing the screen door while I slide in between her and the frame and straight over to the couch. His body rolls off and I make no attempt to get him comfortable as he lies there with his knees on the floor and his stomach pressed against the couch. His head rests sideways on the cushion and his eyes are wide open, but he doesn't say anything. Just a few groans and gurgles escape him.

"I should probably help him up the rest of the way," Shay says with her arms crossed over her chest beside the couch.

"Nah, he'll make his way up there eventually." I grab her by the waist and pull her close. My lips find hers immediately and the sweet taste of her Chapstick coats my lips. I dart my tongue out. "Mmm. Cherry."

I'm not sure why I feel the need to do this, but in some vengeful way, I need Wyatt to see that I'm into chicks. I also need Shay to help erase the memories that won't fade.

She smiles slyly and I pull her back to me. Our bodies parallel. This is exactly what I need—a woman's touch. Just a simple reminder that my body still craves a firm ass and tits pressed against me. Sliding one leg up between her thighs, I cup her crotch and begin rubbing my thumb aggressively through the fabric of her blue jeans. She lets out a subtle moan. "Come on. Let's go to my room."

"Uh uh." I shake my head. "Right here."

"But, Wyatt—"

"He's passed out." My mouth trails down her neck then back up, sucking the thin skin of her lobe between my teeth.

"True." She walks my body forward until we are on the loveseat. I drop down with my back pressed to the cushion, but I shake my head. "Uh uh." Grabbing her by the waist, I flip her over so that she's laying down on the small couch beside the full-sized one. Unbuttoning her pants, I then slide them down, taking her panties along with them. I slither down between her parted legs so that I'm eye level with her pussy. With two fingers, I rub circles around her clit. It's a beautiful sight. Two parted lips and a hole that leads to indescribable pleasure. Flexing my tongue muscle, I taste the inside of her. Bobbing my head back and forth while I caress her clit vigorously.

Her back arches and I slide my tongue out and replace it with two fingers. Soft, warm, and so fucking wet. Twisting and digging, I press my fingers in farther. I'm knuckle deep when she lets out a whimper.

"I want you right fucking now," she says as she grabs a fistful of my hair and slams my face into her. I begin flicking the tip of my tongue against her clit while I slide another finger in. My hard cock grinds against the cushion, but it's not enough. My insides feel like they're on fire. Throbbing. Aching. In dire need of a release.

Much like that day. I credit my reckless behavior to just that —need. It should have never happened, and now that it has, I can't go back. I can feel Wyatt's presence all-too close, and now I'm not sure how I feel about it. Do I like the idea that he could be listening? Watching? Does he wish my body was pressed against his instead of Shay's?

Fuck. Why am I thinking about this?

Picking up my pace, I force my fingers in faster and deeper. My tongue sweeps up, from where the bone of my knuckle presses against her, to the tip of her clit. "Oh God, Tommy," she bellows. More long and tasteful strides of my tongue as I lick her so hard that the abrasion causes my taste buds to swell. I try to chase the vision of Wyatt from my head. The way his lips formed the perfect O around my cock. The way his tongue shimmied up my length while his eyes stayed locked on mine for the briefest of moments. *Don't look at me,* I screamed at him. And when he shut his eyes, I wanted him to open them back up just so I could see the reflection of my own hate.

Stop it. Get him out of your fucking head.

Lifting my head, I pull out my fingers. "Get on your knees," I demand as I grab her waist and help her over. Her arms hang over the back of the love seat and she rolls her hips, her firm ass staring back at me. I pull my wallet out of my back pocket and grab a condom before shoving my wallet back inside and dropping my pants. With my teeth, I rip off the top, take it out, then roll it on. I don't even hesitate before slamming my cock inside of her.

Ramming her from behind at lightning speed, my pelvic bone vibrates against her ass cheeks. I look over at Wyatt on the couch and he's awake. Staring back at me with pain in his eyes that feels like a knife to my chest.

"Faster," Shay cries out, and I peel my eyes from Wyatt's. I'm not sure I can go much faster, but I sure as hell try. "Ughh, yeah. Like that."

This is what I like. I like pussy. I like this ass. I slap a hand to her left cheek, leaving a handprint that reddens immediately.

"Fuck!" I groan. My voice husky and ragged.

My eyes close and all I can see is his smooth, bare chest. Water from his shower minutes prior dripping down to where his hand cupped my balls. Beads dropping onto my cock that he sucked dry. Taking every last morsel of my cum as I shot it into his mouth.

Harder. Faster.

Fuck, she feels so good.

When Shay lets out a few more muffled cries of pleasure and her body relaxes, I know she came. But, I don't stop. Not yet. My finger sweeps up her ass as my cock pile drives inside of her. Rimming her asshole, I push my finger in nail deep. My entire body convulses as I fill up the condom still inside of her. "Holy shit." I pinch my eyes shut as I continue to release.

I pause for a minute before dropping my hand that I didn't even realize was digging into the skin of her hips. I'm not surprised that she didn't complain. Shay likes it rough, or so I've heard.

Pulling out slowly, I slide the condom off and bend down to pull up my boxers and pants that lingered around my ankles. When her neck twists around, I press a chaste kiss to her forehead.

I needed Shay tonight because I was desperately searching for clarity. But, in the end, all it did was fuck me up more. I should have known that doing this with him here—next to us—was a bad idea. But something inside of me wouldn't let him go home. That same something wouldn't let me take Shay up to her room. I have a habit of fucking myself and making things worse than they already are.

But, that guy on the couch, he fucking ruined me.

I give him one last look, but his head is turned away. I wanna see his eyes just so I can know how I made him feel, but deep down, I already know. I feel it, too.

It's one o'clock in the morning and I can't sleep for shit. In my own defense, I haven't even tried. Shooting a text to my dad's driver, I get out of the bed next to Shay when he says he'll be here in twenty-minutes.

Making my way through the long stretch of hall in this one-story house, I try to find the bathroom. I open a closet—nope. Another door that leads to a bedroom—nope. I keep walking and pass through the living room where Wyatt is snoring on the couch and I eye a slightly ajar door. That has to be it.

Making no attempt to quiet my steps, I push it open—bingo.

Tugging my pants down past my hip bone, I press a hand to the back wall and do my business. Washing my hands when I'm done, I don't see a towel, so I pat my hands dry on my shirt.

Before I leave the bathroom, I check my phone and Max says he's still fifteen minutes out. I open the door with the intentions of waiting out front for him, but to my surprise, Wyatt is sitting upright on the couch with his phone in his hands. His eyes slide up to me and he smacks his dry lips together. "What the hell are you doing here?" he says, still only wearing one shoe with his other sock hanging off his foot. He looks like complete shit. His sweater zipper must have split at some point in the backseat of the car because it's stuck midway down.

"You seriously don't remember, do you?"

He doesn't lift his head or look at me. His eyes stay glued to the light of his phone. "If you're referring to you fucking Shay over there," he tilts his head to the loveseat, "then yeah, I remember. What I don't understand is *why* you're still here."

"Tried to sleep but I couldn't. Now I'm leaving." I stuff my phone in my back pocket and walk toward the door.

"That was, what, like three hours ago? It's not like you to stick around after you get what you want. You plan on harassing her now, too?" He finally lifts his head and looks me dead in the eye with a look on his face I've never seen before. His eyes are glossed over and I'm pretty sure he's still drunk to have the nerve to talk to me like this.

"Nah, I don't bully the good ones. Just the lying snakes who take something that don't belong to them." My dignity to be exact. Not to mention, a video of me in a vulnerable state.

He laughs. "Thieves believe everyone steals from them."

Dropping my shoulders, I spin around to face him. "What's that supposed to mean? You calling me a thief, McCoy?"

With dipped brows, he leans forward with his elbows pressed to his knees and looks down at his feet. "I am. I don't trust you anymore. In fact, it wouldn't surprise me if you stole my damn shoe."

Bending down, I pick up his shoe off the floor that I ran out and grabbed before going into Shay's room and I chuck it at him full force. He doesn't even attempt to catch it. He just sways his body to the side and lets it fly over the couch.

"Maybe you need to know the facts before you draw accusations. But, mark my words, I plan to steal that smirk right off your face." I don't say what else I'm thinking because I like the element of surprise. *I plan to replace it with a desperate plea. A cry for help. A scream for mercy. You did fucking take something from me.*

Something I can never get back, but revenge is sweet. I point a finger at him. "You can run, but you can't hide." With that, I pull the door open and step out into the night air. Drawing in a deep breath, I stop myself from going back in there and tearing into his mind and heart, shredding any memories he holds from that day.

Why the fuck does he get under my skin like this? More than anyone has my entire life. Better yet, why do I let him?

It's like I keep coming back for more because I can't stay away.

CHAPTER EIGHT

WYATT

My mouth tastes like ass when I open my eyes. Sun shines brightly through the uncovered windows and the smell of bacon fills my senses. My stomach growls at the scent, but the dire need of water overpowers my hunger.

Rolling off the couch, I grab my sock that slipped off in the night. Then I remember—Tommy was here. Not only was he here, but we had a confrontation in the middle of the night while my head was spinning and I was swallowing down the stale beer that was rising in my throat.

He threatened me. *You can run but you can't hide.* Just when I think he can't take up any more space in my heart, he blows the damn thing apart.

"Good morning, Sunshine." Shay walks in with a cup of liquid gold. The contents slosh around as the ice clanks against the full glass.

I lick my lips and grab it from her. "You're an angel." I tip it back and guzzle the water down.

"And how are we feeling this morning?" She smirks. "It was quite a night for you."

Letting out a pent-up breath, I drop my head back on the

cushion of the couch while I sit on the floor with my knees up. "How bad was I?"

When she laughs, it leads me to believe it wasn't as bad as I'm thinking. "You were fine. A little more outspoken than usual, but you passed right out and slept like a baby.

If only that were true. I slept, but woke suddenly when I felt the presence of the devil himself invade the space of the living room at one o'clock in the morning.

"Tommy carried you in and you never even batted an eye."

I feel my forehead crease as my neck draws back. "Tommy carried me in? Like in his arms? Into the house?" It's all coming back to me now. I did bat an eye, more than once.

"Mmmhmm. He's not as bad as you think, Wyatt."

And I laugh. Then laugh some more. "Yeah, ok. He's a saint, Shay." She has no idea who Tommy really is. Then again, he only gives that version of himself to me. I shouldn't feel honored that I get special treatment, but the sick and twisted side of me kinda does.

Dropping down on the couch, she takes the glass from me and sets it on the end table. "I don't get it. Why do you hate him so much? He's not the same as his friends. He even defended you last night to Shane."

Shane.

Oh my God, Shane. We broke up last night. My heart sinks deep into the pit of my stomach, stirring up the beer inside and pushing the liquid up my throat. "Oh, shit." I push myself off the floor and haul ass to the bathroom. *I'm gonna be sick.*

Popping the lid of the toilet up, I bend over and it all spills out.

Suddenly, that bacon doesn't smell good anymore. In fact, it only makes me feel worse. I slap the bathroom door shut so Shay doesn't have to witness this before it all comes out again.

Once my stomach is emptied, I drop back on the floor with my back pressed to the wall. I can't believe I ended things with

Shane in a fit of drunken stupidity. Now, I not only have Tommy on my ass, but I also have the entire varsity football team as well. Shane is their god, and if he begins targeting me and picking at old wounds, they're sure to follow suit. I might as well just quit school and start working for Dad now. If I don't need a degree to work at Magna Tech, I shouldn't need a high school diploma.

Pushing myself off the floor, I flush the toilet and grab a bottle of mouthwash from the cabinet behind the mirror. Tipping it up, I drop some in my mouth without letting the rim touch my lips. Giving it a swish, I stop when I hear voices. I swish a little more then spit it out and run some water in the sink before wiping the back of my hand across my mouth.

When I walk out, the sickness pools again, but the need to throw up isn't there. It's just this twirling ache that has me feeling like I need to get the hell out of this house.

He's here. This is not like him at all. Taking a girl home from a party, screwing her, and then coming back in the morning with...is that coffee and donuts? I shouldn't take notice that there's only one coffee, but I do.

Tommy whispers something in Shay's ear then looks at me and waves his hand over his shoulder. "Come on. I'm giving you a ride home."

My eyes dart to Shay. "What?"

"Tommy and I have plans for the day. He's gonna run you home while I get ready."

"I'm not riding with him." And what about the bacon? I'm pretty sure I smelled pancakes, too. My appetite is gone, but still, I don't like this.

"Stop it, Wyatt." Shay laughs. As if I'm the one being ridiculous.

"Hurry up or you can walk." Tommy goes over to the door. He stops right in front of it with his fingers wrapped around the handle and turns around. "You coming, or what?"

Throwing Shay the biggest and worst scowl my face can possibly make, my eyes burn into hers, just so she knows how much I do not like this. Call me childish, but being alone in a confined space with Tommy is the worst idea ever. Not only because I'm pretty sure he wants to chop my head off and use my mouth as his own personal toy, but also, because I probably wouldn't put up a fight if he did.

Once I'm sure I've made my point, I growl with each step that leads me to the door. Tommy smirks at me and gestures me to go first. I shake my head in disapproval of whatever he's pulling here. I can't help but get the feeling this is all part of a screwed-up plan he's had brewing.

Still reeling from the effects of last night, I take a few extra breaths of the fresh air to try and clear my head. I've never been drunk before, but the way I'm feeling right now, I can't tell if it's a hangover or if I'm still intoxicated.

Tommy jumps in the driver's seat of his truck and as awkward as it feels, I open the passenger side and get in. My body is totally against me right now. My heart feels all warm and fuzzy being in this position. I hate that I'm so attracted to this guy.

Even the smell of his truck and seeing his personal belongings thrown around has me feeling some sort of way. I watch as he shifts the truck in reverse, taking note of the way his fingers wrap around the shifter.

Everything he does is so graceful and with such confidence. Looking up, I shiver when his arm drapes over the headrest of the passenger seat. His hand mere inches from touching the back of my head. The smell of his deodorant rolls out from his pits and goddamnit, even that gives me butterflies. His neck twists as he looks over his shoulder and backs the truck up.

As he turns back to look out the windshield, he catches me watching him. He gives me a throaty roar. "What are you looking at?"

I snap my head around quickly and peer out the passenger window. "Nothing."

Out of the corner of my eye, I continue to watch him as the fingers of his right hand grip the steering wheel—his veins prominent—while his left hand lays gently on top of his lap.

"Why are you so fucking weird, McCoy?"

I look over at him. "Why do you keep calling me, McCoy? You've always called me, Wyatt." It's true. He always did until a couple months ago.

"You're ignoring the question."

I shake my head. "No. You are. Why not call me by my name?" Is it too personal for him? Does it make what happened between us feel less real if he calls me by my last name?

He doesn't respond. He flicks the blinker up and looks both ways before turning onto the main road toward our street.

Changing the subject, I attempt to break the tension. "What are you and Shay doing today?"

"None of your damn business."

My mouth forms a wide O. "Okaaaay then." I tap my hands to both legs in a nervous manner. "Did you have fun at the party?"

As if I pissed him off, he shouts, "Would you quit asking so many damn questions?"

With wide eyes, I direct my attention to the passenger window again. I bite back a smile and really try hard not to laugh, but I fail miserably.

"What the fuck is so funny?"

"You. You're such an ass—"

"Only to those who deserve it."

"I wasn't finished. You're such an ass to me but so kind to everyone else—well except Shane, but that's a different story. So, why? Why do I get the special treatment?"

"As I just said, I'm only an ass to those who deserve it."

Turning my entire body toward him, I tuck one leg under

the other. "Ok, tell me then, why do I deserve it? Let's get the elephant out of the...truck. What did I ever do to you?"

"Shut up, Wyatt."

"Ohhh, so now I'm Wyatt again. You're really confusing, you know that."

"I said, shut up!" he shouts louder.

"If this is because of what…."

His foot slams on the brake and my entire body flies forward. If it weren't for the seatbelt, I'd be out the windshield right now.

In an instant, his seatbelt unlocks and he's leaning over the seat. Taking my chin between his fingers, I breathe in his scent, getting drunk all over again. Fuck me if I don't like it when he's rough. Man, I really hate the effect he has on me.

His jaw clenches as he bares his white teeth. "Don't you dare say it. Don't you ever fucking say it. Do you hear me?"

I really shouldn't say it. But the urge to push him further is painfully real. "Because of what happened in the locker room?"

"It's in your best interest to forget about that day."

"You expect me to forget about it. But I can guarantee it's all you think about it. Isn't it? You liked the way my lips felt around your dick."

His expression freezes. I swear I can see the beating of his heart through the fabric of his all-white t-shirt right beneath the silver ball of his nipple piercing.

"You want the truth? I feel dirty. Disgusted. I fucking hate myself for what happened. So yeah, I think about it and it makes me fucking crazy."

"Then why'd you carry me in the house last night? Why am I here right now?"

His grip slides down to my neck while his eyes land on my lips. We're stopped right on the side of the road as cars fly past. One of the drivers lays heavy on the horn, but Tommy doesn't budge. "Because I want the truth. I want you to admit you were behind that SD card that was sent to me. And I want you to tell me it was the only one."

His hold on me loosens enough for me to breathe and speak. "We both know that would be a lie. But if you need me to tell you that so you're convinced no one else knows, then yeah, I set up the camera and I sent the card," my brows raise and my lip curls upward, "which has the only proof that I sucked your dick and you liked it."

Giving my head a shove back, he retreats and I assume he's satisfied with my lie. But then he turns off the truck, pulls out his keys, and swings his door open before getting out and closing it. Walking with heavy steps across the front of the truck and over to a cemetery that sits outside my window.

Pushing through a black, wrought-iron gate, he keeps going. *What the hell is he doing?*

Pulling the door handle, I hop out. There's a dry spell in the state and drawing in a deep breath, my throat feels coarse. It could be attributed to dehydration, but blaming the weather is more feasible than the reminder of my drunken stupor last night.

"Where are you going?" I shout as Tommy continues on his way. The gate slams behind him and I look over my shoulder to see if anyone is watching—lurking. A shiver trails down my spine and this dark cloud cascades over me. Eerie and unwanted as I follow Tommy through the gate.

This is no modern-day cemetery. With vintage stones set from the early nineteen hundreds before Redwood grew from village to town status. Tumbleweeds lie across the ground of the cemetery and the landscaping hasn't had attention in years.

It's not the first time I've been here. When I was younger, some of the neighborhood kids and I used to walk down here in the middle of the night for kicks to try and scare the shit out of ourselves. In fact, I'm pretty sure everyone in this town has been here at least once in their lives.

"Would you stop," I holler, louder this time as he keeps on walking farther into the maze of stones. "Shit," I sigh as I pick up my pace until I'm full blown running toward him. It's no lie that I don't handle creepy situations well. Death, ghosts, spirits —not my thing. I can handle a good slasher movie, but throw in an exorcist and I'm out.

A cool breeze hits my side and my entire body shudders. It's seventy degrees out. There should not be a cold gust coming from anywhere but a damn freezer.

When I finally catch up to Tommy, I grab him by the wrist, spinning him to face me. Two hands take hold of my arms, pushing me back farther and farther until my calves hit—I turn around to look—Meredith Kemper's resting place. "Tell me the fucking truth, Wyatt. I need the truth." He looks fearful. Another new expression.

"You want the truth? I didn't do it. I don't know who recorded us. I wish I could say it was me, but it wasn't." All bull-shit and anger aside, we're on the same team when it comes to this. But, I can't tell him it wasn't meant to shake his world. It was meant to blow up mine. Someone knows that I saw Josh that night, and I'm pretty sure they were in the locker room that day. I just don't know who it is or what they want from me.

Exhaling a deep breath, his chin drops to his chest. "Fuck!" he screams, gripping the sides of his head. He looks me in the eyes. "So someone knows?"

Looking left, then right, I make a suggestion and point over my shoulder. "Can we go talk about this in the truck?"

His head shakes, no. "If someone was watching us then, they could be watching us now." Looking around in every direction, he takes me by the wrist and begins leading me alongside him as we walk over to the old mausoleum. Stacked blocks with trickled black stains descend downward due to aging and a cement slab roof make up the small nine-hundred square foot structure.

Tommy pushes open the tin door and it recoils off the inside wall, causing a loud clink that has my body tensing up. It's completely empty with rows of coffin-sized slots in the walls.

"I don't know about this," I tell him before realizing I'm holding onto his arm with both hands. Once we're inside and the door shuts, he drops my arm immediately and shakes off my hold on him.

His back presses to the door and his arms cross over his chest so tightly that his veins descend down his forearms. Bluish purple, bulging, and intimidating. "You wanna leave here? Then you're telling me everything." His voice rises. "Everything!"

My voice cracks. "I told you. I didn't do it."

"Did Shane?"

Shrugging a shoulder, I'm honest with him. "I don't know. I didn't think so, but now I'm not so sure. He's pretty adamant about me staying away from you, so it's possible."

"Did you tell him?'

"What? No. Well, not about that. He knows the extent of your bullying. Saw the artwork you left me. Notices the way you..look at me. The way I look at you."

Forcing his eyebrows together, he scoffs. "You're delusional. I barely even notice you."

"Why do you do this? It's just you and me here. No cameras, no classmates, no friends. For once, just own up to what happened between us. Admit you feel something so I don't feel like I'm going crazy, day in and day out."

His tone drops and he begins picking at a rock that sticks into the cement of one of the open slots in the wall. "I don't know what you're talking about."

Dropping my shoulders, I surrender to defeat. "Fine. Then let's get the hell out of here. This place is creepy."

"Uh uh." He takes a step toward me. "I'm not done. I told you, we're not leaving until I get answers. If it wasn't Shane, then who was it?"

I could tell him I have my theories, but it would only raise more suspicion on my behalf. There's no way he can know about Anderson. Or that I saw Josh dead in the road before his body miraculously ended up in the pastor's basement. "Your guess is as good as mine." I swallow hard when he takes another step.

Tipping his head up, he scoffs. "You're lying."

I take a step backward. Then another. And another. Until my back hits the far wall and we're completely immersed inside the enclosed mausoleum. I'm just grateful it's empty, but it's still dark and suffocating.

Being this close to Tommy in this confined space has me gasping for breath as my heart beats at an unprecedented rate.

Caging me in, Tommy presses his hands on either side of the wall. "Is there something you need to tell me? Something you've been hiding? A secret, perhaps?"

I chuckle. Something I do often when I'm nervous. "I'm an open book. No secrets here." God, how I wish that were true.

"Someone has a reason for watching us. I doubt it was because they're into porn. No, they had a…" his voice trails off and he straightens his back, dropping his hands like he had an epiphany, "it was Shane." Snapping his fingers, he screams, "Fuck! I knew it. It was him."

"What? Why do you think that? What happened?"

"Motherfucker." He draws back his fist and my body heaves when it flies straight past me and plants itself right in the cement behind my head. "God damnit. He was on that app." He shakes his fist and I feel the slap of fresh blood hit my cheek. My fingers slide down my cheek and I try to look at my hand, but it's too dark. Though, I feel the sticky liquid between my fingertips.

Wiping them on my pants, I grab his hand to try and get a look at it. "Why the hell did you do that?" Normally the sight of blood would make me queasy, but it helps that I can't see it.

"I'm gonna kill him, but first…" His words trail off.

I don't even see it coming when his hands grab ahold of my face and he pulls my mouth to his. I'm pretty sure my heart stopped beating and I might as well just crawl into one of those coffin holes. His soft lips press so firmly to mine, spilling hate into my mouth as his tongue slides in and wages war with mine. I fear his jaw will clamp down and tear off the tip of my tongue if I don't put some space between us. But, I don't—I can't. He tastes so good and his touch—this kiss—has taken over my entire body.

Strong fingertips dig into the side of my face. I couldn't escape this if I wanted to. Lifting my arms that were draped at my side, I wrap them around his neck and succumb to our mutual desires. Giving him back everything he's giving to me. A kiss meant to be laced with anger and shame, but feels like fate. It feels like everything it shouldn't be.

All my willpower and modesty fly out the door as I stretch my hand down between us and cup his dick in my hands. At the risk of getting murdered in this dilapidated structure, I take my chances. He doesn't push me away, instead he grinds back against me while our mouths continue to engage in a ferocious mess of unwanted emotions. Twisting, pushing, biting as our hearts pound against each other's chest.

Just when I think that a thousand cameras can't stop what is coming, he eases up. Slowly, our mouths detach while our lips still linger together gently. His eyes open and while it's dark, I can see the glow of his ocean blues. Dropping his hands, he takes a step back.

Then I see it. Like a knife to my chest. A repeat of the events in the locker room that raised hell. The shame returns. His head shakes. Starting in slow nods back and forth, picking up speed. "No," he deadpans. "I shouldn't have done that. It can't happen again."

Once again, I'm mind-blown because, just like last time, he

set this in motion. He cornered me and he kissed me. Not the other way around. Instead of feeling pain, I pull the knife out of my chest and I fire back. "You did this!" I shout, "You came on to me." I laugh, but it's sarcastic and airy. "Don't try and pretend I did something wrong...again!"

"Why didn't you stop me?" he shouts.

"Me? Stop you? As if that is even an option. First of all, I like you. For some fucked-up reason, even though all you do is treat me like I ruined your life, I really like you. Second of all, you scare the shit out of me, Tommy."

He shakes a finger at me. "You're smart to be scared of me."

That's all he has to say. I just told him I liked him and he agrees I should be scared.

"Yeah, you've made that very clear with your history of home invasion, vandalism and creepy notes."

Furrowing his brows in the sliver of light that passes through the crack in the door, his head twists. "Notes?"

"Don't play dumb. I might look stupid, but I'm a master chess player, reading my opponent is what I do."

"I didn't leave any notes."

Calling this a dead-end conversation, I stalk past him. Tucking my erect dick up in the waistline of my shorts, so it's not bulging out, I go to walk out of this death-ridden place.

Jerking me back by my shoulder, he slams me against the row of crypts. "Show me the note."

"I don't have it with me."

With angry eyes and a stern voice, he, once again, behaves like *I* did something wrong. "What did it say?"

"I don't know. Something like 'change your path. If it happens again, I'll feel their wrath.' But, it was you. So, don't try and throw me off and make me believe it was someone else. You know damn well what it said."

He shakes his head. "Wasn't me."

Searching his expression for a reason to doubt what he's

saying, I come up empty-handed. Maybe he is telling the truth. It's possible he's as clueless as I am.

But, am I really? There are two possible suspects that are capable of doing this. Shane, and the person who is likely blowing up my phone right now as it vibrates in my pocket —Anderson.

CHAPTER NINE

TOMMY

"Ignore it." I jerk his hand out of his pocket as he goes to pull his phone out. "We have to figure this out."

Rubbing my battered knuckles, I think.

Someone left Wyatt a note. This whole time he's thought it was me. And this whole time, I thought he was behind the video. I'm more certain than ever that my secret has been exposed. A deep and painful secret. One that has been lacerating my soul. Causing me to drink heavily just so I can sleep. I've been working out like an animal just to try and shut off my thoughts. If I could reach into my brain and pull out the memory, I'd do it. I'd erase it and never let it happen again. But, since it did happen, and I do remember, it's all I think about. *He* is all I think about.

"I have my guesses who it could be," I tell him as we stand mere inches from each other. Shane was on the WatchMeNow app. It's possible he's planning on sharing the video on there. I'll fucking kill him if he does so.

Wyatt licks his lips and I try really fucking hard not to notice the way the tip of his tongue wets them. *Fuck. Why is this happening to me?*

Better yet, what does this mean? I've never had an interest in a guy before. Sure, I've been curious. But I always thought it was normal. Wyatt, though, he doesn't just seduce my body, he seduces my mind.

Shaking the thoughts away, I regain my focus. Someone is leaving mysterious notes for Wyatt. Someone also did something similar to Willa. It's very possible these cases are connected. Which means I need to do what everyone asked and track her phone.

Chewing on my bottom lip, I think for a second before I say what I'm about to say. "I need something from you." The corner of his lip curls up and I scoff. "Not that." I wanna smack him for even insinuating what I know he's thinking. Then again, I just did fucking kiss him, which was a huge mistake. What kind of guy just goes around kissing guys? I refuse to admit it to myself. I won't. I like women.

Fuck. Quit thinking about it! I wanna scream at myself and if I were alone, I'd probably let it all out at the top of my lungs.

His arms cross over his chest. "And why should I give you anything?"

"Seriously? Someone is leaving you threatening notes. Don't you wanna know who it is?" This would probably be an appropriate time to ask him what he was doing on Marni's road the night Josh was killed, but I don't trust him—not yet.

Admitting I know, also means confessing that I know Josh was out there. I'm not yet ready to raise suspicion in his mind. Trust doesn't come easy to me. Not because I've been wronged, but because I'm a firm believer that one must earn it. Wyatt hasn't done that. In fact, he's further away from it than most strangers. For all I know, this is all just a ploy between him and Shane. They could be working together to try and get to all of us because Wyatt killed Josh. They could know more than we think. They could know everything.

"Ok. What's your plan and how am I supposed to help?"

"We need to get into Magna Tech and trace a phone."

I know exactly what's coming next.

"Who's phone?"

"It doesn't matter. But, there's a good chance once we know who made a call on it, we'll also know who was watching us—and left you the note."

Pressing his fingertips to his temples, he rubs in a circular motion. "I don't think I can get you in there. You'd have to give me the phone."

"No. I'm going with you." It's not even a question. I have no idea what could come up and I need to be the one to get the data first.

"You know this is illegal, right?"

"Really?" I huff, "that's your concern? You're not worried at all that you're about to feel someone's wrath? As the note stated."

"Honestly? Now that I know it wasn't you—assuming I believe you—I'm not worried at all. I have nothing to lose."

Biting down hard, I grind my teeth, seething. "Well, I have everything to lose. So get me in that goddamn building." My shoulder nudges hard against his as I push the door open. I don't even hold it open or wait for him, I just take long strides toward my truck.

"I'm sorry I'm not good enough for you," he shouts. I turn around to look at him as he stands in front of the door with his hands in his pockets. "I'm sorry that when you look at me all you feel is shame and regret."

There's a pang in my chest that has me questioning everything I say and do, but I fight like hell to ignore it. Mistake after mistake has landed me in a mess of emotions. If I'd just fought harder against temptation, or the urges that overcome me, I could have just continued on with my damn life. Graduate high school, leave Redwood for art school, get me a studio apartment and eventually a girl to settle down with—but he came and shook things up. It's easier to blame him than accept what I feel may be true. No. It's just a phase. Eventually, I will rid my mind of him.

As Wyatt draws closer, I look down at the ground as I dig the toe of my boot into the dirt. His eyes hold immense pain and I know it's because of me. There's no denying this guy likes me. I'm pretty sure he has for a while. Why couldn't he like Zed, or Talon, or Lars. Why me?

"Give me a couple days. Given my new title at Magna, I should be able to get in there and check things out. It'll give me a chance to know exactly what I'm doing before we track the phone."

Nodding, I press my lips into a thin line. "Let's get out of here."

"Yeah. You've got a date to get to."

We walk over to the truck and both get in. "It's not a date. Shay knows this isn't going anywhere." I start the engine and shift in drive.

Wyatt's body sways a bit as we pull back onto the road. "Was that before or after you screwed her last night?"

Scoffing, I look at him. His eyebrows are drawn up in question and I'm not sure if it's because he's ready to defend his best friend or because he's jealous. "It's Shay. Trust me, she's fine with this."

In a perfect world, I'd be attracted to Shay. She's friends with Marni and the guys seem to tolerate her. She's not their biggest fan, but with some time, she could join the family. But, I don't have those feelings for her. She's a cute girl with a nice ass, but we lack chemistry and a connection. I don't have that gnawing need to be around her. To show up somewhere just because I know she'll be there. Stealing glances at her. Shielding my heart out of fear that she'll find a way in. There's only one person who's doing that to me right now, and I fucking hate myself for it.

Leaning forward, I look both ways before turning at the stop sign. Wyatt is being unusually quiet. Normally, he's a chatterbox. Anytime I see him out, he's always smiling and cracking jokes. It's strange how a person can become someone else under different circumstances. For example, my behavior toward Wyatt is not normal. Nor is my behavior toward Shane. I'm not a bully. I despise bullying. Probably should speak up more when my friends do it, so I guess I'm guilty in that aspect, but these two guys are different. Shane deserves it —but does Wyatt deserve as much hate as I'm throwing his way?

Glancing over at him, I catch him looking out the window. He's deep in thought and I wanna claw my way into his brain just to know what he's thinking about. Is it me? Shane? Does he miss him?

His head pivots and his mouth opens to speak, but he stops when he realizes I was looking at him. "What were you gonna say?" My eyes swerve from him back to the road.

Solemness washes over his face. As if he feels like he just caught me stealing a glance, as he's mentioned before. Which is absurd. Sure, I notice Wyatt, but I don't check him out.

"I was gonna ask where you and Shay are going?"

"Actually, I have to cancel with her. Forgot something came up."

"You forgot something came up?" A deep laugh escapes his throat. "Lame excuse."

"It's not an excuse. It's true. I've gotta talk to the guys about all this. If Shane is the one behind the video and the note left for you, he needs to be stopped."

"Hold up just a minute. *If* Shane is behind it all, then it has nothing to do with you. It's me he's after. You guys need to just leave him alone."

Cocking a brow, I sneer, "Are you still into this guy? He's a grade-A douchebag."

"You don't know him like I do."

Yeah, I'd say so. After the other night, I know a lot more about these two than I care to. "I know enough. Come on, Wyatt. The guy treats you like you're an inconvenience in his life. Pushes you around, tucks you under his arm around his friends but doesn't let you speak. Not to mention, he had you pinned to the wall in the bathroom."

"Yeah, well you just did the same inside a building that houses rotting corpses, and here I am."

"But I'm nothing to you. It's not like you and I are even friends, let alone—"

"What? Come on. Say it. Let alone, lovers?"

"Lovers?" I laugh. "Is that what it's called?"

"Ok. Fuck buddies, partners, boyfriends. Is that better?"

"All of the above. Never have been and never will be. I did what I did for a reason. Treating you the way I have been isn't just for kicks. Regardless of whether or not you are behind that video—which I'm still considering—you fucked me up."

"I fucked you up? Please, tell me how I did that, Tommy, because I'd really like to know." His body shifts and he orbits around so that all of him is facing me. Curling one leg under the other, he taps his chin. "Go on. Explain."

This is a different side to Wyatt. I'm not sure I've seen him get fired up before. I kind of like it. "Alright, it's just us in here. No one is watching or recording. You broke me."

"I *broke* you?"

"Would you quit repeating what I say, it's really annoying."

"I'm just curious how I did any of these things when everything that happened between us was consensual. If anything, I'd say you're the one who broke me. You practically forced me on my knees in that locker room."

"Ohhh, so now you're saying I made you do it? Not a chance in hell. You wanted to do it."

Raising a shoulder, he smirks. "And you liked it."

"In the moment, maybe. Who doesn't like getting their dick sucked. The minute it was over, I hated myself. For the rest of my life, I will hate myself." It's the cold hard truth. I feel dirty and wrong. Wyatt wasn't lying when he said that when I look at him I feel shame and regret. I feel it so deep it literally pains me. There are times he's near and I question why I get so worked up and agitated, and I contribute it to what happened.

Silence wraps itself around us and squeezes, making the small space of this truck feel suffocating.

"You don't have to explain it to me. One of the reasons I put up with what you do and don't tell anyone is because I get it. I don't play victim because I'm not one. You are."

"That doesn't make any sense. How am I a victim?"

"Because there's a war inside your head and until it's over and you accept your identity, it's holding your heart hostage." He turns away, avoiding eye contact. "I've been there and it's lonely as hell."

He's wrong. I know who I am. I know what I want. Ok, maybe there is a small possibility that I might find him attractive. Not just his body, but his mind. A very small part, but that doesn't mean I'm gay. I'm not attracted to all men, just him. I don't know what that means.

Fuck. There is a war in my head—but he started it.

On impulse, I shout, "Why couldn't you just stay the fuck away!"

"Look, Tommy. It's not black and white at first. You're gonna be really fucking angry and confused—"

I cut him off, shouting even louder, "Would you shut the hell up!"

The rest of the drive is silent.

When I pull through the gate to Wyatt's driveway, he already has his fingers wrapped around the handle. "One more thing," I tell him. "When you see me around, you don't see me. Got it?" He doesn't even look at me when I say the words.

Before I even come to a complete stop, the door is swinging open and he's out. He slams it shut, jogs up to the house and doesn't even give me a second look. Why would he?

I'm a fucking asshole.

CHAPTER TEN

WYATT

Closing the door behind me, I press my back to it. My eyes close while my heart aches. It's an indescribable pain and not something I've felt before. As if I'm grieving the loss of something I never even had.

For a brief moment today, I felt like I may have broken through Tommy's rock-solid barrier. For a split second, I was envisioning a future with him. A sliver of an instant where I physically felt like I was tangled in his arms and belonged in his heart.

But then reality slapped me in the face. It was wishful thinking—a daydream. But, hell if I wouldn't rip out a chunk of my heart just to make his feel whole. I know he's fighting himself and I know that pain more than he thinks.

I don't blame him, and I certainly don't hate him. A couple days ago, I may have been close. But now, more than ever, I'm convinced it's not me he has a problem with…it's himself.

In an attempt to push these thoughts away, I pull my phone out of my pocket and review the chain of missed calls from Anderson. Tapping the button on the side, I close the home screen and stick it back in my pocket.

It's been months and I still haven't told Marni anything; I don't know why he thinks I will now. She's the last person I'd ever want to find out what I did. I can barely stand my own reflection. There's no doubt she'd never be able to look at me the same again.

The house is quiet, which leads me to believe Mom is still on her 'trip' and Dad is working, as per usual. Kicking my shoes off, I give them a shove to the side of the door. I'm still feeling the effects of my little binger last night and my empty stomach isn't helping matters. "Elsa," I yell out. "You here?"

There's a shuffle in the kitchen. With light steps, I walk through the corridor to where Elsa is drying her hands on her apron. "Hey, would you mind making me something light to eat."

With wide eyes, she presses the back of her hand to my forehead. "Oh, Wyatt. You don't look well. Are you sick?"

"I'm fine. Just a late night."

She smiles. "Oh yes. I remember those days." Reclaiming her place in front of the sink, she continues, "What would you like? Soup? Salad?"

"Soup and an extra-large glass of water with ice sounds good. Could you bring it up to my room when it's ready?"

"Right away. You go rest."

"Thanks, Elsa." I tell her with a half-smile.

"Oh, and Wyatt, you have company waiting for you." She winks while my eyes pop wide open.

"Company?"

"Mmhmm. Your guy friend has been waiting for about thirty minutes."

Without another word, I walk briskly out of the kitchen. My white socks slide across the freshly waxed hardwood floors, sending me to the steps faster than planned. I grab the banister to stop myself and hurry up the staircase.

I know exactly who's waiting for me on the other side of that door. I'm just not sure what version I'll be getting. The Shane who wants to belittle me and make me feel dumb, or the one who is crazy obsessed with my body and sweet talks his way into my bed.

Turning the handle, I push the door open, and sure enough, there he is. Kicked back on my bed with his hands pretzeled behind his head and ankles crossed in front of him. As soon as I see the look on his face, I know exactly how this is going to go. "What are you doing here?" I hiss.

"Enjoy your night?"

Reaching into my pocket, I pull out my keys and my phone and drop them on my desk. "Not really. You pretty much ruined it for me."

"Don't blame me for that shit. You're the one who called it quits and chose your side."

"My side?" I chuckle. "What the hell is that supposed to mean?"

His back slides against the headboard as he pushes himself up. "You know exactly what I'm talking about. In your head, you think you actually have a chance with Tommy. You're fucking delusional."

I meet his stare as I stand at the end of the bed. "Ending things between us has nothing to do with Tommy and everything to do with you treating me like I'm an inconvenience in your life."

"How'd you get home, Wyatt?" His thumb grazes his chin. "Hmm? Tell me who the fuck brought you home." I can sense that he's getting angry and I need to defuse the bomb before things escalate. But, there is no sense in lying, considering that my window faces the driveway and I'm sure he was watching and waiting.

"Tommy dropped me off. So, what."

"Thanks for not trying to deny. Appreciate that. Where did

you stay last night?" He holds up a hand. "Wait. Better yet, where did Tommy stay? I know you were with Shay."

Shrugging a shoulder, I tell him the truth. "He stayed there for half of the night and then left. Listen, if you're so convinced Tommy would never give me the time of day, why are you so damn jealous of him?"

"Jealous?" He laughs. "You think I'm jealous?" His legs swing over the side of the bed and in one big step, he's at my side. "Of that douchebag?"

Taking a step back, I avoid eye contact. "Just calling it like I see it." I'm not sure why he feels so threatened by Tommy. Unless….unless he knows more than I think he does. Turning, I level with him. "Why do you hate him so much?"

"Hate's too light of a word. I despise him and all of his scoundrel friends."

"But, why? There has to be a reason." Shane and those guys have never gotten along. I'm not sure why, but things have gotten more tense this year. Tommy can't stand Shane's pompous attitude and Shane acts like he's jealous of Tommy. I'm not sure why, but he does.

"I've seen the way you look at him. I've also seen the way he acts around you. He can call us fags and snub us, but he does it for a reason—to hide the fact that he's the exact same."

"Wait a minute, are you telling me you think Tommy is gay?"

"I *know* Tommy is gay."

"How can you be so sure?" I already know this to be true, even if Tommy hasn't admitted it to himself, but how would Shane know this? Sure, I've heard gaydar is a thing, but Tommy definitely does not put off gay vibes. "Have you fooled around with him?" I spit out, with no thought behind it.

"Fuck no!" he shouts before dropping his tone. "But you have, haven't you?"

I shake my head. "No. I haven't." I'd never betray Tommy in

that way. He'll out himself when he's ready. "Look, Shane. We've had some good times, but this is too toxic for me and I think we need to just go our separate ways like we decided last night." I try to be as nice as I can about it without pissing him off.

"You're serious? *You* are dumping *me*?" He laughs, like I said something funny. There's a beat of silence before he grabs me by the face and presses his closed lips to mine. Our mouths crash firmly and hold tight with little to no movement. Trying to pull out of it, he presses harder. Sliding one hand down between us and cupping my dick in his hand.

With his lips still ghosting mine, he mutters, "I don't fucking think so."

In an attempt to assuage his temper that's rising, I place a calming hand on his shoulder. "Let's just talk about this."

"Uh uh. We have nothing to talk about. I fucking made you. You're nothing without me. A ghost in the halls, Shay and Marni's third wheel at parties. With me, you shined. I can break you just as fast as I gave you a name. You think you're too good for me now because you're running around with Tommy boy and his deranged friends?"

"I don't think that at all. I told you, this has nothing to do with Tommy. We're just...I'm just not happy anymore."

"He'll never give you what I can. He'll never make you feel as good as I make you feel." Grabbing me by the waist, he spins me around and pushes me face down on the bed. He's fully equipped to toss me around like I'm a child. I'm not skin and bones, but he's got me by about fifty pounds of solid muscle. When I go to turn over to my back, he shoves my face back down into the plush comforter. "If I'm leaving, I'm taking something with me to remember you by."

There's no sense in trying to fight him off when his hand slithers between my body and the bed and he undoes the button on my pants. Still face down, he slides off my pants, taking my boxers with them.

"Never forget who your first was." He lifts me by the waist until I'm on all fours. With his arm stretched underneath me, he pats my chest. "Because of that, I'll always be in here."

I'll let him believe that, and sometimes I let myself believe it, too.

I'm still on all fours when he walks over to the side of my bed and pulls open the drawer of my nightstand. "No, Shane. This isn't happening." I flip over and get to my feet. I go to reach for my pants, but he snatches them away and tosses them at the wall. I watch as they slide down it in slow motion.

A knock at the door stops us both. "Wyatt. I have your food, hun," Elsa says from outside the room.

Shane leans in, his breath hitting the lobe of my ear. "Get rid of her."

"Just leave it at the door, Elsa. Thanks." I return my attention to Shane. "You need to leave." Pushing past him, I go to retrieve my clothes off the floor.

I'm not exactly sure what happened next, but the sting in the back of my head leads to believe I was struck. Cold fingers wrap around my neck as I'm dragged back to the bed and shoved hard onto the mattress.

Shane crawls on top of me on all fours. In my face, he snarls, "I tried to protect you, Wyatt. You're no good to me now. You're tarnished. An embarrassment. A disgrace. And I plan to make your life hell for making me out to be a fool. But, I'm the least of your worries because they'll sink you first. Just wait and see."

He kisses me one last time, hard and painful. So deep that I feel my bottom lip bust open and a metallic taste seeps into my mouth. "Goodbye." He gives my cheek a tender pat and backs off the bed.

Undressed from the waist down, I lie flat on the bed and stare at the ceiling. Unable to comprehend what just happened or what he just said. He tried to protect me? Bullshit. Shane only protects himself.

Minutes pass, maybe even an hour before I force myself up. Grabbing a pair of gym shorts out of my dresser, I slide them on and open the door to find my cold soup on a tray with a dozen packs of saltine crackers next to it. I grab the water first and slam half of it. Then I pick up the tray and set it on top of my dresser before kicking the door shut.

Picking up my phone, I dial Dad.

It goes straight to voicemail, naturally.

Once it beeps, I leave a message. "Hey, Dad. I've thought a lot about what you said, and I'm ready to jump in head first. I think a future at Magna Tech working beside you is the best plan for me. I'd like to come by tomorrow and get a feel for the place, maybe pick out my office." I end the call and drop my phone back down.

It was all a lie. Working for Dad will give me a nice firm cushion for the future, but it's not my dream—it's his. But, I told Tommy I'd help him and now more than ever, I wanna know where that note came from. If it's in any way connected to whoever's phone he's tracing, then I have to try. Not just for him, but for myself.

CHAPTER ELEVEN

TOMMY

Expecting Talon's house to be full, I'm surprised when I walk in and see that it's empty. "Talon?" I holler. "Lars? Anyone?" With my shoes still on, I drop my keys into the front pocket of my jeans and walk into the kitchen.

No one. But voices coming from downstairs grab my attention. There's a bout of laughter, followed by some hooting and hollering. Pushing open the door that leads to the entertainment room, I head down the carpeted stairs.

Talon and Lars are engaged in an intense game of *Call of Duty*. Both leaned forward and thumbing their controllers like madmen. "What's up, boys?"

"Shh," Talon hushes me. "One more kill and I win this shit."

"I'm happy to see you guys are enjoying yourselves, but since when do we have time for anything fun. We've got business to tend to." I drop down on a black recliner and pull the lever on the side, kicking my feet up.

"Fuck yes!" Talon beams with excitement as he slams the controller down next to him. "And that's how it's done." His attention shifts to me like he just realized I was here. "Oh hey, Tommy."

"Double or nothing?" Lars asks, and I can only ascertain that there's some sort of wager being made. No good can ever come out of any kind of bet between any of us. Last time, Lars knocked up Willa and in three months, he's gonna be a daddy to a little girl. I feel sorry for any guy that tries to win her over when she's a teenager.

"Nah, I'll take my hundred and call it good."

"You would. I've got a baby on the way and you wipe your ass with hundreds, but sure, take it all."

Talon laughs. "Yeah, you're really hurting for money."

Lars shrugs his shoulders. "Kids are expensive."

Lars is definitely not hurting for money. All four of us guys have hefty trust funds that will take care of us for life, but most of us still prefer to work hard and build our own foundation for our children. We have dreams that are not our parents'. Talon does not. And his kids will be just fine. As will their kids.

Interrupting their banter, I cut in, "Speaking of the future. There's been a change in plans. This one's for you, Lars."

All eyes shoot to me and Lars sets his remote controller down next to him on the sectional. "What kind of change?"

"I think I convinced Wyatt to trace Willa's phone."

"No shit. You playing nice now?" Talon asks.

"I'm playing the *no questions asked* card on this one. I still need the party Friday night, though. I'll take care of the rest."

Talon grins. "If Wyatt's tracing the phone, does that mean he's not the problem?" He'd like that because it means keeping his girlfriend happy. My boys have been softened up by these chicks and I'm not sure how I feel about it.

My shoulders shrug. "I still don't know. I don't exactly trust him, but it seems someone else is a bigger problem for me than Wyatt."

"Who?" Lars asks.

"Shane."

Lars snaps his fingers. "I knew it before you even said his

name. After that encounter at the party, I knew something was up with you and Wyatt's boyfriend."

"He's not his fucking boyfriend," I snap, unintentionally. Lightening my tone, I recant my outburst. "He's not his boyfriend. They broke up." The idea of Shane even being near Wyatt rattles something fierce inside of me.

"Well, let us hear it. What did he do?" Talon says.

I wanna tell them I think he's on the app for another reason than just a good time. I also could tell them that I think he left Wyatt a threatening note and recorded me and Wyatt in the locker room, but none of that's possible. They can never know.

As much as I trust these guys, there are some things I just can't share with them. So instead, I give them one piece of truth. "I think he's the one who left Willa that message and was watching her. I don't know why, but that's what I need to find out."

Lars' eyebrows hit his forehead as if he'd have never guessed it was Shane who was stalking his girl. "What makes you think that?"

I throw my hands up and smirk. "No questions asked." I'm glad we made this rule because we've all had to use it. Some information is not meant to be disclosed. That's why they're called secrets.

Lars springs to his feet and shouts, "Fuck the rules. If Shane was harassing Willa, I wanna know it. I'll take care of him myself."

"Sit your ass down. Your turn is over. This is my shot and I get to do things the way I want. I've played the puppet too long. Now I get to pull the strings. I'll let you know once we have a trace." I stand up and brush off my pants. "Start planning that party."

AFTER I LEFT Talon's house, I went home and passed out as soon as my body hit the bed. My eyes flicker open and the sound of the vacuum running in the hall has me getting up. I grab my phone and check the time and realize it's past dinner time.

I pull open my door and see Madeline pushing the vacuum up and down the runner in the hall. "Hey, Madeline. Are my parents back yet?" I speak loud enough that she can hear me over the noise of the vacuum.

With a solemn expression, she shakes her head no. I nod in response. I didn't think they were, considering Mom texted me this morning asking me the twins' room numbers at the dorm. Which means they were popping in for a visit with my brothers.

I'm standing at the doorway, wearing just a pair of gym shorts, deep in thought, when Madeline kills the vacuum. "Everything ok, Tommy?"

"Huh." I pull my eyes off the floor and look up at her. "Oh yeah, I'm fine."

"Would you like to talk about it?" She smiles warmly. Madeline knows me better than anyone. Better than my own parents.

I respond politely, "Nah, I'm fine."

She straightens up the vacuum and walks toward me then pats the side of my head. "Something's going on up there."

"That obvious?"

"In the bedroom. Come on." She walks right past me and over to my unmade bed. I think she's going to sit down and start drilling me, but instead, she pulls the comforter off and starts straightening the grey fitted sheet.

Standing beside her, I cross my arms over my chest. "Have you ever felt like if people knew who you really were, they'd treat you differently?"

She doesn't even give herself a moment to think about it. "Did you know I used to sing?"

In typical Madeline fashion, a story is brewing. She loves to tell them at the most opportune times. I shake my head. "No, I didn't know that, but what does that—"

"I did. Oh, I loved singing. Usually when I was alone. Still do sometimes when I'm cleaning and no one is around. I once told my mother I was going to sing at The Grand Ole' Opry one day. You know what she did? She laughed at me." Madeline chuckles and brings a fluffed pillow to her chest. "My own mother laughed at my dreams." Returning to making my bed, she continues, "She told me dreams do not pay the rent and that only hard work can do that. As if singing was simply a hobby. So, I listened to her. Never took lessons. Never chased that dream because at that point, I knew it was just that—a dream."

"I still don't understand—"

She cuts me off again. "To answer your questions, yes. If I would have ignored my mother and chased that dream, she would have treated me differently. But, you know what?" Madeline takes a step forward and places her overworked hand on my cheek. "I regret it every day of my life." Dropping her hand, she gathers up some dirty laundry on my floor. "But it also would mean I wouldn't have found my way here and I like to think this is where I'm meant to be. With you, and your brothers."

"For what it's worth, I'm glad your singing career didn't take off because I'm a selfish asshole and I need you here."

Madeline smiles at my response and I know she feels the same way. I know she loves our family just as much as we love her.

"Every choice leads us down a different path. But," she shakes her finger with a stern expression, "no matter what choice you make, just be true to yourself. As someone very smart once said, *those who matter don't mind, and those who mind don't matter.* This may come as a surprise, but the ones who matter probably already know the real you, even if you haven't revealed yourself." She winks and walks out of the room with an armful of clothes.

CHAPTER TWELVE

TOMMY

Shuffling my feet, trying not to trip over them, I hurry into the kitchen to grab a water before hauling ass to class. Even if I were already in my car at this point, I'd be late. "Morning, Madeline," I say as I pull open the refrigerator. I close the door and stuff my water into the pocket of my back pack.

"Woah, woah, woah." She stops me. Pivoting around, I stand in the hand-carved door frame. I throw my hands up and catch a banana just in time before it smacks me in the face. "You're a growing boy, you need to eat."

Holding up the banana, I chuckle. "Thanks," I skedaddle over to her side and press a chaste kiss to her soft, wrinkled cheek.

"Those tattoos and piercings aren't fooling anyone, Thomas." She cups her mouth and hollers as I hurry into the mud room, "You're as sweet as they come."

"Only to you," I tell her. Dipping one foot in my shoe, then the other. "Just don't tell anyone. I have a reputation to protect." I toss her a wink before I pull open the door and step into the garage.

I get in my truck, and at this point, I don't even try to make it on time. There's no way I'll make it to school—let alone my first class—in three minutes.

Once I'm on the road, I peel back my banana and bite off half of it. Driving past Wyatt's house, I look down his narrow driveway. I'm not sure what I'm looking for because he's already at school, but for some reason, I always look.

I make it four minutes after the final bell, so I put no hurry behind my steps as I walk up to the school. The house of a million memories. If these walls could talk, I could only imagine the stories they'd tell. It's bittersweet that it's almost over. I, for one, am ready to get the hell out of this place. But I know once I'm gone, I'll wish I were back.

People will tell you to embrace these years and not rush them. Savor every moment and appreciate life before responsibility and worry take hold. Well, those people didn't grow up with my friends, and they've likely never been a stranger to their own thoughts.

After a quick stop at the office for a pass, I walk into European History, interrupting Mr. Bing's lecture. I pass him my note then slide between the desks to make my way to the back. Wyatt has his head down in his notebook and I can't help but feel like he's purposely avoiding looking at me. When I slide my chair back, I bump the table where he sits just to grab his attention. I'm not sure why I did it, but it worked.

He looks up at me with puppy dog eyes and then straight back to his book. I take a seat and flip open to chapter twelve.

"Go ahead and get a piece of paper. We're having a pop quiz on this morning's discussion."

What the hell? I just got here.

It wouldn't surprise me one bit if Mr. Bing was purposely doing this because I was late. Not to mention, I ran out of class last week without a word.

Tearing a sheet of lined paper from my notebook, I go to

grab my pencil that's always in the binding, but it's not there. I look around on the table, then to the left and right on the floor.

"Number one, The Industrial Revolution increased demand for what item?"

Fuck. I don't have a pencil.

Just as I go to raise my hand, there's a tap on my shoulder. I turn around and see Wyatt handing me one. "I want that back," he tells me.

I raise it up with a smile, my way of saying thanks.

Ten questions later, and I'm pretty sure I failed. Not because I don't know the material, but I can't fucking focus in this class.

When the bell rings, I'm the first one up, ready to get out of this suffocating room. Once I hit the hall, I draw in a deep breath and convince myself that I'm not gonna let irrational thoughts consume me today.

"So, I know you asked me not to acknowledge you, but I'm gonna need that pencil back."

"Oh, right." I push my finger down into the binding and nudge the damn thing right into the middle. Pinching my fingers together, I try and pull it out, but it's not budging. I wish my own pencil would have had this problem, then I wouldn't be standing in the middle of the hall with Wyatt breathing down my neck, waiting on me. Slapping the back of my neck, I give up. "I can't get it out. I'll buy ya a new one."

Before he can respond, I start walking forward but ram right into Shane, who stops me in my tracks. "Well, isn't this cute. New besties? Or something more?"

"Fuck off." I walk past him and once I'm about twenty feet away, I glance over my shoulder and notice Shane and a couple of his buddies have Wyatt cornered.

He's a big boy. He can take care of himself.

Hell if I don't wanna keep walking. Damn it, I really should. But, I don't. Spinning on my heels, I slam my books down on the hall floor and haul ass full force straight into the back of

Shane, taking him down. I'm oblivious to the crowd watching as I crank my fist back and plant it square on his nose. "Now do you feel tough?" I shout, "Huh?" Gripping him by the collar of his polo shirt, I lift his shoulders off the floor. "What did I tell you about bullying my classmates."

I can feel multiple hands on my back—pulling, tugging, trying to get me off of him as my legs strangle around his torso.

"Tommy!" It's Marni's voice and she's pissed. "What the hell are you doing? You're gonna get expelled." My focus shifts and in that moment of weakness, she's able to jerk me backward with the help of a couple other guys—including Wyatt.

I get to my feet with my fists still balled at my sides, ready to take further action if need be. Shane lies on his back with his head elevated and a death glare shooting straight at me. Blood trickles down the side of his face and it's a picture I need to paint one day.

Steering me away, Marni keeps a firm grip on the back of my shirt. "Come on. We need to get out of here before Principal Scott makes an appearance."

Shane doesn't dare speak about what just happened. Neither does the rest of the student body who witnessed it. We have a saying around here, *snitches are bitches.*

Looking over my shoulder, my eyes catch Wyatt's staring back at me. He looks dumbfounded while I'm sure I look the same. Our gazes hold tight until I round the corner with Marni, who takes the reins by walking me like I'm a disobedient child.

Once we're down the freshman hall, Marni shoves me against the wall. "What the fuck, Tommy!"

"What? He deserved it." I speak casually, though my adrenaline is still pumping.

"For the last four and a half months, we've fought hard not to draw attention to ourselves and that seems to be all you're doing lately." She swats my arm. "You need to pull it together before you do something really fucking dumb."

Too late for that.

"It's fine. We're fine. So I got a little carried away and punched Shane in the face. He's an asshole and I was doing a favor for everyone else in this school who have wanted to do the same."

"And last week when you two had a little quarrel. No. It's more than that. What did he do that has you so pissed off?"

The halls clear and the second period bell rings and it looks like I'm late for the second time today. Five more classes to go, I wonder if I can keep this up all day. It'd be a record for me.

"Nothing. I just don't like him. It's no big deal."

"Does it have anything to do with Wyatt? Because he's been getting special treatment from you, too."

My eyes pop wide open. "What's that supposed to mean?"

Her arms cross over her chest and she pops a hip up. "You know exactly what it means. You scream *don't bully* and yet that's exactly what you're doing to those two."

"First of all," I lean close and whisper, "in case you've forgotten, Wyatt was on the camera at the time that Josh was hit. He very well could have hit and killed him."

"Even if that were the case, which I don't think it is, so what? How is it our problem?"

An airy laugh escapes me. "Are you serious right now? It's a big problem. Whoever hit Josh is likely trying to put the pieces together. We tampered with that body, had possession of Josh's vehicle, got rid of said vehicle. He could fry us all for breakfast."

Her head shakes back and forth. "No. Wyatt wouldn't do that. If it was him–which, like I said, I doubt—then he's probably scared out of his mind. I'm sure it would have been an accident."

This entire conversation is moot because I also don't think Wyatt killed Josh. He's too good and honest. He would have called 911. However, it's better to shift the conversation to this subject rather than her drilling me about why I can't stand Shane or Wyatt.

Shane deserves my hate. I'm starting to second guess things with Wyatt now that I know and believe he wasn't behind the mysterious video of us in the locker room. It doesn't change the fact that I'm still not accepting of these feelings that have suddenly sprouted. I can't make out what they are. Mostly because I won't allow myself to go there.

"Regardless, Shane's an ass. The end."

Her chin tips up and she grins. "What's up with you and Shay? Heard you two," she air quotes, "hung out."

"It's Shay. Nothing is up with us. Come on, you know better than that."

"I think she likes you."

"Most women do. They can't resist this." I rub my hands down my puffed out chest.

I wish I could feel something toward Shay. Even more so, I wish I didn't have sex with her just so I could try and erase the memories of Wyatt's mouth around my cock. I'd give anything to unfeel the imprint of his touch on my skin. He's forever etched in my thoughts and I just wanna go back in time and take back what happened so life could be somewhat normal again—so I could feel normal again.

"Your ego is far too big for that little head of yours." She tilts her head toward the end of the hall. "Come on, we better get going."

"See ya at lunch." I wave over my shoulder before heading back to my locker.

"Tommy? Be nice to him, please. He's better than us."

I don't even have to ask who she's talking about. I know. And she's right.

Marni disappears out of sight and I drop my head, running my fingers through my hair then looking down at my hands. These knuckles can't take much more. First a brick wall and now Shane's face. When I lift my head up, I'm surprised to see Wyatt standing at my locker. He has one foot kicked up and his face in his phone. As I get closer, I notice my books tucked under his arm.

"Hey, I could've grabbed those. Thanks, man." I take the books out from under his arm.

"Yeah, you could have. But you couldn't get this, so…." He holds up his pencil.

"Nice." I chuckle. "You better go. Mr. Peterson doesn't take tardiness lightly."

"How'd you know I have Mr. Peterson for second period?"

I shrug my shoulders. I honestly have no idea how I know that. I just do. He's got European History first period, then Calculus, Chemistry, English Lit, Health, and then Physics. Second semester just started a couple weeks ago and I can barely even remember my own new schedule.

"Alright then," he says. "See ya around."

"Wyatt. Wait." I surprise him and myself at the same time.

"Someone probably ratted on me about the fight. I don't really feel like explaining myself today. I think I'm gonna head out. Wanna go?" I can feel my chest tense up. Like the weight of an elephant is sitting on it. It was spontaneous and not thought out whatsoever, which is very much me. I really need to start thinking before I speak. But suddenly, everything has changed. I have a new plan and while Wyatt is no longer a part of it, there is something I need to do.

His shoulders rise and then fall. "Ok."

Pulling my locker open, I toss my books inside and grab my backpack. In complete and utter silence, we walk down the hall and out the front door. The fresh air hits me square in the face and something swirls in my stomach. Biting back a smile, we head for my truck.

For the first time in a long while, I feel excited. Reckless.

Careless. And for another first, it's not because I'm helping the guys.

This might be wrong. But fuck if it doesn't feel right.

"Go ahead and get in. I have to make a call," I tell him. Once he does, I pull out my phone and make a silent prayer that he answers. If anyone can pull off what I plan to do, it's Zed.

CHAPTER THIRTEEN

WYATT

Here we are again. Front seat of Tommy's truck. Two days ago, he told me to shut the fuck up and made it clear that he didn't want me to acknowledge his presence. Yet, here I am. Hands folded in my lap. Sweat pooling in my palms as I rub them together nervously. I've always considered myself somewhat of a pushover, but when it comes to this guy, I'm weak—plain and simple.

Once we're out of the high school parking lot, my shoulders drop and I try to shake off some of this pent-up tension. "Where do you plan on going?"

With his elbow resting on the windowsill and his fingers tapping the top of it in tune with "My Own Prison" by Creed that plays quietly through the speakers, he glances over at me. "I've gotta take care of something in Jester Creek. You up for a little road trip?"

Jester Creek? That's over an hour away. "I'm supposed to be at Magna Tech after school. Will we be back by then?"

He flashes me a devious smirk that sends chills swimming down my spine. "Oh yeah. This won't take long."

"Why Jester Creek?"

"My family has a cabin there. I need to prep it for a guest."

I nod in understanding, though I don't understand at all. "And you thought you might just invite me to tag along because you don't wanna go alone?"

His expression drops. "Do you wanna go back to school? Because I'll take you back."

"No. No. That's not what I'm saying. I guess I'm just really confused as to why you invited me to go with you." It needs to be said. Tommy is mind-fucking me and I'm not complaining because it's giving me insight as to who Tommy Chambers really is, but it's confusing as hell.

"Honestly. I didn't put a whole lotta thought behind the plan. One minute I was planning on going to class and then I saw you at my locker, you were already late, and everything changed. Let's not make this a big thing, alright?"

"Ok." I nod again. "No big thing." Switching to a more casual conversation, I use this opportunity to just enjoy the day with a *friend*? Is that what he is? "Got any plans after graduation?"

"I'll probably stick around town for the summer then I'm heading to State for their Arts Program."

"No shit? You're going to State?" I had no idea. It almost makes the sudden change in my future all the more dreadful. I say almost, because I'm not sure it can feel much worse than it already does.

"Yeah. Aren't you going? I saw your name on the roster for 2020 grads."

I look out the window at the passing fields and begin chewing on the skin on my nails. Fighting back the self-pity I'm feeling. "Not anymore."

He huffs. "You're not going?" Almost as if he's disappointed, which eases the ache inside of me.

"I don't get to decide my future. It's been decided for me."

"Your dad?"

"Yup. The plan was always to go to school, get a degree, live a little, and then step in next to my uncle as CEO. My uncle is out, and now I'm taking the position straight outta high school."

"Damn. That's awesome."

Spewing sarcasm, I roll my eyes at the reflection of myself in the window. "Right. Awesome."

"It is. An eighteen-year-old CEO making big money straight out of school. Who wouldn't want that?"

With a half-suppressed laugh, I drop my hands back in my lap. "Well, how about an eighteen year old who spent half of his childhood being an adult and wanted to be youthful for a couple years before becoming who he's meant to be." When he doesn't respond, I can see that he's deep in thought. "I guess you're not the only one who has to pretend just to please the people around you."

Twisting his head, he scoffs. "What's that supposed to mean?"

"Parents. Friends. Society. Isn't that the reason why you're pretending?" I immediately eat my words and wish I'd just kept them to myself.

"Don't fucking do this again. I know what you're getting at," he speaks loudly. "I just need time to figure out this shit in my head. It's why I wanted you to stay away from me. It's why I can't—"

There's a long pause that has me holding my breath. "It's why I can't stay away from you."

Still holding my breath, with my eyes straight in front of me, I watch as the yellow lines ripple on the road as we pass them. I don't blink—I don't think. I just replay his words in my head. *It's why I can't stay away from you.*

I wanna ask what that means. I need to hear more. My heart craves it. The reassurance, the hope, the light at the end of this tunnel. The long nights because I can't stop thinking about him. The days filled with him trying to convince himself how much he hated what happened between us. Taking it out on me just to replace the fact that he didn't hate it all. I just need to hear him say he feels something toward me. Anything other than pure hatred. I'm hungry for words he can't give me. Not yet, anyways.

Until then, I'll just wait. Because I know now the reason I am, is because he trusts me enough to show me his depth. He gets close without fully giving himself to me. Temptation is gnawing at him and I can see the fight he wages against himself. He's bottling this up and his thoughts are spilling over and he needs a reprieve. Fighting a battle all on his own, he's chosen me to be his confidant. It's not because he's angry with me; it's because he's angry with himself.

"Ok. Well, I'm here when you're ready to talk about it. As a friend."

We drive along in silence. Staring out the window, I watch as we pass by houses and wonder what secrets live inside each of the walls surrounding them. We all have them. Secrets that could hurt us, secrets that could hurt others, and then there's the ones you'd rather die than expose.

An hour into the drive, my phone buzzes in my backpack. I unzip the front pocket and pull it out.

Marni.

"Hey, Marni. What's up?"

I catch Tommy looking at me. "I need to talk to her before you hang up."

"Who was that?" Marni says from the other end of the call.

"Umm, Tommy," I say slowly, feeling like I'm betraying him in some sort of way if I admit we're together. But, she'll know anyways if he talks to her, so I assume it's safe to share.

"Wyatt, get out of the car now! You have to get away from him."

My eyebrows pinch together and I look over at Tommy who keeps side-eyeing me. "What are you talking about?"

"Just do it. Trust me. You have to get as far away from him as you can. Don't listen to a word he says." She continues to ramble off nonsense. "He's out to hurt you, Wyatt. Please, just get out and run. Where are you? I'll come pick you up."

"Woah, calm down, girl. I'm fine. We're heading to—"

Tommy shakes his head no and mouths, "Don't tell her."

"We're heading to the city to get a....new tire." Fuck. I don't know what the hell to say. I suck at lying on the spot.

I'm still looking at Tommy who's giving me a weird-ass look. "A tire? Really?"

"Tommy's tire popped earlier and he's driving on a donut and they don't have his size in town." I shrug my shoulders. I need to get the hell off this phone.

"Turn your location on as soon as I end this call, Wyatt. Don't tell him, just do it."

"Ok," I tell her, just to stop her from worrying. "But hey, Tommy wants to talk to you first."

I hand him the phone and listen intently. Marni is really worried for some reason and she's acting very strange. I don't know what's going on, but I know Tommy isn't out to get me.

Or is he? Things have been moving forward suddenly. Is this just all some sort of sick plan to hurt me? Maybe he still thinks I sent that video. Or, maybe he really did send me that note.

I can hear Marni shouting in the distance, but I can't make out what she's saying. "Would you chill the fuck out. I'm not doing anything stupid. Listen, just rally everyone together because things have changed. *My* plans have changed." He ends the call and hands me back my phone. "Damn that girl is a handful."

Thumbing through my phone, I play it safe and turn on my location, then send Marni a share invite. "She's just looking out for me." Turning my body toward Tommy, I humor myself. "Why would she think I was in some sort of danger?"

"Because it's Marni and she thinks everyone is out to get you. Like you said, she's just looking out for you."

Tommy flips his blinker and takes a left down a dirt road. The terrain is smooth and there's a sign with an arrow pointing down the road that says, Jester Creek. I've heard of this town, but I've never been here. The scenery paired with the remoteness is supposedly breathtaking.

"Do you come out here often?" I ask him, as my nerves begin to unsettle. Marni put me on high alert and even if I don't think Tommy would hurt me, I feel like he's definitely up to something.

Extending his arm out and gripping the steering wheel tightly, he stretches his back. "When I was a kid. My brothers and I used to fish up here with my dad quite a bit."

We continue down the road and so far I've only noticed one house that sits back in the wide open space. My eyes skim my surroundings, taking note of markers, just in case I need to pull them from memory if Tommy decides to hold me captive out here.

"Who's this guest you're getting the cabin ready for?"

"Just an old acquaintance who needs a little time-out to recount his sins and recollect his thoughts."

We're about two miles down the road when Tommy takes a sharp turn down another dirt road. Then he turns abruptly into a driveway. Ash trees surround either side of the paved path. A log cabin comes into sight and it's probably one of the most beautiful homes I've ever seen. Sure, I've seen some nice houses, but the landscaping and surrounding area just really give this place a home-like feel.

The grass is pretty dried out and there's a couple dead hanging baskets on the front porch, so it's apparent the place has been neglected. I can't imagine why anyone would own this and not visit often. A retaining brick divides the house and the endless rows of trees. There's a skinny, beaten trail in the mix and I assume it leads to the creek. "This place is gorgeous."

"Yeah. It's all right." Tommy shrugs his shoulders and it makes me wonder if he has some bad memories here.

Tommy takes the truck right up to the front door and for a moment, I think he's going to plow straight through the front porch. Throwing it in park, he grabs the handle of his door and opens it. Once he's out, he stretches his arm straight up in the air and releases a drawn-out yawn. Clapping his hands together, he beams. "Alright, let's do this."

"Ok. I have no idea what we're doing, but let's do it." I get out of the passenger side and fill my lungs with the fresh clean air.

Instead of going inside the two-story cabin, Tommy walks around the side. I follow about three feet behind him and notice a baseball lying next to a tree. It's old and dirty and half of it is submerged in dirt. Tilting my head toward it, I notice the initials *TIC*—Thomas Isaac Chambers.

"You don't play ball, do you?" I ask out of curiosity. I know he played football, but don't think I've ever heard of him playing baseball.

His head twists around to look at me, but he keeps walking. "No. Why?"

I nod my head behind me toward the tree. "There was a ball back there with your initials on it. Just wondering."

Turning back around, he stops when he reaches a shed. "That ball's probably about twelve years old." There's a padlock on the shed, but it's not locked together. Tommy slides it off and pulls open the double tin doors. "We used to play catch out here when we'd come up and stay. It's been awhile, though." He grabs an empty box and just starts pulling things out of the shed and dropping them in. There's duct tape, a rope, a handsaw, a toolbox, and some other things I don't even know the names for.

My eyes stay focused on each item that drops in the box.

"Yeah, I guess we outgrow some of the things that were once fun to us."

"Guess so. Even if you outgrow them when you're only six years old. Like I said, it's been awhile."

"So your family doesn't come up here and stay anymore?"

"Not together. My dad was here a couple times last year. My brothers had a party out here after they graduated. But, no. We don't stay here together."

"Then why not just sell it?"

Bending down, he picks up the full box. It's nothing for him to lift the eighty pounds of cargo. The veins in his arms flex out and his biceps bulge and it's hot as hell seeing his muscles strain. "Because selling the house means selling our secrets."

"Secrets?"

"We all have them, don't we?" He winks. He actually fucking winks. Electricity ignites every cell in my body, settling in my stomach where it continues to flicker. Then he walks right past me like he never did it.

Once we're back out front, he positions the box under his palm and holds it up like it's nothing, then taps in a code on the keypad that's mounted next to the door. Once it beeps, he pulls open the door. I feel like I should be helping, doing something, other than just following him around like a puppy.

We step inside and it's no surprise that the inside is just as beautiful as the outside. Vaulted ceilings with skylights fill the open space with natural light. There's a staircase that leads up to a wraparound loft and though the structure is impeccable, it smells old and musty. Just like one would expect a cabin on the creek to smell, but not one this extravagant.

Tommy drops the box on the floor at his feet with a thud. "This shouldn't take long." He walks over and grabs a chair that sits in front of the oak dining room table—positioning it in the middle of the room beside the box.

My entire body jolts when I hear the shutting of another car door. "Is someone here?" The front door is wide open, so I lean forward to look outside. "Zed King?" I mumble under my breath before stealing a glance at Tommy.

He doesn't seem surprised when Zed walks in the house with heavy steps beneath his black combat boots. A lit cigarette hangs from the corner of his mouth and he doesn't even bother to put it out before coming inside. "Fuck, man, this place brings back some memories." He tugs the cigarette from his mouth and gives it a flick out the door. The cherry still burns brightly as it lies on the wooden porch. I wanna go extinguish it before the entire place catches fire, but I also don't wanna seem like a pussy.

"Hell yeah, it does. Rotten memories,' Tommy says as he lays a long rope loosely over the back of the chair. And then it hits me.

Fuck. I need to get the hell out of here.

Zed chuckles. "Rotten is a pretty good word for it." His eyes skim up and down my body as if he just now realized I was standing here. Dipping his eyebrows, he keeps a watchful eye on me. "How's it going, McCoy?"

I don't respond. I just look at Tommy in hopes of him giving me any inclination that he's not planning to tie me up in that chair. What the hell am I thinking? Of course he is. That's exactly why Marni tried to warn me. Why else would he bring me here? It's not like he suddenly grew feelings for me when just yesterday he spewed hatred in my direction.

"You're fucking shaking, Wyatt. Calm down, this isn't for you." Zed smacks a forceful hand to my back and lets out a boisterous laugh.

I breathe in a sigh of relief. "Ok. Well, it's apparent it's for someone. Dare I ask, who?"

"You dare not. Once you know, you'll never be able to not know. Take it from me, you don't want that shit on your conscience."

Running my fingers through my hair, my eyebrows hit my hairline. Whoever they're planning this for is in for a hellish ride. Tommy pulls out some vise grips and my stomach churns. It's like he's prepping for surgery. Only, it's not medical equipment—it's tools that can do just as much harm, only much less sanitary.

Once it appears everything is set to his liking, he turns to Zed and looks at him for the first time since he's stepped foot in the cabin. "You look like shit. How the hell are ya?" He pulls Zed in for a hug and they both give each other a bro-tap to the back.

He really does look like shit. Last time I saw Zed, he was still an eighteen-year-old boy with a bad attitude. I can tell the attitude is still there, but now he's got a stubble of facial hair and looks like he hasn't had a hair cut in months. Not to mention the bags under his eyes that make it apparent he needs a good night's sleep.

"That's irrelevant. I told you, no personal talk. This is all business."

"Alright. Alright." Tommy nods in agreement. "I'm just thankful you made it. I know things haven't been—" He trails off when he remembers I'm standing here. Or, because Zed made it clear this is strictly business. Whatever business that is.

"McCoy," Zed angles his head toward the door, "be a good helper and go fetch me my cigarettes off my front seat."

Like the pushover I am, I go.

I pull open the door to his black Suburban and notice the keys are in the ignition. If I wanted to make an escape, this would be my chance.

They said that chair's not for me. But can I really trust Zed King—or even Tommy?

This must be the year for bad choices because I snatch up the cigarettes and shut the door. I'm sure it was a ploy just to get me away so they could talk about whatever the hell they have planned.

Flipping open the box, I count the cigarettes inside, just as a distraction as I try to listen to the voices carrying out the front door.

"Because we can't talk about this shit over the phone. There've been enough phone calls, videos, and lurkers around. I knew you wouldn't come back to Redwood so this was the only way."

"What about your friend?"

"He won't talk. As a matter of fact, he's a part of this. We just don't know how much of a part yet."

Pushing my thumb down on the top, I close the pack of cigarettes but stare down at it. *He's a part of this. We just don't know how much of a part yet.* How am I part of any of this? What the fuck are they talking about?

My phone sounds in my pocket and somehow I must have switched it off silent mode. Pulling it out, I look at the door while I stand to the side of the porch steps. Tommy and Zed both stare out at me with cautious eyes. "Here." I toss Zed's cigarettes onto the porch. They land about a foot from the door and he steps outside and picks them up while I fumble with my phone.

"Put that away!" he orders me.

Squinting, I question what he's telling me to do. "What?"

Zed eats up the space between us and snatches my phone out of my hand. Without even looking at the screen, he holds his thumb over the power button until it shuts my phone down then he tosses it back at me. It rolls down my chest and I catch it just before it drops.

"Why'd you do that?"

"Are you fucking dumb? Can't you tell there's a reason we're out here. We don't need you telling all your friends where they can find us. In fact, you mention that you saw me and I'll tie you to that chair myself and let the critters feast on your remains after you rot."

Swallowing hard, I look at Tommy who refuses to make eye contact with me. So much for being my friend. He can't even stand up for me. Though, I should be the one standing up for myself. Not many people push back when Zed beats them down, but surely his friends would be able to put him in his place.

Zed looks at Tommy. "We done here?"

"We're done. Just remember, timing is everything." Tommy walks outside and finally looks at me. His eyes seek something I'm not sure I can give him. *An indication that I'm ok, maybe?*

Tommy makes a fist and stretches his arm toward Zed. "Start to finish."

Zed bumps it back while Tommy holds tight like he's waiting for Zed to say something.

When he doesn't, Tommy retreats.

"Alright then. Peace out, fuckers." Zed turns around and flips his middle finger in the air.

With that, Zed hops in his truck and burns out, kicking up dust behind him as he flies down the driveway.

I look at Tommy with displeasure. "Alright, explain what the hell that was about." I'm not keeping quiet this time. They were talking about me and I need to know why.

"We better get back to Redwood. You have a meeting with your dad." He begins walking up the steps, but I stop him by grabbing him by the shoulder.

"Not so fast. I heard you say I was part of a plan. What plan is that?"

"Ah, you heard? I thought you might have been listening."

"In my defense, I was right outside the door and you two weren't exactly quiet."

"What else did you hear?"

"That was all. But I wanna know what you meant."

Coming down a step, his eyes level with mine and his blue ones looking back are enough to drive me wild. Standing here like this—in seclusion—makes me think of everything we could do together that no one would know about.

"You'll know soon enough."

I lick my lips as my body trembles. "That's not good enough. I need to know now."

His head leans forward, and he whispers in my ear, "Be patient with me. That's all I can say right now."

Taking a few steps backward, his eyes stay locked on mine. The scowl on his face is replaced by a half-smile that does nothing to calm the growing bulge in my pants. I wonder if he'd stop me if I ran up and shoved him inside the cabin then kicked the door shut while ridding him of his clothes.

Once the back of his ankles hit the bottom step, he turns around and jogs up them. Curiously, I follow.

When I get inside, I close the front door halfway. Tommy keeps on walking and I have no idea where he's going. I stop myself from trailing behind him. He could just be going to the bathroom. Gnawing on the inside of my cheek, I look around the room and take everything in. There is no sign of family life here. No family pictures, no wall hangings that say things like *home is at the cabin* or anything similar. The walls are empty and there's nothing that screams, *fun summer vacation,* to me. The longer I stand here, the more eerie the place begins to feel.

A few minutes pass and Tommy still hasn't returned, so I take it upon myself to go find him. The doors to all the rooms down the long narrow hall are open, so I start with the first one and work my way down. When I look inside the bathroom and don't see him, I turn around, and there he is. Lying on a bed with his boots still on and his ankles crossed. His hands are folded under his head and his eyes are dead set on me. "What are you doing?" I ask him as I take a step inside the room.

This room, too, is pretty basic. Just a full-size bed with navy blue bedding, a white dresser, and a matching nightstand.

"Thinking."

I take another step closer to the bed. "About?"

"Life."

And another step. "Oh yeah? And what have you come up with? Is it as unfair as it seems?"

"Very much so."

Against my better judgment, I take a seat on the end of the bed. Half of my ass hangs off and I put weight on my legs to keep me up. "You don't like this place, do you?" It's just a gut feeling, but I'm pretty sure it's accurate.

"I fucking hate it." His eyes pinch shut while he speaks. "We came here a lot when I was a kid. It was my favorite place in the world. It was the summer of my sixth birthday, my grandpa flew in from California and we had just come inside after having a fire and roasting marshmallows. Mom was washing my hands in the bathroom because they were covered in marshmallow goo. I'll never forget the sound of the first pop. Screams smoldered and cries rang out. They were the loudest and most deafening pleas for help that I'd ever heard."

His eyes open, and in them, I see his six-year-old self. Scared, helpless, confused. "Damn, who was it? What happened?"

"When someone rises to the top quickly, there's usually an unethical reason behind it. In my dad's case, there were many. My dad loves his kids, loves his wife—but others see him differently. Mom stuffed me under the sink cupboard and told me to be quiet. I was six, I didn't know how to sit still. So once she left the bathroom, I followed her out. I'll never be able to erase the picture in my head of my grandpa lying in a pool of blood with half of his head blown off. Blood and tissue scattered around the room and the casing from the deer rifle was stuck in the wall behind where he stood. Mom shielded my brothers' eyes, but mine were wide open when dad grabbed that rifle from the masked man and returned the favor. I watched in slow motion as the lifeless assailant dropped to the floor and created another puddle of fresh blood. It poured out of him like leaking water in a fish bag."

I don't even know what to say. So, I place a comforting hand on his ankle. "That must've been awful."

"Another man came charging in and took my dad down right on top of my grandpa's body. There was a brief brawl and everyone just stood there. Mom hiding her face and my brothers. So, I grabbed a metal baseball bat that was perched against the wall and I took it right to the back of the man's head. I was only six, so it didn't completely knock him out, but it gave Dad a chance to gain the upper hand. He shouted for Mom to get us out and as she was, he tied the man to a chair. *Kill or be killed.* My dad looked me in the eyes with blood-stained skin and whispered those words. They've stuck with me every day since. Maybe that's why I'm always on the defense. Anyways, I still don't know why it happened. All I know for sure is dad pissed off the wrong man and they thought my grandpa was him."

"Were any charges ever pressed?"

His head shakes. "Nope. Dad got his answers and I'm pretty sure he killed the other guy, too. Dad called in help to clean up the mess and the next day, three fresh plots by the creek appeared. My guess is that they're all three buried there and that's why dad will never sell the place. Like I said, too many secrets."

I can't believe he's telling me this. This is some deep stuff. "That's fucked up."

"That's when I took up drawing and painting. Dad said we needed to find a quiet outlet for the emotions we were feeling. Art has always been my outlet." He scoots himself up into a sitting position. "Needless to say, this place has some harrowing memories, so I'm not too concerned about adding a few more to someone who might deserve a little reality check."

"Is that someone Shane?"

"You don't wanna ask any more questions. Trust me."

"Ok, how about something lighter? Aside from vandalizing bedroom walls and school property, what do you like to paint?"

He halts, then scratches at his head with a shrugged shoulder. "Everything. I'm a mood artist. I create what I feel. If I feel anger, I express it through angry art. If I'm happy, I create things that make me happy."

Inching closer, I position myself so that I'm fully on the bed. I tuck one leg under the other and shift to face him. "If you were to paint a picture right now, what would it be?"

His blank gaze leeches onto me. Observing as if he's drawing my body in his head. "I'd start at the bottom. An array of lines resembling a knotted rope. Overlapping, meeting, and forming the brain in my head. Two strings on each side running up to a hand holding onto either side of the string. Fingers pinched together tightly, pulling and puppeteering the hold it has on me. My thoughts, my emotions, my logic."

Titling my head to the side, I paint the picture in my head. "And who do the hands belong to?"

"Everyone. My friends, society, my parents—you."

I move closer, his leg brushing against my hip and sending heat throughout my body. "Do you feel like those hands are controlling you?"

He comes up on his knees but never breaks our cemented gaze. "Didn't you?" My eyes shimmy down to his lips and I watch as he speaks. His mouth opening and closing so gracefully. "Didn't you feel like the world would disapprove if they knew who you really were?"

"The world already knew who I was. My sexual orientation doesn't define me. It doesn't define you, either." Admit it. Just admit to me. I need this. More than anything, I need him to talk to me. Not just for reassurance, but so he can begin to accept what we both know to be true.

"It's only you, Wyatt. No one else does this to me."

My voice cracks as my arms begin to tremble while bracing my body upright. "What do I do to you?"

Straightening up, he takes my hand in his and places it on his cock. "This. I don't know what it means. It's not just my body that reacts to you, it's more than that. It's like you've found a home in my head and you never leave. No matter how hard I try to kick you out, you're just...always there."

This is everything I have ever wanted and now that I'm here and he's opening up, I don't know what to do. I'm scared if I say too much, I'll push him away, but if I say nothing at all, he'll feel humiliated.

So, I do the only thing I can think of and I get on my knees and put my body parallel to his. Taking his face in my hands, I tilt my head to the side and let my lips collide with his. What starts off slow and passionate, escalates quickly into full-blown tongue tangling making out.

His breaths are labored and I know he wants me just as badly as I want him. He lets out a subtle moan that has me wanting to hear more. To feel the vibration rumble against my tongue that unleashes from deep inside of him.

Moving slowly, I drop his back to the bed and top my body with his. I can feel his erection pressed against mine. I unequivocally start grinding against him. His hands slide up the back of my shirt and his open palm squeezes my shoulder blade. His touch leaves an imprint that will forever be tattooed on my skin. Even if this never happens again, I want to remember it for the rest of my life.

Our kiss holds tight and begins to pick up, until we're like two wild animals tearing into each other. Breaking the suction, I lift his shirt over his head and toss it to the side. He doesn't stop me. Instead, he does the same to me. I take in the view of his beautiful body. Trailing my fingers down the artwork on his collarbone before pressing my lips to the snake-like infinity symbol on his neck. I wanna ask him what it means. I wanna know every story on his flawless skin.

When I come up on my knees, with my legs straddling him, we both freeze. Our eyes search one another's and I can see his heart beating thunderously in his chest. His stomach rising and falling with each rapid breath.

Searching for approval with a skeptical expression, he begins to unbutton my pants. I bite the corner of my lip and move my hands to the side to let him take the lead. Once my zipper is down, I come forward, and he pushes my pants down, springing my dick free, and I shake my legs until my pants are all the way off. Using one foot on the other, I remove my socks.

His eyes slide down to my dick and when he licks his lips, I know he likes what he sees. I've never seen Tommy in such a vulnerable state. Like a virgin who's ready to take the leap into a new world of sexual pleasure.

"Touch it," I tell him. His hand rises, then falls back to his side as he questions himself. So I take it upon myself to pick it back up and put it on my cock. I can feel his fingers shiver as he locks them around me. With my hand still on his, I slide up and down, until he begins stroking my shaft on his own. It's not like he needs instruction, every eighteen-year-old guy knows how to stroke a cock.

Watching his lips while he watches the motions of his hand, I imagine his plump, wet, tight mouth wrapped around my cock as his tongue flicks under my shaft and drives me to an orgasm that spills down his throat.

"I wanna suck it," he says, as if he read my mind.

I'm taken by surprise, but don't show it.

His hand drops and he pulls himself out from underneath me. Before he gets too far out of reach, I take his pants down and he frees his legs, but his boxers stay on. I take his place with my back pressed against the mattress.

On his knees, he doesn't hesitate before taking me in his mouth. My eyes close and ecstasy ripples through me, taking over my entire body. His tongue stretches and slides up and down my length and holy fuck, it feels so good. I've had my dick sucked, but there is something euphoric about Tommy being the one to bring me this intense pleasure. We're connecting on an entirely different level and because of it, we'll always be intertwined.

"Shift this way," I tell him. When he goes on his side with his legs near my torso, I stick my hand down his boxers and graze my thumb over the smooth head of his tortured cock. He stops sucking me off and lifts his head. Just as I think something might be wrong, he takes his boxers off. His cock is freed and it's a beautiful sight.

I begin stroking his length while he returns to sucking me off. My eyes close as I take it all in. His warm lips around me. I place a hand on his head as it bobs up and down.

"Holy shit," I cry out in a raspy croak. Guiding his movements with my hand, I rock my body in rhythm with his upward-downward motion.

My body takes control and I don't even put any thought behind my actions when I take my hand off his dick and pop my finger in my mouth to wet it. I slop it up really well then rub the excess saliva around his entrance. I repeat the process, getting it more lubed up, then slide the tip of my finger inside of him. He doesn't stop me; in fact, it only arouses him further as he begins sucking harder and faster. I stop stroking his cock and grab a fist full of his hair then push my finger all the way inside of him, sliding it in and out.

He releases a moan when I reach his prostate. Using the pad of my fingers, I massage in a circular motion then slide another finger in. He lets out a throaty rumble that causes a vibration in his mouth as he takes all of me in, and then out again. His tongue does laps around my head, then works my cock back in as far as he can take me.

My fingers pump inside of him. Prodding, twisting, turning. I keep going because the way his doe eyes look up at me, I can tell he likes it.

When his head lifts, I freeze, thinking I did something wrong. "Fuck me, Wyatt." His voice is husky and warranted.

"Are you..are you sure?" He immediately nods in response, so I pull my fingers out of him and stretch my arm down to try and grab my pants off the floor. When I come up empty-handed, he begins searching for me.

I watch intently as he bends over my body to the side of the bed and fishes for my pants. When he comes back up, he hands me them and I pull my wallet out of the back pocket. As I begin rummaging through it, he starts stroking my cock again, keeping me hard and ready. Not that I could possibly go limp with his sexy, naked ass cradling me. "Ok, lie on your back," I tell him. Once he does, I climb on top of him with his legs bent on either side of me.

Tearing the top of the wrapper off with my teeth, I spit it to the side, unsure where it went. I roll the condom on then pinch the top of it, leaving a little space at the tip. My eyes skim the room for something we can use as lube, but I see nothing. I grin back at him, hoping I'm not ruining the moment here. I know this is all new to him. "Don't get grossed out, but I'm gonna spit on you."

He gives me a look of concern, but then nods. "Ok."

Bending my head down, I spit directly in his hole then rub it around. The condom is lubed, but this is his first time, so I wanna make sure it's not super painful. I line my head up with his hole and slowly slide inside of him, watching his expression for anything that tells me it's uncomfortable for him. His fingers clench the sheet tightly at his side, and he flinches just a tad.

"You ok?" I ask him, easing myself back out a little bit, without losing all of my headway.

"Mmmhmm." He grumbles under his breath.

I slide in slowly, giving him only a centimeter at a time. Each time he stiffens his back, I stop my movements.

"You sure?"

His head nods, but his hands bunch the sheet even more. I slide in a little bit farther until my head is fully inside and we both breathe a sigh of relief.

His body relaxes a bit more and his fingers slowly ungrip the sheet and slide up to my waist.

He's so fucking tight and it feels so good inside of him. Pushing farther, I search for the spot while watching his face.

His body shifts slightly, giving me better access as his back arches off the bed. I continue to thrust inside and when he trembles slightly and lets out an airy breath, I know I've found it.

I can feel him tense up a bit as he sucks in his stomach. "You ok? "

"Mmhmm." He pulls his lip between his teeth, biting down on it pretty hard.

"Relax, baby. Just tell me if you want me to stop."

With my dick all the way inside of him now, I begin vibrating my pelvis against his ass while taking his cock in my hand and giving it firm strokes.

"Fuck!" he bellows. His body jerks beneath me as he experiences this new kind of pleasure. A high like no other. It's safe to say he's not feeling discomfort anymore, so I pick up my pace. Jerking him faster and thrusting deeper. His tight ass swallows up my dick and attempts to force me out as his muscles clench tightly around me.

To me, this is so much more than sex, it's beautiful and enlightening seeing Tommy come out of this shell he's tucked himself inside for so long. I can't help myself when I lean forward and press my lips to his. Gently, with my mouth closed. Butterflies flutter through me and my heart doubles in size. His open eyes stare back at mine, and I don't see a man full of shame and regret; I see someone full of hopes and dreams.

My back steels when I come back up on my knees and I take one of his legs under my forearm and continue to stroke his dick with my free hand. Tightening my hold around his cock, I rub up and down his length as I lunge inside of him, hitting a spot that drives him wild.

"Oh God," he moans, driving me further as I take both of us to the height of our orgasms. Just as I spill inside of the condom, his cum shoots out and I continue to stroke him, lathering his cock up as I slide my fingers up and down.

My cock twitches inside of him as I slowly slide out. I immediately pull the condom off and tie the end of it.

When I look up at him, I expect him to smile or show some sort of sign that this was everything he wanted, but instead, I see those eyes of regret again, causing my heart to drop deep into my stomach.

One step forward, two steps back. It wasn't supposed to be like this.

"Tommy?" I say his name as a question. "What's wrong?"

"There's towels in the bathroom." He tilts his head to the side and gestures me to an open door in the room.

I push myself off him and go inside to grab one. Tossing the condom in an empty trash bin, I feel faint and off-balance. On the verge of tears, because I'm not ready to face what's going to be thrown at me when I walk back into the room, I wash my hands and grab a hand towel hanging on a rack, wondering how long it's hung there without being used.

Drawing in a deep breath, I walk back to the bed where Tommy still lies fully undressed with a pool of semen formed around his belly button. I drop the towel on him and stand there, waiting for something—anything.

When he just wipes himself off and doesn't say a word, I take it upon myself to pry. "Are you ok?"

"I'm fine," he deadpans.

The towel drops to the floor, but he still lies there. His legs flat out in front of him and his arms at his sides. "I guess I just didn't expect to like it that much. Was kinda hoping I'd get it out of my system and you'd escape my head."

I chuckle, trying to make light of the situation, though it's not funny. "Of course you liked it. What's not to like?"

He smiles.

Finally. He fucking smiles.

I continue, "As for me taking up space in your head, I'm not sorry for that because you've invaded mine, too." I take a seat on the bed. My body longs to lie next to him, to feel his arms wrap around me, but I know this requires baby steps. Instead of pushing him further, I grab his clothes off the floor at my feet and lie them on top of him. "We better go. I have to get to Magna Tech, so we can get started on tracing that phone of yours."

He nods his head, but doesn't say anything more. I don't need him to, though. He'll open up more when he's ready. And I'll be here waiting, as long as it takes.

The slamming of a car door has both of our eyes widening.

"Fuck!" Tommy springs up. "Get dressed now!"

CHAPTER FOURTEEN

TOMMY

Tripping over my pant legs, I finally get them up. My eyes scan the room in search of my shirt. *Fuck. Where is it?*

"Wyatt?" Marni yells from outside the room. "Tommy?" How the hell does she know we're here. My eyes dart to Wyatt—wide and angry.

My jaw clenches, and I mutter, "What did you do?" He looks apologetic and worried, so I know he got her here somehow.

Wyatt tosses my shirt at me then proceeds to pull up the zipper on his pants. Running my fingers through my hair, I attempt to tame the loose strands falling carelessly over my forehead. I give Wyatt a once-over and make sure he's decent before gripping the handle. *Ready or not.*

As soon as I pull the door open, I'm face to face with Marni, who's got her hands on her hips and a grimace on her face. "What the hell are you doing here, Marni?" My heart is pounding in my chest and my palms are sweating like rain clouds.

"I could ask you two the same thing?" She points between Wyatt and me. "What is this?"

"Well, I'm not killing him if that's what you're thinking?" I slide past her and walk into the kitchen to avoid her seeing the apprehension that's written all over my face.

"Are you ok?" I hear her ask Wyatt.

Their voices carry into the kitchen while I stand there with my palms pressed to the counter.

"I'm fine. Why did you come here?"

"Because you never listen to me. And when I noticed your location came on, I figured you did it because you needed help."

"Everything is fine. Do you know something I don't, because you're acting really weird lately?"

"Marni," I holler. "Can I talk to you? Alone."

Once she rounds the corner, I nod toward the door. "Outside."

Her eyes roll, but her feet move and I follow behind her. "Care to explain to me what the hell is going on?" I step outside and pull the door closed.

"I was worried about him."

"Ok," I nod, "so, you decide to track him down and drive an hour just to make sure he's ok?"

"What's going on with you lately, Tommy? You've been a mess and this vendetta against Wyatt is getting out of control."

Grabbing her by the arm, I point to the tattoo on her wrist. "Do you see this? It's a fucking oath. A pact you took. So let me ask you again, what the fuck are you doing here?"

She jerks her arm back and snarls, "He's my best friend! I won't let you hurt him."

"Would you let him hurt me? Or Talon? Or Lars and Willa? Huh? Answer that."

She shakes her head. "What? No! I wouldn't."

"And what makes you so sure he hasn't already? He could have been the one who hit Josh. He could know what we've all been doing this entire time. How do you know you can trust him?"

I don't think Wyatt knows any of this and I don't think he's out to get us, but I'm still not one-hundred percent sure I can fully trust him. There are still so many unanswered questions.

"Because I know him."

Tilting my head to the side, I press harder. "If you two are so close then why hasn't he come to you and told you he saw Josh in the road that night?"

"I don't know. Maybe he's scared. But I know he's not trying to incriminate any of us. He would never do that."

"And how do you know?" I keep digging and digging because the truth is, she doesn't know. None of us do.

"Because Wyatt helped me. Remember when I stole Talon's phone? I took it so I could see what he was up to. Wyatt helped me download the information off of it. He never asked questions and he never told a soul. I know I can trust him."

Holding up a hand, I stop her. "Wait a minute. You fucking told him?"

"No. I didn't tell him anything. He didn't bother to ask because he didn't want any part of what I was doing. He knew it involved you all and he didn't want you on his ass even more than you already were."

Pressing my fingers together, I hold them against my face and think. I know that Wyatt is a dead end. It was just easier to find a reason to hate him, so I didn't have to focus on how much I really don't hate him. How he makes my heart beat quicker and my legs feel weak. How just being in the same room with him gives me a feeling of contentment—now more than ever.

Marni's phone beeps in her hand, at the same time mine buzzes in my pocket. She looks at her screen then up at me while I pull my phone out. "Who is that?" I ask her.

"I don't know. Who's yours from?"

I open the message and it's an incoming image that's downloading. "It's a picture from an unknown caller. Service is sketchy out here. I'm not sure it'll download." I hold my phone up in the air and try to get a better signal.

"I got a picture, too."

I lean forward to get a better look at her phone and it's the same thing.

"Wyatt!" I shout, "come here."

Three seconds later, he's out the door with his phone in his hand. "Get in the truck. We have to drive down the road to get a phone signal."

We all pile in my truck and drive about a half mile when Marni stops me. "It's loading."

"What's loading?" Wyatt asks from the backseat.

Neither of us respond because whatever this is could be something he can't know about.

I glance in the rearview mirror and Wyatt's face suddenly looks as white as a ghost. "What's wrong, man?" I ask him.

His wide eyes find mine and his jaw drops. "Um, nothing," he lies. I know he's fucking lying.

"Tommy. Pull over," Marni demands. "You're not gonna fucking believe this."

Swerving to the side of the road, I don't even shift in park before opening my phone back up. "Holy shit! Who sent this?"

Wyatt leans forward and tries to steal a glance at my phone, but I flip it over in my lap.

"If it's a copy of Josh's death certificate, you don't need to hide it from me. I got one, too."

My foot digs into the brake as I shift in park. My upper body turns quickly to face Wyatt in the back seat. "What are you talking about?"

Sinking back, his complexion becomes even more chalky than when I caught him in the rearview mirror. "Oh, wrong message. Never mind, just ignore me." He tries to play it off like I have no idea what he's talking about. Or at least making it appear that way because he's hiding something.

"Why would you get a text with Josh Moran's death certificate?"

"Tommy, just stop it. We need to figure this out," Marni says, right before her phone begins ringing. "It's Talon. Hello," she says in the same breath. I watch her intently as she talks. "I know. I know. We got it, too. And apparently so did Wyatt." She looks over her shoulder. Wyatt's eyes shift from hers to mine. "We'll be there soon. Well, about an hour. Ok. Love you, too." She ends the call. "Everyone got it."

Still watching Wyatt, searching for something that gives me insight into what he might be feeling. Is it guilt? Is he scared?

"Damnit." He slaps his hands to his legs. "I'm sorry, guys. This is my fault."

Marni and I exchange a glance. "Go on," I tell him.

"Something happened. I should have said something sooner. Went to the cops. Hell, I don't know. But this has nothing to do with you all. It's because I saw Josh the night he was killed and I think someone knows. And now I've dragged you guys into my mess." His face drops in his hands as he rubs aggressively at his temples.

"It's ok, Wyatt," Marni says, as she stretches her arm back and places a hand on his leg. "Just tell us everything."

Is this really happening right now? Are we finally getting the answers we've been searching for so long?

Wyatt lifts his head and his eyes shift back and forth from me to Marni. "It was two days before Halloween. I was driving down the road pretty fast and I saw something, in front of your house actually. I slowed down a little bit to get a look and I realized it was a person. It looked like someone hit him and drove straight over his body and just left him there. Then I saw his face. It was pretty messed up, but I knew it was Josh. I panicked and left. I should have stopped and called for help, but I was worried the blame would be put on me. So I kept going and left him there."

Fear washes over Wyatt's face. His eyes dampen as he sniffles. "I went back the next day and he was gone. I figured someone found him. A couple days later, he was reported missing and then a week later, they found his car. I didn't know what the hell was going on. But then they found him in Pastor Jeffries' basement. I assumed he killed him and set this whole thing in motion. Maybe he was one of his victims and Josh was planning to go to the cops. Shit, I don't know." He rubs his palms up and down on his pants and I can tell he's nervous as hell.

"Ok. So, what makes you think the dirty pastor didn't kill him?" Marni asks.

"I got a note. I thought it was from Tommy, but he swears it wasn't, so I thought maybe it was someone who knew I drove past your house the night Josh was hit."

Marni questions me with her eyes. I hold my hands up in surrender. "It wasn't me."

Wyatt continues, "And now this text. Someone else must have done it because the pastor sure as hell isn't sending messages from the grave."

"Wyatt, it's not—"

I hold up a hand, stopping Marni from saying too much. "Don't. Don't involve him more than he needs to be."

Her eyebrows pinch together and I can tell she's getting upset. "Can't you see now that we can trust him?"

"This has nothing to do with trust. I don't want him dragged into this mess any more than he needs to be. Knowing too much can put him in danger."

Wyatt leans forward in the empty space up front. "What are you guys talking about? Is there something more to this that you're not telling me?"

"I'll figure this out," I tell him. "Just lay low and don't draw any attention to yourself. We need to get you back to Redwood, so you can go to Magna Tech and find the control room to track the phone."

Marni looks at me with puzzlement. "You think this is connected?"

"I'd bet my life on it. It's too much of a coincidence not to be."

"Someone needs to tell me what the hell is going on," Wyatt bellows from between us.

"Just don't say anything. Don't run to the cops. Do not mention this to anyone." I grab my phone and read over the death certificate.

WHO PRONOUNCES OR CERTIFIES DEATH 12 22 201 6:32PM

26. SIGNATURE OF PERSON PRONOUNCING DEATH (Only when applicable) Martin Reams
27. LICENSE NUMBER 023-00
28. DATE SIGNED (Mo/Day/Yr) 02 16 2020

29. ACTUAL OR PRESUMED DATE OF DEATH (Mo/Day/Yr) (Spell Month) 10 28 2019
30. ACTUAL OR PRESUMED TIME OF DEATH 9:00 PM
31. WAS MEDICAL EXAMINER OR CORONER CONTACTED? ☑ Yes ☐ No

CAUSE OF DEATH (See instructions and examples)

32. **PART I.** Enter the chain of events--diseases, injuries, or complications--that directly caused the death. DO NOT enter terminal events such as cardiac arrest, respiratory arrest, or ventricular fibrillation without showing the etiology. DO NOT ABBREVIATE. Enter only one cause on a line. Add additional lines if necessary.

		Approximate interval Onset to death
IMMEDIATE CAUSE (Final disease or condition resulting in death) --------->	a. Rolling injuries sustained from an automobile	TBD
	Due to (or as a consequence of)	
Sequentially list conditions, if any, leading to the cause listed on line a. Enter the **UNDERLYING CAUSE** (disease or injury that initiated the events resulting in death) **LAST**	b. Internal hemmorahing of the cerebrum. Blunt force trauma to the head and spinal cord	
	Due to (or as a consequence of)	
	c. Postive for Methamphetamine	
	Due to (or as a consequence of)	
	d. Possible homicide	

PART II. Enter other significant conditions contributing to death but not resulting in the underlying cause given in PART I

Note 1A: Victims body was significantly tampered with.

Note 1B: Tire tracks left on victims arm. White paint chips found in samples of the victims hair. Possibly from the vehicle

33. WAS AN AUTOPSY PERFORMED? ☑ Yes ☐ No
34. WERE AUTOPSY FINDINGS AVAILABLE TO COMPLETE THE CAUSE OF DEATH? ☑ Yes ☐ No

"Positive for methamphetamine? Possible homicide? What the actual fuck! Was Josh into drugs?"

"Oh my god," Wyatt chokes out. He drops back in the seat. "What if someone does think I killed him? I'm done for. What the hell do I do?"

I attempt to calm him down, while trying to reassure myself at the same time. "Nothing. You do nothing. Let me handle this. Like I said, lay low and do not talk. I mean it, Wyatt. You can't say a word to anyone about this."

With his fingers gripping both sides of his head, he nods. "Ok."

"It'll be ok, Wyatt. These guys know what they're doing," Marni says.

But, do we really know what we're doing? Because, most days, I feel like I'm just winging this shit. I do have a plan, though. If all goes according to it, we might have answers sooner than everyone thinks.

One thing is for sure, Wyatt didn't kill Josh. But someone did, and that someone is well aware we know it wasn't Pastor Jeffries.

Let's just hope they aren't trying to pin this on Wyatt.

CHAPTER FIFTEEN

WYATT

It's all coming out. For four and a half months, I've agonized over seeing Josh. He was there, and then he wasn't. He just sort of vanished without a trace. As his picture began popping up on every lamppost in town with *MISSING* in big, bold letters, I knew he wasn't actually missing and he was dead.

What I never could have anticipated, is the reaction I got from Marni and Tommy. It's like they weren't surprised at all. Sure, they were surprised to get the text, but when I recounted my part in this, they remained calm—too calm.

"I've gotta run inside and lock the place up before we head back to Redwood," Tommy tells me as he hops out the driver's side door.

Marni opens the front door and I get out of the back seat and take her place. I roll down the window and her arms press on the windowsill. She looks exhausted just from that brief bout of stress.

"Why don't you ride with me? I think we need to talk about this," she says.

Talking about any of this with Marni is the last thing I want to do. This secret may have been exposed, but there are more where that came from. If she knew the rest of the story or who I was trying to get away from that night, she'd never speak to me again.

"Actually, I'm gonna ride back with Tommy. He and I have a few things to discuss, too."

"Are you sure? He's not your biggest fan, Wyatt. I still don't trust whatever he has planned."

Placing a hand on top of hers, I try to reassure her that I'll be ok. "I might look like a pussy, but I can take care of myself."

She laughs. "Alright. I'm a text a way and I'll be heading in the same direction if you need me." She throws her thumb over her shoulder. "I have to use the bathroom before we hit the road."

I give her a nod and watch as she walks away.

Tommy said he's handling things. I have no idea what that means, but I have no choice right now but to trust him and keep my mouth shut like he said.

I pull up the text message on my phone again and read over the death certificate. *Possible homicide.* This means the case will reopen and the investigation will resume. Even though the cops already assumed it was a murder/suicide on the pastor's behalf, I'm sure they are working out a timeline. Maybe the pastor did hit and kill him. It's possible, and I can only hope that's what happened. Case closed. Everyone moves on. But we all know it won't be that easy.

Minutes later, Marni walks out of the cabin and Tommy follows behind her. Tommy pulls open the door and jumps in. "Alright, let's get the hell outta here." He throws the truck in drive and heads down the driveway that we just came up.

I don't even know where to start here. Do I talk about us and what happened in that cabin? Or jump right into the situation with Josh?

Tommy starts talking, making my mind up for me. "Is there anything else you haven't told me. Anything that I should know before I try and figure out what we're doing about this text?"

I shake my head no in a big, fat lie.

He side-eyes me and questions my response. "Nothing at all?"

"Not that I can think of."

"Ok, start from the beginning. I need to know everything. You were driving down Marni's road—where were you headed? Better yet, where were you coming from?"

"I was going to see Marni."

He glances over at me with an off look on his face, as if I just tossed a million questions into his head. "Wait. You were going to Marni's house? How fast were you driving before you saw him on the road?"

"I don't know. The speed limit. Why?"

"I'm gonna be straight with you, Wyatt. We knew you saw Josh. We've known for a while."

He knew? They knew? Horrified, I turn to face him slowly. "What?"

"Nothing you said came as a surprise. We knew you were out there."

"Marni knew?"

His lips press together in a thin line and he nods.

"Marni fucking knew and she never told me?"

"For what it's worth, she couldn't tell you. We have a pact."

I can feel myself getting more fired up with each word that he says. "So what? She and I have a lifelong friendship. She could have told me. Someone should have come to me. I've been holding this in for months, out of fear, and all this time you all have been...what? Following me and trying to see what I know? You did leave the note, didn't you?" I sink farther into the seat. "I fucking knew it."

"Where were you going, Wyatt?" His voice is solemn and lacks any emotion. "You're lying to me."

"I told you. I was going to see Marni."

"You were driving at least sixty miles an hour when you tapped your brakes and came to a stop for a second. There is no way you were preparing to turn into her driveway."

"What the hell does it matter where I was going? It doesn't matter at all. The point is, I saw Josh and then someone must have picked up his body shortly after. Probably that pastor."

"If the pastor picked up his body, then who sent us those messages? Hmm? Who left you that note? Surely not him."

He's right. Someone else knows that I was there. Likely the person who found Josh and put him in the pastor's basement.

"Where the fuck were you going, Wyatt?" he howls. His knuckles turning pale from his tight grip on the steering wheel. "Just answer the damn question."

Damnit. I can't tell him where I was coming from or where I was going. I just can't.

"I know you're lying to me. You've got two seconds to tell me the truth or I'll call the cops myself."

I still don't respond. I don't know how.

His foot slams on the brake and my body flies forward. This has been happening way too frequently.

Unbuckling his seatbelt, he leans over the center console and invades my personal space. "Where were you going?"

"I was emotionally distraught over a fight with someone and I was trying to get as far away as I could. Ok?"

"So someone was following you?"

"No." I shake my head. "At least I don't think so. Fuck," I drop my face in my hands, "I don't know. I can't say any more, Tommy. It'll ruin me."

"*This* will ruin you. If you were running away from someone, they could have been the one that hit Josh."

It's possible, but not likely.

"Who was it?" he asks again.

Chewing on my thumbnail, I just shake my head. I can't tell him; I won't.

"Fine. It's obvious you're not talking, but tell me this...was it Shane you had the fight with?"

"No," I say quickly.

"Ok." He nods his head. "Does Shane know about this fight?"

"There's no way Shane could have known. At that time, Shane and I had only hung out a few times. We didn't even talk that often."

"You'd be surprised at what people in this town know."

"Well, there's an easy solution. I track the message we just got from my phone."

"We can try. But something tells me this person is a lot smarter than we're giving them credit for."

We continue to drive in silence. Me in my thoughts, Tommy in his. The *Welcome to Redwood* sign appears and part of me wishes we could just go back to that moment in the cabin and stay in it forever.

As we inch closer and closer to the school where my car is, questions I wanna ask scramble in my head.

Where do we go from here? What happens next? Do you regret what we did?

We turn down the road to the high school and I glance over at Tommy, who does the same to me. "What?" he asks. It's what he always says when he catches me looking at him. Tommy isn't one to hold back what he's thinking, unless it comes to personal matters of his heart and mind. "Why are you looking at me like that?"

"I'm just wondering what this is between us. Am I still the enemy?"

"You're slowly moving out of enemy territory, but as far as an *us*, there isn't one. I need time to sort this shit out in my head. Probably shouldn't have let things get that far."

"So you regret it?"

His truck stops next to my car that sits alone in the parking lot. Tommy hits the unlock button then dangles his wrists over the steering wheel while staring straight ahead. "Nah, no regrets. Not this time."

Something tickles the insides of my stomach, working its way up to my heart. I can't even try to hold back the smile that raises my cheekbones to my eyelids. Grabbing the handle, I pull the door open. "See ya tomorrow."

He doesn't say anything, so I get out and shut the door. For the first time in a while, I don't need a response.

I ARRIVE at Magna Tech later than I planned, wearing my school clothes from the day, looking like a washed-up teenager there to step in as CEO and shake things up. I'll probably screw up at first, but eventually, I'll get the hang of things. Anyone else here for this position would probably dress the part, but I'm not an aspiring CEO; I'm just the guy who was born to the founder of the company.

I look around the main entrance of the building. It's obvious it was designed by my dad. White marble flooring, glass wrapped walls, elegant chandeliers hung overhead, and skylights in the vaulted ceiling.

I've been here a couple times, but was never invested in learning about the place. Figured I had some time before I really cared about the logistics of the company.

"Wyatt, how are ya, Hun?" Glenda, from front desk support asks as I walk casually up to her with my hands stuffed inside my pockets.

"Fine, thank you. Is my father around?"

"He sure is. He's been expecting you." She presses a button on the phone and the speaker comes on. "Mr. McCoy, Wyatt's here."

"About damn time. Send him in." I hear my dad say from the other end.

Great. I can already tell he's in a pissy mood. I just need to get this over with and find out how I'm supposed to trace my damn phone.

With no hurry behind my steps, I drag my feet down the hall. Trailing my finger along the glass walls that surround the place. This entire building looks like a disaster waiting to happen. One reckless toddler and the entire place could collapse.

Stepping in front of Dad's office, I take a look at my future. One day this will all be mine. The white curtains are wide open behind the glass wall, so I'm able to see the entire space. A large desk sits in front of the wall window that overlooks the entire town. Desert landscape in the distance, the sun sinking behind fluffy white clouds. This isn't exactly my dream, but I know I have the potential be successful here. It's a good paycheck and a job to be proud of.

Dad tucks out of the door to his private bathroom and acknowledges my presence. Waving a hand, he motions me inside.

I turn the handle on the glass French doors and before they even close behind me, Dad starts tearing into me. "Jesus, Wyatt. School let out an hour and a half ago. Where the hell have you been?" He looks me up and down, taking in my attire. "You sure as hell weren't changing into something more appropriate for an incoming CEO."

"Sorry, Dad. I, err, had a tutoring session I forgot about."

He pushes a button on his phone, similar to the one Glenda has at the front desk. "Glenda, send Marty in." Buttoning up the jacket of his three piece suit, he steps out from behind his desk. "Marty will be your go-to person. He sort of runs the show around here. He's gonna show you where your office will be and give you a little tour of the building. When you're done, come back up to my office and we'll go over a few things."

Standing there awkwardly, we wait for Marty. Dad begins jotting something down on a notepad and I know it's because he feels the same tension I do. Dad doesn't show emotion well and he's all work, no play.

"You heard from Mom?" I ask, trying to break the ice.

"She should be home this weekend."

Pinching my lips together, I nod. My eyes scope out the place, though there isn't much to see. No family pics, no artwork that might give a stranger any insight as to who Royce McCoy is.

A couple minutes later, a gentleman wearing navy blue dress pants and a white three-button polo walks in and I could hug him for saving me from this suffocating situation.

"Marty Jenson. You must be Mr. McCoy Junior." He extends a hand to me, and I return the gesture, giving him a firm squeeze. One thing dad always taught me is that you can tell a lot by a person by the way they shake your hand. Soft and fast shows intimidation. Firm and prolonged shows self-assurance.

"Nice to meet you, Marty." He lets go of my hand first, and my dad gives me a look of recognition.

"Alright," Marty claps his hands together, "let's get started. We've got three months to teach you the ins and outs of this place. No time to waste." He looks at my dad. "I'll return him shortly."

I follow Marty out of the office, and as soon as the doors close, he breathes a sigh of relief. I'm not sure if he noticed that I caught it, but I did.

"That bad, huh?" I ask him.

He side-eyes me and shakes his head. "Your dad is good at what he does. Let's just leave it at that."

I chuckle. "No need to beat around the bush; he's brutal."

"Right? A fucking browbeater."

"Worse." I laugh. I think I'm gonna like this guy. He's only about ten years older than me. Tall, slender, glasses, and hair so blond it's almost white.

"Alright, Wyatt," we turn a corner and he gestures to an open and empty room, "this will be your office."

From the outside of the glass wall, I look around the room. Not much to see, but the view is the same as Dad's, so it works for me. "Very nice."

"It is. There are only a couple people who get that view. Your dad, you, and his assistant."

"My dad's assistant has an office this nice. Wonder what she did to earn that?" I shake my head in disgust, because I know exactly what she did, or does. I might be following in the old man's footsteps, but that's one road I'll never go down. I never want to be that man.

"Oh, I'm sure you'll hear the rumors eventually." He zips his fingers across his lips. "But not from me."

Marty finishes showing me the offices and then we tour a couple other wings that are just as boring, before going down to the lower level where the magic happens. We only go as far as security, but that's ok, I know all I need to know. This is where I need to get to when I come back.

CHAPTER SIXTEEN

TOMMY

When the final bell rings, I'm out of class before anyone else. Usually I hang around for a bit and let the halls clear, but I need to get to Wyatt's locker before he leaves for the day. Pushing through the crowd of students who linger in the hallway, I spot Shane. Standing directly where I intended to go—Wyatt's locker.

I could turn and walk away. Let him have this time to try and sway Wyatt back into his bed, but I don't. Instead, I stand directly next to him with my back pressed to Wyatt's neighbor's locker. I kick my foot up behind me, taking the same stance as Shane. I can feel his eyes burn into the side of my head and it makes me smile inwardly.

'What are you doing?" he asks with displeasure in his tone.

I don't look at him. I just stand and stare straight ahead. Watching as students gather their belongings and leave for the day. "Waiting. Same thing you are."

"Get lost. Wyatt has plans after school that don't involve you."

"Oh," I chortle, "and I assume his plans are with you?"

"As a matter of fact they are."

Something bites my insides and I wanna spin around and pin him to the locker and throw threats in his face, but I refrain. Keeping my cool, I don't react. He's probably lying anyways. Besides, I'll have my moment with Shane where he will feel the full wrath of my hatred for him.

Wyatt comes walking down the hall toward us and the minute he spots us both standing there, his eyebrows shoot to his forehead. His books hang freely from his right hand and I take it all in. Everything about him. His honey brown eyes, his disheveled hair that looks like he's had a busy day, his choice of clothes that I've always thought were too sophisticated, but now suit him well.

"Umm, this is different. What's going on, guys?"

Shane steps aside so Wyatt can get in his locker. "You know why I'm here. No idea what he wants."

So, it wasn't a lie. They do have plans. What the hell? Pushing my foot off the locker, I try to catch a glimpse of Wyatt's expression to see if Shane is making this shit up. But he avoids looking at me and pulls open his locker, dropping his books into his backpack.

"I need to talk to you," I spit out. My voice is strangled as I try not show how upset this whole situation makes me. Yesterday I let Wyatt see me at my most vulnerable. I gave him a part of me that I haven't even accepted myself. It felt refreshing. Like a weight had been lifted off my shoulders and everything was starting to make sense. I'm still sorting through things in my head, but in some crazy way, it gave me hope. A reason to believe that I'm not damaged and that maybe I am interested in him. Not maybe. I am. Plain and simple. I like him. There, I said it.

I can feel anger rising inside of me, heating my cheeks and disturbing my thoughts. "Do you mind going somewhere, Shane. You're not wanted here."

"Dude, are you fucking deaf? I told you that Wyatt and I have plans."

Wyatt slams his locker shut and turns to face Shane. "Not plans. A tutoring session. One that I didn't want to begin with because I know damn well you don't need a tutor for a freshman algebra class."

Shane's face flushes with embarrassment. He's taking freshman algebra as a senior? I wanna laugh, but I don't.

Wyatt looks at me. "I just need an hour. That's all he gets. I can text you when I'm done."

Eyeing Shane, I clench my jaw. "Nah, I'll come back in an hour."

"Really?" Wyatt's eyes light up and the look he gives me offers all the reassurance I need that there is nothing going on between these two.

"Yeah," I point my thumb over my shoulder, "I'll be in the parking lot."

He smiles in response and then walks away while Shane follows behind like a lost puppy, shooting daggers at me with each step. Even once he's past me, he eyes me over his shoulder. I smile back at him. *Kill em' with kindness*. Until I get my hands on him that is.

Using this time wisely, I figure I should catch up with the boys. We didn't get a chance to talk last night and I really need to make sure they're on the same page as far as my plan goes.

Pulling my phone out of the side pocket of my bag, I shoot Lars and Talon a group text.

Me: Meet me at Briarwood ASAP

Lars: Leaving Willa's doc appointment. We'll be there in ten.

Talon: Your timing sucks ass!

Me: Take her from behind, you'll finish faster.

Talon: Fuck you.

Me: Sounds like Marni's already got you covered.

Lars: You guys are so immature.

Talon: Says the dad.

Me: Boom! He told you.

Lars: Speaking of, Willa wants a co-ed baby shower. I expect you both to be there. Two weeks.

Me: And you agreed to that shit?

Lars: You try arguing with a seven month pregnant chick. I will not.

Talon: Marni and I will be there.

Me: I guess. Gotta drive now. See ya soon.

Whoever came up with that co-ed baby shower stuff was a pussy-whipped bitch. Then again, me agreeing to attend means I'm not much better.

Seven minutes after leaving the school, I'm pulling up to Briarwood. This place holds so many memories. Good and bad. There was a time when it was solely visited for a good time. Smoking weed, drinking beer, and banging chicks. Now, we only come here when we need to plot destruction—or hide a body. Chills wash over me at the thought. It was only four months ago that Josh's body lay on the basement floor wrapped up in Zed's grandma's blanket.

So much has happened since then.

I wait in the car until I see the flicker of headlights bounce down the gravel drive. Lars and Willa pull up first, and Talon and Marni trail right behind.

Killing the engine, I jump out of the truck and shut the door. "Hey, fellas. Miss me?" I throw my hands in the air.

"Wanna know what I miss? Normalcy." Lars holds up his phone with Josh's death certificate pulled up on the screen. "This is fucked up." He taps out of the message and sticks his phone in his back pocket.

"Yeah, no shit. Any guesses on who sent it?" I ask.

"I have a few," Talon chimes in and starts counting off fingers, "Zed. Zed. Oh, and Zed."

I shake my head in disagreement. "Really don't think it was him."

Talon puts an arm around Marni's waist and pulls her close. "Ok then, what's your guess?"

"Shane Velmont. Anderson Thorn, maybe?" I look at Marni. "Sorry Marni, but after everything we did to him, it's possible."

She rolls her eyes and shrugs her shoulders. She doesn't wanna agree, but deep down, I think she knows it's a possibility. Anderson is a smart man with connections. It very well could have been him. "But, my bet is on Shane."

"Is that because you think it's him? Or because you want it to be him?" Marni asks. She gives me a weird smirk that has me questioning what she's implying here.

"Why would I *want* it to be him? I don't *want it* to be anyone."

She cocks a brow. "Oh, I dunno. Maybe because it would be a chance for you to get revenge on him for everything else he does to piss you off."

"Whoever I get my revenge on will get it because they deserve it. Not for the simple matter that I don't like them. I don't like a lot of people but that doesn't mean I go around torturing them or bullying them. Shane's a fucking asshole. If he did do this, he will pay." I can feel myself getting fired up and I have to take a few deep breaths to calm myself down before I lose my shit.

Lars huffs in agitation. "Alright. So what's the plan? It's getting late. Willa's hungry and we're getting nowhere."

"Party on Friday like we planned. I'm talking huge. I'll make an appearance, appear drunk, and then I'll go pass out..or so everyone will think. That's all I need. I have someone else helping me with the other side of things."

Talon drops his arm from around Marni's waist and balls his fists at his side. "What the fuck do you mean you have someone else helping you?" He takes a step toward me. "You let an outsider in on this?"

"No outsiders. He's one of us."

Lars joins Talon's side. "Wait a damn minute. Have you been talking to Zed?"

I tsk. "No questions asked, remember?"

Talon lets out an airy chuckle. "Oh I see how it is. You're taking his side now."

"Didn't know we were on opposite sides. Just last month, you were letting him crash at your house to get what you wanted from him. Now I'm getting grief because I asked him for help?"

"Dude," Lars throws his hands in the air, "we would have helped you."

"I needed someone ruthless. You're having a baby soon. Talon is still reeling from his revenge against his dad. Besides, it's a good chance to see where Zed's loyalties lie. Regardless of the shit he's pulled, he's still one of us. Everything in between, remember?"

Talon sweeps the air with his hand and walks back to his SUV. "Whatever, I'm outta here." Once he gets to the driver's side, he shouts, "I'll have your party because I'm a man of my word, but don't bring that shithead back to Redwood."

Marni holds up a finger and hollers to Talon, "Wait a minute." Her attention then shifts to me. "Tommy, can I talk to you for a minute?"

"Yeah, sure."

Side by side, we walk away from Lars and Willa and closer to the building. "I know that we've had a bit of a rough patch because of your vendetta against Wyatt, but that's in the past, right?"

"Of course. We're cool." I slap a hand to her shoulder.

"Ok, good. Also, I want to stress this as much as I possibly can, don't hurt him, Tommy." Her expression grows solemn and her eyes soften in the light of the bright sun.

"Plans changed. Wyatt isn't the issue anymore."

"That's not what I meant. Don't hurt him, Tommy. And I'm telling him the same thing about you. I care about you both a lot."

Trying hard to read into what she's saying, I can only come up with one conclusion—she knows.

"How do you—?"

"I can tell. You threw so much shit his way, but he still watched you with lust-filled eyes and a palpitating chest. And when he wasn't looking, but I was, I saw the same reaction from you. Oh, and not to mention the fresh condom that laid on top of the garbage in the bathroom at the cabin yesterday."

My face drops into my hands and I shake my head. When I look up, she's still there. She didn't run and spread the word that I have a crush on another guy—and slept with him. She's not shaming me, shunning me, or turning her back on me. "Don't say anything to anyone. I'm still sorting this all out. I don't know what the fuck I'm doing."

"Maybe you should stop trying so hard to," she air quotes, "*sort it out,* and just let things happen the way they're meant to. We all love you, Tommy. Doesn't matter who you love back, or who you're attracted to. This group of friends is the most loyal and fucking awesome group I've ever had the pleasure of being in. A little screwed up, and a whole lotta crazy, but we've got each other's backs."

I pull her in for a hug. "Thanks, Marni."

When we both pull back, she holds out her fist, just like me and the guys always do. "From start to finish."

I bump her fist back. "And everything in between."

"Would you two wrap up this little moment you're having over there? I've got a pregnant chick who's hungry and if I don't feed her within the next five minutes, you'll all be hiding another body because she'll fucking kill me in the car."

Marni and I both laugh as we make our way back over to them. Talon is standing on the frame of his SUV with his hands hanging over the open door. "Come on, babe. We gotta go finish what we started."

I shout back, "Really, man? You had to do that. She's like a fucking sister to us. We don't need to know that shit."

In true Talon fashion, he flips me off then drops down into the front seat.

CHAPTER SEVENTEEN

TOMMY

I'm back at the high school with five minutes to spare. "Back to Good" by Matchbox Twenty blasts through the speakers as I tap the steering wheel in rhythm to the beat. My eyes laser-focused on the door as I anticipate Wyatt walking out. Naturally, Shane will be on his tail, but he'll go his separate way and Wyatt and I can finally talk.

After my talk with Madeline, then Marni, it's like everything I've been second-guessing or fighting against came to a head and in a matter of days, I've begun to accept what I've always known to be true. It's scary, but it's also bringing me out of the darkness that I've lived in for so long.

It wasn't long ago that I hated Wyatt, or at least I thought I did. Now I know that I never hated him; I was just afraid to *not* hate him. It also helps that I know he hasn't been toying with all of us and lurking in the shadows trying to out us for our part in Josh's disappearance. But someone is. There's no doubt that that person is the one who hit Josh, stalked Willa, and is now taunting all of us. This person holds so many of our secrets and they need to be silenced.

The doors push open and I straighten up in the seat, turning the volume down on the steering wheel. Sure enough, Shane walks out beside him. I expected Wyatt to be hustling to get away from him after spending a torturous hour tutoring him, but they seem to be laughing. Shane's talking with his hands and says something that has Wyatt curling over in hysterics.

Something twinges inside me. I guess I just thought that when things ended between them, that they ended badly. Maybe it was just wishful thinking. Maybe Wyatt still has feelings for Shane.

Nausea pools in my stomach at the thought of them getting back together. Irrational thoughts swirl in my head. What if Wyatt has just been protecting Shane this entire time? What if he's playing me? What if they're both playing me?

Those irrational thoughts and the nausea dissipate quickly and are replaced with fury. One of my biggest fears is being made out to be a fool. Ever since I was a kid, I've always been in constant defense mode. I'm a listener, not a talker. I rarely let my guard down. Never let anyone see me vulnerable—in fact, I prefer to bring out the vulnerability in others. Kill or be killed.

But I showed Wyatt a side of me that I never wanted to, and the idea of him using that against me has me clenching my fingers around the steering wheel so tightly my palms begin to burn.

Wyatt catches my stare and waves Shane off. Shane looks in my direction and scowls as Wyatt makes his way to my truck. I click the unlock button, so he can get it, but he comes to the driver's side instead.

Rolling the window down, I draw in a deep breath then exhale slowly. "What the hell was that all about?"

"What?" he asks. His arms fold over the window frame and I fight hard not to notice how good he smells.

"You and Shane. You looked pretty chummy a minute ago."

"Oh," he chuckles, "we were just talking about the time I went to one of his games and he threw a curveball and hit Leon

Michaels right in the balls. Guy's an ass, but he's got a killer arm."

I don't return the smile he gives me with his response. Instead, my expression stays stern. "I thought you two were over."

"We are. But I had to tutor him today."

"So you said."

"Wait a minute. Are you...jealous?" He smirks.

"Fuck no, I'm not jealous." I'm not. Not even a little bit. So what if the idea of them getting close again feels like a knife slowly penetrating my spine. Shane's a snake. Wyatt might not see it right now, but he will. "Are you gonna get in or what?"

"You want me to?" He seems surprised. I'm pretty sure I told him I wanted to talk. Did he think I just wanted to catch the weather report for tomorrow or something?

I can feel myself getting even more agitated. "Yes, I want you to. That's why I'm here."

He seems a bit taken aback. "Ok. I didn't know." Rounding the truck, he opens the passenger door and gets in. "Sorry to keep you waiting. I didn't even know I was tutoring him until after lunch. I'm sure he did this on purpose."

And now I feel like an ass. "No, it's cool. I just know that you don't deserve the shit he put you through and seeing you two laughing made me think….I don't know. Just forget about it."

"That we were getting back together? No. Not a chance in hell."

Relief washes over me. I really should give Wyatt more credit than what I do. He's a smart guy. Knows an asshole when he sees one. Well, except for me. But I like to think I'm the exception.

"So, what's up? Everything ok?" he asks.

"Yeah." I comb my fingers through my hair, pushing it off my forehead. "We didn't really talk much about what happened and I know that I sort of left things hanging."

I turn to look at him and our eyes meet. His fluffed brows furrow and his brown eyes ignite electricity into mine. "I get it. I know you need time. I'm good with waiting until you're ready."

"You wanna get out of here?" I spit out on impulse.

He smiles back at me. "With you? Yes."

Shifting in drive, I roll my window up and pull out of the parking lot. A few minutes later, I'm pulling back down the drive to Briarwood. This is the only place I can think of that we can get some privacy to finally talk. Though, my mind is elsewhere right now.

"Really? This place gives me the creeps. I hope you don't plan on us going inside there."

I don't respond. I pop the door open and jump out. "Come on," I say, before shutting it. Then I walk with long strides up to the asylum.

Wyatt follows behind with his backpack flung over his shoulder but is in no hurry to catch up. I don't look back but jog up the cement stairs two at a time and push open the old wooden door, leaving it open behind me.

I take about six steps in and press my back to the wall beside the door and wait for him to make an appearance. Once his feet hit the floor, I grab him by the arm, slam the door shut and spin him around so his back is to the wall. Then I devour his mouth with mine. "You're fucking killing me, Wyatt," I mutter into his tantalizing mouth. Sucking his bottom lip between my teeth then sliding my tongue between his lips. He tastes so damn good.

Pushing down the sleeves of his unzipped sweater, it hangs freely from his forearms. My hand slithers up his shirt and over the smooth skin of his chest. "Ever since the locker room, this is all I can think about. It's all I wanna do."

"You're all I think about, too." Our mouths reconnect and it's everything I want and more. His touch, his scent—the nervousness in his bite as he nibbles at the lobe of my ear. Wondering if

I'm going to lash out or throw a tantrum. I can't quit him. Not this time.

Bony fingers snake down my pants and my body reacts with a shiver. The feelings washing over me are like nothing I've felt in my entire life. Even my first time with Jackie Henderson in the ninth grade when I came as soon as my cock slid inside of her. The stimulation alone had my body feeling like I was on the verge of convulsing. But I never felt connected to her. Even as years passed by and I'd see her in the hall.

What once was a loud girl with big tits who skipped class and smoked cigarettes under the bleachers during football games, grew into our class valedictorian. She alone is proof that people change. Or maybe we don't. Maybe we just find ourselves.

Goosebumps cascade down my back and Wyatt swallows up all my thoughts, leaving me with nothing but a dire need to touch him back. Tearing his sweater off all the way, I press his shoulders against the wall and trail my lips down his neck. "This hold you have on me. Do I have it on you?" I have to know. Do I disrupt his sleep? Wake him during his dreams? Haunt his thoughts?

"You've been holding onto me longer than I'll ever admit. This," he takes a step back and looks at me, "is all I've ever wanted. It feels unreal."

Our lips crash together again. This time, there is nothing tender in our kiss. It's unrestrained and grating. Articles of clothing shed one by one and our lips separate only to pull our shirts over our heads, then they find their way back to each other.

Sliding down together, Wyatt fluffs a shirt out behind me and my back falls to the cold, dirty floor. His warm body presses against mine, making me forget where we are. It doesn't matter. Nothing matters but this—us. I'd give anything to pause time and live in this moment where the world isn't waiting outside. No one to answer to. No one to put on a mask for. With Wyatt, I can be myself and he embraces all that I am.

"I'm sorry," I choke out, my emotions getting the best of me. "I'm sorry I was such an ass to you."

He presses a finger to my lips. "You didn't know any better." Dropping his finger, his mouth replaces it. Soft, subtle, agonizing.

All I want is to feast on him like he's my last meal. I want him to show me everything. I want it all from him.

His cock digs into the crease of my thigh and he reaches down and takes both of ours into one of his hands. Rubbing them together. Stroking up and down as his smooth skin melts with mine. A low groan releases from deep inside me and spills into his mouth.

Body to body, we lie there. My pelvis grinding against his knuckles as he lifts his chest off mine and peers down at his hand that holds us. His thumb grazes the head of my cock, sweeping up a bead of precum and using it as lube.

"I want more," I tell him. His wide eyes stare back into mine as I talk. "I need more."

"What do you want?" His voice is husky and he holds this confidence that I've never seen before. It's sexy as hell watching him take charge. Teaching me things he already knows.

"I wanna fuck you this time."

He seems surprised, but doesn't say it. "Ok. I've got a condom in my backpack." He pushes himself off me and reaches over to grab his bag. He digs inside and pulls out a condom in one hand and some lotion in the other. His eyebrows waggle. "It's our lucky day."

"Darn, I was hoping to spit on you this time," I tease with a smirk.

"Oh, I'm sure you'll have your chance at some point." Taking my hand in his, he squirts some lotion on the tips of my fingers.

With my hand held out, I try not to smooth the lotion into my skin.

He pulls the top of the wrapper off and rolls it down my cock. Once it's on, his lips press to mine quickly before he takes me by the hand and pulls me to my knees. His body turns and he gets on all fours in front of me. We're still right in front of the door and at any point, anyone could walk in, but it doesn't stop me.

I'm hesitant to make a move here. This is all so new to me.

I line a finger up with his entrance, but refrain from putting any pressure on him. His head twists back and he looks at me. "Just like you'd finger a girl from behind, he tells me.

Ok. I can do this.

Rubbing some of the lotion on his hole, I dip inside of him up to the joint of my finger. Sliding in and out while slowly adding more, until I fill him up. My cock throbs with the need to be inside of him. To feel him wrapped around me while I pound him from behind.

Another finger joins and sweeps in and out, stretching him for what's coming next. He begins swaying back and forth with his ass tipped up as he tries to get me to hit a certain spot, and once I do, I prod my fingers against it and he lets out a low groan that has my dick quivering.

"Alright, I'm ready," he says.

Pulling my fingers out, I stretch my hand up to Wyatt who's holding the lotion. He squirts some on my hand and I rub it up and down the condom. I place my slippery hands on his hips and move mine forward slightly; my head lines up with his hole and I slide it in. He doesn't whimper or jolt; instead, he pushes his ass back and takes more of me. Moving back and forth, I give him the shallow end of my cock—afraid to go any further. I once tried to stick my dick in a girl's ass and she punched me. To say that I don't have a little PTSD from that moment would be a lie.

"I'm ok. Trust me," he says.

Pushing farther, my pelvic bone hits is ass. Slowly, I glide in and out until I get into a rhythm. Then, I pick up my pace. Wyatt drops to his elbows with his arms spread in front of him. His ass rocking back and forth against me. He's so tight and it feels like heaven inside of him. I can feel my cock throb relentlessly.

Smacking my hands to his hips, I get a good grip and dig deeper. Thrusting faster until I'm slamming in and out of him. I throw my head back and close my eyes, relishing in this intense pleasure.

"Baby," he groans, "you're doing so fucking good."

Giving me the confidence I need, my head falls forward, my mouth agape as I squeeze his sides tighter and pound him from behind. Vibrating off his ass in quick and sudden thrusts.

Wyatt reaches back and grabs one of my hands and pulls me forward. My chest presses to his back while he drops my hand on his cock. I continue to fuck him while stroking him from underneath.

Untucking my knees, I get to my feet. Slouched down with my legs spread on either side of him. Using all of my lower body strength, I roll my hips in a circular motion, feeling every wall on his insides.

"Fuck!" I cry out. "I'm gonna come." Just as the words leave my mouth, I feel myself fill up the condom. Electricity zaps every cell in my body as I come undone. I don't stop. I keep going as he begins ramming himself against me. Moments later, his cum shoots all over my hand. I continue to stroke him through his orgasm until his body twitches.

Sliding out slowly, I let go of his dick, and he turns around. The condom hangs from me so I pull it off and set it down next to us. Making a mental note to clean up the mess that just spilled from it.

Wyatt sits on the floor in front of me and leans forward to

steal a kiss from me before I go to clean up. "You did awesome. That was…amazing," he says.

I smile in response. My mind is reeling from all of these emotions hitting me at once. Taking in a deep breath, I stand up and scoop up the dirty condom. I don't even put on clothes before going to find somewhere to throw this thing away.

There's a black trash bag that's likely filled with old keg cups, so I pull it back and drop the condom inside. There's no running water or electricity, so I step out the back door to take a piss. The sun has set and there's a chill to the night air.

"Tommy? Where are you?" Wyatt asks as he comes walking down the hall. I give myself a shake and turn around. He pushes through the screen door and stands beside me. "This place is terrifying. I swear I just heard someone crying. Don't ever leave me again."

I laugh. "You probably did. Rumor has it there's a girl who haunts the place."

Grabbing me by the arm, he pulls me close. "Stop it!"

"I'm not kidding. Zed says he's seen her a couple times."

"Alright. Clothes now. We're getting the hell out of here."

"Really?" I turn to face him. "Was kinda hoping we could stay."

"Like all night?" His head shakes in disagreement. "I'd love nothing more than to stay the night with you, Tommy. But I draw the line at haunted asylums."

I pull him close, our naked bodies pressed against each other. "If you get to teach me new experiences, it's only fair that I get to return the favor." My hands trail up and down his arms, goosebumps following behind my touch.

His eyes widen in surprise, and he frowns. "You're serious?"

"Dead serious."

He drops his head to my shoulder. "Alright then. I guess it's only fair."

"Come on." I take him by the hand and pull him back inside.

We get cleaned up and dressed—me without a shirt because mine was used as a mat on the floor—then I run out to my truck to grab a blanket from the back seat that's been there ever since I got a license. During my search, I also find a hoodie that I throw on.

Once I'm back inside, we go upstairs to the most comfortable room in this place. Nothing about this building offers comfort, but the guys and I hang out in this room a lot. There's a blanket over the window and a couple butane lanterns. The walls are covered in artwork by yours truly. Some might call it graffiti or vandalism; I call it art. Doesn't matter where the picture is painted, it's the story behind it that matters. It could be on the side of a building, beneath some bleachers, or the bedroom wall of a guy you've been trying to push out of your head—art is art.

"We're actually sleeping up here?" Wyatt asks as he takes in his surroundings.

With both ends of the blanket gripped in my hand, I swing it up and let it fall to the floor. "Yup."

"Ya know, I can pay for a hotel if you wanna stay the night together. No need to wake the spirits in this place. They might get pissed that we're in their home."

I laugh. "Nah, they don't care." I watch as he stands there, unsure of whether or not he really wants to do this. "Get over here." I pat the blanket next to where I lie on my side.

Getting on his knees, he finally drops down next to me on his side. With my elbow pressed to the floor and my fist under my chin, we're face to face. I place a hand on his side and pull him closer. This is what I've wanted. To just lie here with him, get tangled in his arms, while digging into his heart and finding out what makes it tick.

Once he seems to let his guard down a tad, he slides closer and wraps an arm around me. His lips brush gently across mine before he nuzzles his head to my chest. I drop my hand down and position it under his head, pulling him even closer. And we just lie there quietly in each other's arms.

"Can we just stay here forever?" he whispers.

"If only that were possible."

"What happens when we leave? What does tomorrow bring?"

"Not sure. I guess we just take it one day at a time." I'd love nothing more than to explore this further, but I still have so much to figure out. I'm far from being ready to share this with everyone else.

Right now, it's just for us.

My eyes slowly start to close as my thoughts feel like they are getting further and further away, when all of a sudden, there's a blow to the window. We both spring up and Wyatt screeches. "Holy shit!" His hands slap to his chest. "What was that?"

Glass shatters beneath the black blanket over the window. Dropping slivers of crystals to the floor. They glisten in the dim light of the lantern and a ball rolls away from the wall.

"What the fuck!" I grumble, "Someone's here." Pushing myself off the floor, I get to my feet and bolt to the window. I bend down and pick up the ball that has a note tied around it with a rubber band. Pulling back the blanket, I try to get a look outside, but it's dark and I see nothing.

I let the blanket fall back in place then unravel the rubber band before dropping the ball to the floor.

"Whoever did this is an excellent throw," Wyatt says as he joins my side.

I unfold the small white paper and read the words written in black ink while Wyatt hovers at my side.

Are we playing hide and seek? I found you. Your turn.

We both look at each other. Fear in his eyes, and anger boiling in mine.

I bend down and pick up the ball. I plan on keeping every

last bit of evidence that son of a bitch has given us. "He better hope I never find him. I'll kill him."

"Maybe we should go," Wyatt says. "My parents are gone. We can go back to my place."

"I don't think that's a good idea. But, you're right, we should get outta here. I'll come back tomorrow after school and scope out the area to see if he left anything behind."

Wyatt pulls on my arm, all too anxious to leave this place. "Come on."

I follow behind him. Snatching up the blanket from the floor as we head out.

Whoever this is, they're getting brave. I hope they keep it up because, eventually, they'll slip up and I'll nail them…right in the fucking head.

CHAPTER EIGHTEEN

WYATT

Dragging my feet, I walk from my car to the front doors of the high school. My eyes do a sweep of the parking lot, but I don't see Tommy's truck where it's usually parked. It wouldn't surprise me if he skipped today; we had a pretty late night.

My heart flutters at the memories of last night. It was everything and more. My lips tug up in a smile before I feel the force of a body hit my side. I look over abruptly. "Hey, Shay."

"What are you so happy about?" she quips.

"Oh, nothing." I avoid looking at her because I know she'll see more of my giddiness and dig further.

"No one smiles like that this early. Spill." Just as the words leave her mouth, I catch Tommy driving across the parking lot. His window is down with his arm resting on the sill. He looks at me, then Shay.

In an attempt to read Shay's thoughts, I study her.

"Why are you looking at me like that?" she nudges me, "you creep."

I laugh. "I saw that smile grow on your face when he pulled

in." I really did. As much as I don't wanna admit it, I think Shay likes him.

"Who, Tommy? Nah. He's cute and all, but it was just a quick fling."

We step into the school and the chatter of students has me raising my voice. "Oh yeah?" I say, wondering if she'll elaborate further.

"Besides, even if I were interested in a relationship, Tommy's too closed-off and not very affectionate."

I feel an immense amount of relief hearing her say this. I would have been the asshole who tried to pretend that my best friend wasn't pining after the same guy as I was. Sadly, it wouldn't have stopped me. Now that this thing has started with Tommy, I don't think I'll ever be able to let it end. I just hope he feels the same way.

"Yeah. You're probably right."

Shay stops in the hall. Stands directly in front of me, and this time, she's the one studying me. "Wait a damn minute. Wyatt McCoy, you have a crush on him, don't you?"

"What?" I grimace, "No way!" I try to walk around her to avoid her seeing the *lie* written all over my face. If she sees my expression, it might as well be in capital letters with permanent marker, because I'm such a terrible liar.

"Do so!"

Before I can respond, Tommy walks past us. In a pair of straight cut black jeans with fringe hanging from the holes of his knees, his everyday black combat boots, and a snug fitting black t-shirt with some graphic on the front that I didn't catch. His sandy blond hair is flipped over to one side and the tattoos on his arms flex out with his veins as he walks. My heart jumps as I hold in a breath, feeling faint while a swarm of butterflies attack my stomach. His gaze follows over his shoulder while he keeps walking. "Hey, Wyatt." He smiles with a flash wave, before turning back and continuing down the hall.

I completely forgot Shay was even standing here, let alone the entire student body. For that sliver of a second, it was just me and Tommy. "Oh my god, Wyatt!" Shay slaps my arm. "Since when does Tommy say hi to you...and when did he start putting smiles like that on your face." She pokes my cheek and I swat her hand away.

"You're delusional." I keep walking, while she follows and continues to prod.

"And you have a secret."

I can feel my cheeks flush with warmth. It's not embarrassment; it's the weakness in my knees and the attempt to hide everything I'm feeling, while ultimately failing.

We reach my locker, and Shay is still talking. "Ok, I'll drop it for now, but if there is something going on with you two, then it all makes sense and definitely helps my self-esteem. I was starting to think there was something wrong with me."

"Why would you ever think that? You're perfect, baby girl." I give her a kiss to her cheek then continue to unload my backpack, tossing books on the top shelf of my locker.

"That morning he took you home, he called and canceled our plans. I texted him later that night and he sent me a response, explaining that it wasn't me, it was him. I never said anything because I was embarrassed, but I think I know why he did it now. It really wasn't me. It *was* him, and maybe you."

Closing my locker, Shay and I walk to hers next. "You'll find someone eventually, and when you do, you'll know he's the one."

"Is that how you feel about Tommy? You just know?"

"Well, it's..." I stop myself. I almost gave myself up. Almost. I chuckle. "Nice try. I've gotta go. See ya at lunch."

FOUR DAYS DOWN, one more to go and the weekend is here. I slam my locker shut and turn around to find a very unhappy Marni glaring at me from a foot away with some papers in her hand. "Uh oh, who do I have to hurt?" I tease.

"It's a little late for that, the damage is done." She slams the papers to my chest. "Care to explain what the hell this is?"

I look down at the papers. They're printed pictures that look like they came from a security camera at a hotel. A hotel I visited a few months ago. What's worse, is who I'm with. Wrapped in his arms while we kiss in front of the elevator. I look up at her. Her eyes filled to the brim with tears that threaten to spill over. "Marni, I can explain—"

"My dad! Really, Wyatt?" Her fists plant into my chest continuously. "You were having an affair with my father?" I grab ahold of her hands to try and stop her. To try and calm her down. Something—anything.

"How could you do this?" She jerks her wrists away in one swift motion. "How long has this been going on?"

I don't respond. I just look into her eyes and hope that this isn't real. Wish, rather. But it is real, she knows.

"How long?" she shouts even louder.

"It's over now. It lasted a couple months, but I haven't even seen him since before Halloween."

"And these pictures." She knocks the papers from my hand and they fall all around my feet. "When? Where?"

"At the end of last summer. We took a trip to LA."

"This is why you didn't come to my birthday party, isn't it? Because things ended badly between you two." She grabs the sides of her head. "I cannot believe this. My dad? You? He's....gay?"

I look past Marni, and I see him. My heart sinks into the pit of my stomach. Tommy is standing directly behind her. He bends down, picks up the papers and takes one look at them before tossing them back down again. He heads down the hall without a word, pushing through the crowd of students who are just as eager to escape this place as he is. "Tommy! Wait!" I shout. I go to walk after him, but Marni stops me.

"We're not done here."

I collect the images and crumble them into a ball. "Where did you get these?"

"They were in my locker."

"Well, someone put them there to try and hurt you. To try and hurt me."

"Who cares? You slept with my dad, Wyatt!" Her head shakes continuously while her entire body trembles. Her cheeks are tear-stained and the tip of her nose is tinged pink. "I have to go."

Just like Tommy, she walks away. I don't chase after her. Instead, I uncrumple the papers and take one last look.

This has gone too far.

CHAPTER NINETEEN

TOMMY

Are you fucking kidding me? Marni's dad?

Forceful steps lead me through the parking lot, moving as quickly as I can. My mind is full of questions that I don't even wanna ask, let alone know the answers to them.

Was it Anderson that he was trying to get away from that night? Is Anderson more a part of this than we thought? How long was this thing going on between them? Is it still going on?

Ripping the door open to my truck, I jump inside. Turning the key, I shift into drive before the engine even comes to life.

One last glance at the door has me screaming internally at myself for even looking to see if he was running out after me. Of course, Marni is his best friend and his priority and I don't blame him for sticking around to try and feed her some lame ass excuse as to why he was banging her forty-year-old dad.

"Fuck!" I shout, slamming my hands to the steering wheel. I was such a damn fool. Wyatt grabbed my attention out of nowhere a few months ago and every time I saw him, he took a little bit more of me. Until I gave him everything. Let my guard down, let him in, and he was probably making jokes behind my back with this full grown, experienced man.

He's a fucking whore, that's what he is. And I was just another side piece while his main piece was away on business.

With no destination in mind, I keep driving.

An hour passes and I've lapped around the entire town lost in my thoughts. Wyatt hasn't even tried to call me. Why would he? He got what he wanted.

My mind continue to run rampant. Wyatt drove down Marni's road right after Josh was hit, or so he says. He claims he was trying to get away from someone. I know now that person was Anderson. We all know Anderson was there.

Whipping a U-turn in the middle of the road, I drive toward Briarwood. I need to look around the place like I planned. See if I can find anything that the person outside last night may have left behind.

It's almost like this person wants to be caught. They're not being very careful anymore. It wouldn't surprise me if they left behind another clue.

Reaching over to my glovebox, it drops open and I grab the ball from last night.

Whoever threw this has really good aim to make it in a window that high up on the first try.

We were just talking about the time I went to one of his games and he threw a curveball and hit Leon Michaels right in the balls. Guys an ass, but he's got a killer arm.

"Yes!" I toss the ball up and down in my hand. "I fucking found you, you son of a bitch. You can run, but you can't hide."

It seems that my suspicions were right all along.

I grab my phone off my seat and shoot a text to Zed.

I've had my guesses that it was Shane. Even if it wasn't him, I still need to have a little chat with him about unsportsmanlike conduct. He's gotten under my skin for the last time. If he wants any future in sports, he's going to listen to me or I'll report his steroid use to Coach. His scholarship will go down the drain faster than his pills would.

Me: Still on for tomorrow?

He doesn't respond right away, so I head back down the driveway. There's no need to look around now; I got what I was looking for.

I don't go home; instead, I go to Talon's. There's a small chance that Wyatt will come looking for me and I know damn well he wouldn't dare show his face here.

Checking my phone before I go inside, I see a response from Zed.

Zed: All set.

When I go in, Marni is a ball of tears on the couch as Talon holds her tightly to his chest. Shutting the door quietly behind me, I try not to disturb them, but it does no good. Marni's eyes shoot up to mine.

"Can you believe this shit, Tommy? My dad?"

"Yeah, it's pretty messed up." I don't say more and I really hope Marni hasn't said anything about her knowledge of me and Wyatt. Sometimes emotions get the best of us and we throw people under the bus without even realizing we're doing it.

"All the times he spent the night at my house. When he'd wake up in the middle of the night to use the bathroom or get water and take forever coming back, I bet he was sneaking into my dad's room."

Holding up a hand, I stop her, not just for her own good, but for mine, too. "Don't let yourself go there. Please."

"I'm sorry—" she begins, but I shake my head no. *Don't say anything. Please just stop talking.* "This is why he stopped coming over and why he never even came to my birthday party. Because he couldn't stand to see my dad."

I assumed that this thing between Wyatt and Anderson was still going on. Was I wrong? Taking a step farther into the room, I ask her this one question. "So, he said this thing with him and your dad is over?"

She huffs. "That's what he says. It could be a lie. I don't know what to believe anymore."

I'm not sure what to believe either. I shoot a thumb toward the basement door. "Willa and Lars downstairs?"

"Yeah, they're down there planning the baby shower," Talon says.

"Alright. I'll let you two talk. Holler if you need anything." I rub the top of Marni's head as I pass by.

Each step that brings me downstairs feels heavier and heavier. It feels like that dark cloud that hung over my head for so long has returned. I thought Wyatt carried me out of the storm, but in the end, he just pushed me farther into it.

"Hey," I say, as I walk straight for the mini bar. I've been trying to cut back on my drinking, but I'm making an exception. I grab a glass and flip open the lid on the ice maker behind the bar. Digging the spoon in, I drop a few rocks into the glass and pull the top off a glass carafe full of Bourbon.

"You're drinking? It's five o'clock on a school night."

"Listen, *Dad*," I emphasize, "I don't need a lecture. It's been a shitty day."

Tipping the glass back, I take half of the contents and relish the burn. A few more of these should kick Wyatt out of my head for the night.

I walk over to the couch and sit down next to Willa. She's got her legs folded in a pretzel with a notebook in her hand.

I peer over her shoulder. "What's that?"

"We're making a list of guests for the shower." She points to my name with her pen. 'Looks like you made the cut."

I sigh with sarcasm. "Lucky me."

"If I have to be there, you all have to be there," Lars says.

"Well, I can say that this will be my first time attending a baby shower." I look over her shoulder again, searching for one name in particular. "Might wanna cross him off." I point to Wyatt's name. "Marni won't be too happy if he's there."

Willa laughs. "Wyatt is one of her best friends, of course she'd like to see them there."

Dropping back onto the couch, I take another drink. "You obviously haven't heard."

Lars comes forward to get a better look at me. "Heard what?"

"Marni just found out that Wyatt has been screwing her old man." I tip my drink back and let every last drop fall into my mouth until the glass is left with only ice. Before either of them respond, I'm on my feet again for a refill.

Lars gasps. "No fucking way."

Grabbing the carafe, I pour myself another. This time filling it to the brim. "Way. She's upstairs soaking Talon's shoulder over it."

"Well, that sucks, but we've already determined that Wyatt is useless to us," Lars says, as he taps the notebook on Willa's lap. "Let's finish this."

Rounding the bar, I walk over and stand in front of the couch where they sit. "Is he, though? Think about it. Anderson was part of this at one time. Maybe he didn't hit Josh, but both of them were on that road within minutes of each other. We're missing something here. Something big."

"I don't know, man. I really think it's all just a coincidence."

Feeling defeated, I drop back down onto the couch with my drink in hand. There was another car on that shitty footage seconds before Wyatt. The only reason we were able to make out Wyatt's vehicle was because of his neon pink hubcaps.

If Wyatt was trying to get away from Anderson, who was trying to get away from Wyatt?

Everything keeps coming back to Shane. I can feel it in my gut. He hit Josh—maybe it was an accident and he panicked and kept going so that Wyatt didn't know he was there. Somehow Shane got pictures of them at a hotel. He must have known

Wyatt and Anderson had a relationship to go snooping around like that.

Someone is lying, and time's running out. I need to get to the bottom of this before more secrets are exposed and we're all swimming in a pool of shame and humiliation.

CHAPTER TWENTY

WYATT

"Hello, again," I say to Glenda. "Is my father around?" I already know the answer, but for added measure, I play dumb.

"Actually, he left this morning for a meeting in Washau. Anything I can help you with?"

"Oh darn. I was hoping to see him. I'm sure you've heard that I'll be joining the team shortly after graduation."

Her eyes light up as she begins gnawing on the end of a pen. "I did! We're all so excited to have you join us. I suppose I should begin calling you Mr. McCoy now, huh?"

I chuckle. "No, please don't. Wyatt is fine." I'm not ready for that title just yet. I need a few more years on me before I'll even respond to that name. Mr. McCoy is my father. "Well, he knows I was coming in today to take a look around. Can I get one of those access card thingies?"

"Of course. Let me just try and get your dad on the line to get his approval. Wouldn't wanna lose my job for handing out cards to the wrong person."

"Oh sure. I totally get it. But, Glenda, it's me." I pat my hands to my chest. "I'll be taking control of security, not to mention the staff. I could hire and fire anyone I want at the drop of a hat. There's no reason to bother my dad, is there?" I hate to be that person, but if I'm stepping in as CEO, then it's time to start running shit around here. "I'll need unlimited access as well."

Her jaw about hits the desk and I assume she caught on to my nonchalant threat. Dad has no idea I was coming in today. But, even he knew I was, he'd question why I need an access card. Dad is a smart man and he wouldn't hesitate to drill me as to why I needed it.

There are a few different departments here and while Magna designs the products, they're manufactured at a factory in California. From there, they are distributed to warehouses all over the country, and a big majority are also sent back here for quality checks and software upgrades. I need to get into the control room where these upgrades and quality checks take place. Security is top notch here, but with a card, and my head hung low, I can easily blend in.

She pulls a card out from a drawer and holds it underneath a scanner. "I suppose I can let you through this one time."

"Appreciate it, Glenda." She hands me the card then sweeps the room with her eyes to make sure no one is looking, who might question her decision to grant me access to every door in this building. "Return the card before you leave, please." She's no longer using the sweet voice she had when she welcomed me.

When I agreed to do this, it was for Tommy. Now, this is just as much for me as it is him.

Pulling the rooms from memory of my visit here earlier this week, I walk briskly through the halls.

Leaving the office part of the building, I take the elevator to the lower level where the control room is. It's a short ride before I'm stepping out into a dim hall that has cameras on every end and doors with scanners in front of them. There's a sign overhead one of the doors that reads *Authorized Personnel Only*. Bingo—that's my room.

During my tour with Marty, this was as far as we went. But I know that the action happens behind these doors.

Holding my card under the scanner, I wait for the light to flash green before turning the handle. I step inside, and it's nothing like I expected. A wall of monitors take up one side of the room and another door inside with a rectangular glass window is on the other side. I catch a glimpse of men walking around inside and the equipment I see leads me to believe that's where I need to be.

"Excuse me. You don't have permission to be here." A very large gentleman says as he walks over to me.

"As a matter of fact I do. Do you have any idea who I am?" Damnit, that sounded pompous as hell. I really hate pulling that card, but I have to be aggressive.

He grabs a hold of my arm and begins pulling the door back open. "I don't give a shit who you are. This room is for security only."

"If you wanna keep your job, I suggest you get your hands off me right now."

"Listen kid, just get outta here before I drag your ass out. Make it easy on yourself."

"Unless you want my father, Royce McCoy, called down here immediately, you're gonna walk right back over to that chair and watch those monitors like you're paid to do."

"Wyatt?" he says my name in question, like he's heard of me. Of course he has. Dad's always talking about his son who will run this place one day. It's probably the only time he mentions me.

"That's right." I jerk my arm out of his hold abruptly. "I need to see the control room. There was an issue with a malfunctioning Nano Tracker and I was sent down for a part number." I might not know much about this company, but I do know some.

"Why not just call? Marty could've got that for you."

"Where is Marty? I'd like to speak with him."

He looks down at the card in my hand. "You got an access card?"

Pulling my phone out of my pocket, I use it to my advantage and raise my voice. "Yes, I've got a card. How the hell do you think I got in here? Now, point me in the direction of Marty before I dial my father and tell him you're the reason that I'm taking so long.

Sweeping the air with his hand, he huffs. "In there. Make it quick."

Drawing in a deep breath, I scan my card again to gain access to the control room. My head feels faint and I do not like this one bit. If only there were another way.

I step inside the room and everyone just carries on with their business like they don't even see me. It's dim inside and most of the light shines from the monitors all over the room. I catch sight of Marty while he uses an authoritative tone toward someone that I take to be an intern.

Greeting him with a wave, I walk over to him. "Hey, Marty." I stretch my hand out and he extends his with a shake. "I need you to point me in the direction of the Nano Tracker devices that are currently being tested for quality."

"Jimmy," he hollers, "he needs to see the Nanos that passed this afternoon."

Trying hard to hide my astonishment that he didn't question anything I just said, I walk over to Jimmy who's waving me in his direction. I'm still surprised at myself for getting the Magna lingo down correctly. I guess it does pay to eavesdrop on Dad's conversations from time to time. I remember when he first started the company from the ground up, it's all he talked about. That was back when we had family dinners around the table and Mom was still home every day.

"Have a seat. Check it out," Jimmy tells me before he gets up and walks over to Marty who's in the middle of explaining SD card placement to the intern. "I'm taking my lunch," Jimmy tells Marty.

Looking all around like I'm expecting someone to jump out and grab me and drag me out of here, I'm taken aback when no one seems to care. All the hoops I had to jump through to get inside, and now it's like it doesn't even matter. I suppose they probably assume if I made it past Mr. Macho out there, then I'm good.

I drop down into the large black chair, and by drop, I mean sink. There's a box of trackers to my right and a bunch of cords connected to it that run from a monitor.

Glancing over my shoulder to the left, and then to the right, I pull my phone out of my pocket. Whoever sent the death certificate to all of us has to be the same person popping up and exposing my secrets.

Rummaging through the endless amounts of cords and connectors, I find one that fits perfectly into the charging port of my phone. The monitor flashes, then beeps loudly. One, two, three beeps. My eyes shoot over my shoulder, but no one pays any attention to me. There's a button on the touch screen that says start scan, but I'm not sure how I trace the actual message.

Fuck.

"Hey, man," I say to a guy who's sitting about three feet down at another monitor. "Can you help me out a minute?"

Pulling off a pair of earphones that hang around his neck, he drops them on the connected desk in front of him and walks over. His palms press to the desk. "Whatcha need?"

"My dad, Mr. McCoy, sent me down to check this device. Figured I'd just mess around and check it with my phone. How do I trace a specific message?"

"Open the message on your phone, tap the screen, and info will pop up." He pats my back and returns to his work.

Seriously? It's that easy?

I do what he said, and wait as the screen loads. *Tracing*

flashes on the screen with a meter bar that fills up pretty quickly. *Almost there. Almost there.* It feels like there's a jackhammer inside my chest and my palms are sweating profusely. I wipe the back of my hands across my forehead and brush away the beads of sweat that are pooling.

Complete.

Damn it! I should have known whoever did this would be smart enough not to use their own personal phone. All I've got is a registered address.

Shuffling things around on the desk, I find a sticky note and a pen and jot down the address in Stanton. It's about twenty minutes from Redwood, so it shouldn't be hard to find out where this address leads.

"If you tap that again, it'll give you the rest of the info." The guy who just helped me appears over my shoulder and my heart jumps into my throat from him scaring the shit out of me. "These devices passed quality but there was an upgrade about an hour ago."

"Oh, thanks," I tell him as I tap an arrow on the screen.

It shows the number, date of activation, and that the call was placed in Stanton. Here I thought that the owner of the phone lived in Stanton. I guess both are possibilities. It still doesn't give me a name, but I need to go to this address.

Unplugging my phone quickly, I jump up and don't even announce my exit. Walking out the door, I go through the security room and back out into the open hallway. Pressing my back to the wall, I take a deep breath.

I'm not telling anyone about this yet. First, I need to find out where this address takes me.

CHAPTER TWENTY-ONE

TOMMY

Wyatt never called last night, and since I skipped school today, I haven't seen him at all. It's safe to say that what happened between us had little to no effect on him. He hasn't even tried to explain himself. He claims that him and Anderson are over, but why hasn't he tried to explain that to me?

All these months of questioning what I was feeling, and then I finally gave in, and suddenly, everything started to make sense and I was on the brink of acceptance. Now, I'm left wondering if it was even worth it to put myself out there like I did. If I could go back and keep this secret a little longer, I would. But it's not my secret anymore. People now know.

I walk through Talon's yard feeling like I'm wearing shades of regret that grab everyone's attention. I can feel their eyes on me and it makes me wonder if they know. Do they know that the best sex of my life was with a guy? That I loved every second of it and wanna do it again, and again, and again? Do they know that I would be perfectly content never sleeping with another chick again because I prefer guys—because I prefer Wyatt? Do they know that I'm gay?

The front door is wide open and people are coming and

going. Taking the party from inside to outside and vice versa. There's girls in swimsuits around the pool and they must be drunk already because it's still too cold for swimming, especially at night. They're probably just trying to catch the attention of some guys. That's what girls do.

"Hey, man." Talon pats a hand to my shoulder then gestures around the room. "How'd we do?"

"Perfect. Everything I envisioned."

"Good. Now take this." He hands me a plastic cup then leans in and whispers, "It's water. Keep downing them."

People need to see me here. Living it up, mingling, drinking, and having a good time. Even if my insides feel like they're being ripped apart. It's all for show.

Looking around the room, I search for him. I should know better, though.

"Who ya looking for?"

"No one. Just seeing who all is here."

"Everyone," he beams with a raise of his glass, "everyone is here." *Not everyone.* "Oh, and my girl is getting a little drunk right now so help me keep an eye on her. She's still pretty pissed off and you never know who she might take it out on."

I nod, still searching the room. Talon was literally just talking about how Marni is pissed over what Wyatt did; yet, I continue to search for him. *What the fuck is wrong with me?*

He's not here. He wouldn't dare show his face and he probably doesn't want to anyways. Wyatt's not a loner, but he's also not big on the party scene.

The plan was always for him to be here. I wanted him here where he'd be safe from incrimination. Because he has a part in this, it would be easy for fingers to point at him. But, one shift in the plan doesn't mean it all falls apart. Hopefully he's somewhere he can get an alibi if needed. Regardless of how hurt I am, I don't want to see his world fall apart.

"Dude. You alright?"

"Hmm? Yeah. I'm good. Just going over the plan in my head."

"I wouldn't know anything about that because you didn't fill us in on your plan with Zed."

Ah, there it is. The guilt trip. "There's a reason why I'm having Zed help me and not you guys."

Lars and Willa are about to be parents. They need out of this mess, not dragged further into it. Talon and Marni are finally at a point where they can be happy. Everyone around me is fucking happy. Zed and I are not on that spectrum yet. We're still searching for what everyone else has. Therefore, we have nothing to lose. It also helps that Zed's a ruthless son of a bitch who lacks the ability to feel empathy.

"Whatever," Talon says, "I'm having fun tonight and not letting all of this bullshit weigh on me. We deserve a night of being reckless teenagers."

Talon picks up a conversation with a couple guys and I mingle through the party, stopping for some small talk with a few of the guests and making my presence known.

I'm talking with Alan when I look over his shoulder and see Marni outside. She's sitting on the edge of the pool with her feet dangling in the water. There are people all around her, but she pays no attention to them.

"I'll catch up with ya in a bit," I tell Alan, with my eyes on Marni. I walk past him and outside through the double doors.

"Tommy!" someone hoots and hollers from somewhere nearby. I feel a hand pat my back, but I ignore them all and keep walking.

I slouch down next to Marni. "Penny for your thoughts?"

She grabs the cup from my hand and takes a drink, immediately spitting it back out into the pool. "Water? Really?"

My shoulders shrug. "It's all about presentation tonight."

"Oh, right. Your revenge. You guys and your stupid games." I can tell she's drunk, but I don't react. I'm just here to listen right now. "Those games are what started this disaster. If you all would have just reported Josh's body and let nature take its course, we wouldn't even be in this mess."

"That's true. But you also wouldn't be with Talon. Lars would have never found Willa. And, I would have…." my words trail off.

"You would have never fallen for Wyatt? Is that what you were gonna say?" She looks up at me. Her squinted eyes rimmed with black liner that matches the black dress she's wearing. "Could have been a blessing if you ask me."

"Come on now, you're mad at him, but I know that you care about him." I can't believe I'm defending Wyatt right now, but it's true. Marni will get over this eventually. There may be some awkwardness for a while, but with some time, they'll be close again.

"Tell me this, how do you feel about what he did?" She asks me.

I shrug my shoulders because, the truth is, I'm not sure how I feel. Betrayed, maybe. Used. Discredited. "Everyone has a past."

Marni pulls her feet out of the water and turns to face me. Her legs curl up under her ass and I give her dress a tug to cover her up better.

"I think I'm just more in shock than anything. When my mom had an affair, I watched my dad suffer. Slowly changing to this cold and callous man who hated life. Then, she died, and I felt like he died with her. For so long, I just wanted him to be happy," she smiles, "and then gradually, he started to show me pieces of the man he was before the affair. And now I can't help but wonder if Wyatt—my best friend—was the reason that he was coming back to life."

Her words carry this indescribable sadness that punctures my heart. Because the truth is, she's probably right. In the same way that our sexuality knows no boundaries, neither does our age. Our hearts beat for our desires. They want what they want.

As I try to convince her otherwise, I try to convince myself at the same time. "Maybe it wasn't Wyatt at all. It's possible that Wyatt was just a small part of the bigger picture."

"Meaning?"

"Meaning that your dad found a part of him that he didn't know existed, and once he accepted it, he was able to find happiness again. Even if you don't agree with it—even if I don't agree with it—he didn't do it for us, he did it for himself."

Marni gives my arm a push and her body sways backward. "I hate when you're right."

"Which is always. So get used to it." I smirk.

"I'm not ready to forgive either of them. They both lied to me for so long. But, I also don't want all the sordid details of what they did. I guess I just need some time to accept it all."

"I think giving it some time is a good idea."

"And what about you and Wyatt? What happens now?"

I let out a sigh and comb my hair back with my fingers. "I guess I'm gonna use a little bit of that time, too. Everything sort of happened so fast between us. One day I hated him because I felt like he was trying to make me into someone I wasn't, and the next minute, I realized that it was just easier to blame him than accept that I was that person."

"I won't hate you if you work things out with him. But, you do need to be careful. Him and Shane just broke up, before that he was with my dad. Take things slow and remember there are plenty of fish in the sea."

I chuckle. "Touché. The thing is, though, I don't want any other fish."

She raises her brows. "Like. Any fish?"

"If you're asking about girls, the answer is no."

She throws her hands around me and pulls me in for a hug. "I'm happy for you, Tommy. I like seeing you smile."

"What's going on over here?" Talon comes out of nowhere. I

look up and he's standing there with a cup in his hand and a grin on his face. "You know she's taken, right?"

"I know. I know." I push myself off the ground and get to my feet. "I missed out on that one." I wink at Marni. "Alright, you two enjoy the night. It's getting late and I think I'm gonna go pass out upstairs behind a locked door."

Talon stops me. "Hey, call if things go bad. I mean it, man. Don't try and be a hero."

We bump knuckles, and I walk away. It's showtime.

CHAPTER TWENTY-TWO

WYATT

Darkness descends over the winding drive as I follow the GPS on my dash. I've been to Stanton when I was a kid, but the area is rundown and has a pretty high crime rate. I'm told to take a turn next to a corner market where a lady stands on the corner wearing only enough to cover her tits and ass.

"Your destination is on the left."

I tap end on the GPS and stop right in the middle of the road. Looking to my left, I see a ramshackle house that is in need of some serious repairs. Shingles on the roof are missing. Pieces of the ivory siding threaten to break loose. Just one gust of wind in their direction would send them falling to the ground.

Backing up my car a little bit, I turn in the one-car driveway. There are no other vehicles here, but light shines through one of the cracked windows where the screen hangs on by a thread.

I'm hesitant to shut the car off, in case I need to make a run for it, but I also don't trust that it'll still be here when I get back.

Against my better judgment, I turn it off and drop the keys in my pocket. I can't imagine that the person who lives in this house knows who I am, let alone sent me threatening notes.

Let's hope this is all worth it and I leave here with some answers.

One foot at a time, I get out. My eyes sweep every direction as I make my way up to the house. I can hear sirens in the distance and they send my heart into a frenzy of rapid beats.

Once I reach the door, I ball my fist, ready to knock, but freeze. *Just do it.*

"God, don't let me get killed," I mutter under my breath, before tapping my knuckles to the door. A few paint chips shimmy onto my shoe, so I shake it a couple times to get them off.

When the door swings open, I gasp.

"Wyatt, sweetie, how are you?"

"Mrs. Velmont? You live here?" Shane's mom surely has changed since the last time I saw her. She's about fifty pounds lighter—practically skin and bones. She looks like she hasn't showered in days, nor changed her clothes. There's a red sauce stain on the stomach of her oversized, baby pink t-shirt and the bags under her eyes could hold a week's worth of groceries.

The last time I saw Mrs. Velmont at Shane's football game, she was prim, proper, and healthy.

This doesn't make any sense. I thought Shane and his family were still in Redwood. Granted, I've never been to his house. He always said that he preferred we spend time at mine. I thought maybe it was because his family was going through a lot with his dad's case. Though it was dropped, I know they lost a lot in the process. It seems that they've lost everything.

"Didn't Shane tell you we moved?"

"Yeah. He, umm, he told me he moved, but I guess I assumed he was still in Redwood." I cock my head to the side, trying to get a look inside. "Is he here by chance?"

"No. He never came home after school today. Haven't heard from him. You can try calling him. I just paid this month's cell phone bill, so he should be good to go."

"What about Mr. Velmont, is he home?" I ask out of sheer curiosity. It's so hard to imagine Shane's dad living in this type of environment.

"Oh no, sweetie. Shane's father is still serving his sentence. He still has three and a half years."

My jaw drops down. I pick it up quickly in an attempt to hide my surprise. "He's in prison? I'm so sorry. I thought those charges were dropped."

"We were close, but the testimony from Harold Moran sent him away for good. That dirty scoundrel really pulled one over on us, after everything we've been through together."

"Harold Moran? As in Josh's dad?"

"Yep. Once his son went missing and his world fell apart, ours came tumbling after."

I'm so damn confused right now.

"Anyways, I'm glad Shane has you. He's been having a pretty hard time adjusting, and he speaks so highly of you and his friends. How's Talon doing anyways?"

"Talon?" I question what she just said. Did she just refer to Talon as one of Shane's friends?

"Mmhmm, I know he spends a lot of time with you guys. Are you all excited for graduation?"

I don't even bother to set her straight. I don't think she could handle the truth if she knew how far from friends we all are. "Oh yeah. Ready as ever." My brows dip and I place a hand on her fragile shoulder. "Look, I've gotta get going. But, if you need anything at all, just let me know. Ok?"

Her shoulder tips and she smiles. "A few dollars for something to eat from the market would be nice."

"Yeah. Of course." I reach into my pocket and pull out my wallet and lay a hundred dollar bill in her hand. Her eyes light up immediately and I just hope that she really does use some of this to buy some food or pay a bill. As awful as Shane has been, I don't like seeing anyone suffer emotionally or financially. "Take care of yourself, Mrs. Velmont."

I turn around and walk away. Looking over my shoulder, I catch her holding the bill up and searching for the watermark. Does she think I gave her counterfeit money? She waves it in the air. "Thanks again. If you see Shane around tonight, tell him I'm making goulash for dinner."

I get in the car, close the door and place my forehead on the steering wheel. Not only has his mom lost her home, her husband, and her money, it seems that her mind is going, too. My heart breaks for her. Her husband made one bad choice and dragged them both down with him. Now Shane is digging the hole even deeper.

It was Shane all along. I'm not surprised.

Tommy is pretty mad at me right now and this is likely going to cause a scene, but I need to go to Talon's and talk to him face to face. There's no doubt he's there. Everyone who's anyone is at that party tonight—possibly even Shane.

THIRTY MINUTES LATER, I turn down Talon's road, but do a double take in the rearview mirror when a truck drives past me. *That was Tommy.*

Shifting in reverse, I back into someone else's driveway then pull out and head in the direction I came from.

I'm not sure where he's going, but I really need to tell him what I know. I tap the call button on the screen on the dash.

"Call Tommy."

It rings. And rings. And ends.

I try again.

"Call Tommy."

Same thing.

I hit end and continue to follow behind him, giving him a

little bit of space. When he turns onto the expressway, I get the feeling that he's leaving Redwood. Minutes later, traffic begins to pick up as people enter the city. I'm a couple cars behind him now, but I've still got my sights set on his truck.

Flicking my blinker, I take the same exit he did and see the sign for Jester Creek.

He's going to the cabin.

All the prepping he did earlier this week, could it have been for tonight?

I keep following, but leave a few car lengths between us, because now I'm curious what the hell is going on.

A half hour later, familiar scenery surrounds me.

Once I turn down the dirt road that the cabin sits off of, I stop my car. If I get any closer to him, he'll get suspicious. So, I give him five minutes and then continue on my way—turning down the long drive to his family's property.

Creeping up slowly, at only five miles an hour, I lean forward to get a better look at the place. Someone else is here. Parked next to Tommy's truck is Zed's SUV. I stop halfway down the driveway and shut my lights off.

My body shivers at the unknown. There is no saying what these guys could be up to and I'm not so sure I wanna find out.

Minutes pass. I take a deep breath and force myself out of the car. Holding the handle up, I close the door quietly then nudge my hip against it so it latches shut.

It's really fucking scary out here. Dead bodies buried by that creek. An owl hoots, causing me to grab my chest. "Shit," I mumble.

On my tiptoes, I walk without a sound. As I draw closer, I try to get a look in the window but can't see anything at all.

I'm gonna pass out. I just know it. I am not cut out for this shit. I'm a simple guy who likes to stay home and watch movies, eat popcorn, maybe a little male/male porn. Dead bodies, kidnapping, and secrets are not my forte.

Once I reach the cabin, I press my back to it and steady my breaths. Breathing in and out while also trying to calm my racing heart. Once I feel just a tad better, a scream rings though my ears.

"Fuccccck!" A familiar voice carries from the entryway. "Ahhhh, stop! Just stop!"

Oh my god, it's Shane.

Long strides take me up the steps and through the front door. My hand slaps to my mouth and all eyes shoot to me.

Shane is bound to the chair with blood spilling down his face.

"What the hell are you doing to him?" I cry out.

CHAPTER TWENTY-THREE

TOMMY

"Get him out of here," I shout to Zed, who immediately grabs Wyatt by the arm. "And don't fucking hurt him."

With my eyes still focused on Shane, I listen as Wyatt puts up a fight behind me. The shuffling of their feet stop and the door slams shut.

"I'm gonna ask you one more time, where were you the night that Josh went missing?" We're so close. I can feel it. I know it was Shane who hit him. I fucking know it.

He doesn't respond, which warrants the loss of another fingernail. With the vise grips open, I clamp down on the very tip of his nail and pull that son of bitch straight off his skin.

"Ahhhhh!" he screams, "you stupid son of a bitch. I'm gonna fucking kill you when I get out of here."

Blood drops down his finger onto the arm of the chair.

I tsk. "Who said you were getting out of here? You're not going anywhere until I have answers. And if you don't give them to me, I'll hand you over to my boy, Zed. He's been known to take care of trouble that arises."

He stares at his bare fingertip, unable to shield it from air and stop the sting of pain I know he's feeling. Dropping his chin to his chest, he seethes, "You know all the answers to your questions. You all did this. Not me."

"We didn't do anything!" I shout. "You're just trying to make it look like we did, aren't you?" Taking his middle finger in my hand, I ask him another question while Zed's not around. "Where is the original video from the locker room?"

Pressing his lips together, he smirks. "Your buddy out there know that you like dick?"

Swinging my hand around, I slap him across the face. "Shut the fuck up!"

"A tight ass beats a loose pussy any day, doesn't it?"

My jaw clenches as I lean forward. Pressing my palms to the arms of the chair he's bound. "I want answers and I want them now."

"You assholes can play dumb all you want, but I know you killed Josh. I've known for a while."

My head shakes. "We didn't kill Josh. You did."

Shane chuckles maliciously. His head comes forward, so close that I inhale his exhaled breaths. "I saw Zed driving his car. I watched you guys push that same car over the cliff at Miner Point." His eyes darken, and his lip curls. "You guys killed him and because of what you did, I lost everything." Spit flies in my face and on impulse, I smack him again before using the sleeve of my shirt to wipe it away.

"We did do those things, but we didn't kill him. He was hit by a car and left dead in the road. Your car. If you lost anything, it's on you."

He draws back, giving me a look of confusion. "You guys left him in the road after you hit him?"

At the top of my lungs, I scream, "We didn't hit him!"

"We're just gonna go back and forth on this. You really think that if I hit my dad's godson, I'd leave him in the fucking road? No! I'd call for help, you fucking moron."

What's he talking about? "Your dad's godson?"

"Yes, my dad is Josh's godfather. After Josh died, my entire world unraveled. Because of you and your idiot friends."

I hold up a hand. "Wait a damn second, you really think we killed Josh?"

"I know you did. I told you, I watched the aftermath. All of it."

The door flies open behind me and Wyatt comes flying into the room. "He did it. He's the one who's been sending the notes and texts," he spits out, before Zed grabs him by the arms.

"Sorry, he's a persistent little shit. If you want him gone, I'm gonna have to be aggressive."

Waving my hands toward them, I gesture to Zed to let him go. I have no doubt it was Shane. Guessed it all along. That's why he's here. But Wyatt could have found actual proof. "How are you so sure?"

His hands drop to his knees and he holds up a finger, trying to catch his breath. "One sec. Your friend is really fucking strong." A few seconds later, he straightens back up. "I traced my phone. It led me to Shane's house," he steps closer to Shane and looks him in the eyes, "in Stanton."

Looking from Wyatt to Shane, I notice the displeasure in Shane's expression. "You live in Stanton?" I ask him. "Why do you go to Redwood? It's a half hour away."

"Yes. I live in Stanton. I live there because when you guys killed Josh, his parents were investigated as possible suspects. During that investigation, it was found out that money was being laundered from Core Associates," he pauses, "by Josh's dad and mine. They were best friends all my life. Worked together for half of it. But his dad didn't reap the consequences of that one. No," he laughs, "he's free as a bird while my dad's sitting in prison and my mom is slowly becoming an agoraphobic. We have no money, and soon, we'll have no home. All because you dumbasses couldn't come forward with what you did. So I followed you guys everywhere. Tried to make it clear that I knew. I dug up your secrets so that I could expose them just like my dad's were exposed. If he has to pay for his sins, so do you."

"Why drag Wyatt into this? If you think we killed Josh, what's Wyatt's place in the threats?"

"I was trying to protect him. The note I left was meant to scare him away from you all. But, he chose his side, so he became another target."

"And Willa?"

"She was sleeping with the enemy. She was just a pawn to get through to you guys."

It was really him. All this time. He may have been behind all of the threats, but I believe him when he says he didn't kill Josh. I'm not sure why, but I do.

I look behind me and notice Wyatt taking steps backward to the door. His face is pale and his hands are shaking. "You guys killed Josh?"

"No," I tell him. Then I look back at Shane. "Dude. We didn't kill Josh."

"Liar!" he shouts so loudly the echo reverberates through my entire body.

"It all makes sense now. All this time it was you guys." Wyatt tries to bolt out the door, but Zed grabs a hold of him and braces him from behind.

I can't focus on that right now. Slouching down in front of Shane, I try to reason with him. "Listen to me. We.did.not.kil-l.Josh. We have footage of the night he was hit. He was killed in front of Marni's house. Yes, we got rid of his body. Yes, we got rid of his car, but we did not hit him. Someone else did, and that someone is out there somewhere."

"If you got rid of his body, how the hell did it end up in the pastor's basement?"

"I put it there." I turn around and look at Zed who's raising his hand. "That pastor was a monster and I framed him for

Josh's death. Not gonna lie. He deserves every name thrown at him. Liar, pedophile, murderer."

"Stop Zed, don't say anything else." One wrong admission and he can be charged with the pastor's murder.

"It doesn't matter. " Zed shrugs, "None of it matters anymore. I'll take any and all blame. Where I'm going, sinners thrive."

I humor myself. "Oh yeah, and where is that?"

His shoulder's rise. "Hell."

I peel my eyes from an emotionless Zed. "Ok, none of this matters. The point is, the person who did hit Josh is still out there. It also means that this fucking asshole sitting here has a pocketful of secrets and we need to do something about that."

There's no saying what all he knows. One by one, he's revealed our secrets, but he could have something else up his sleeve. Not to mention, I'm not ready to be outed. When that time comes, I wanna do it myself.

Shane licks a drop of blood off his lips. "I'm still not convinced it wasn't you guys."

"Would you two give us a minute, please?" I ask Wyatt and Zed. They both just stand there, looking at me like I'll change my mind. My brows raise and I snap, "Like, now?"

"Come on, chess boy." Zed jerks Wyatt by the arm and pulls him out.

Once I'm alone with Shane, I level with him. "You've really made a mess of things, ya know that? But I'm willing to give you an out."

"I'm listening."

"First of all, we did not kill Josh, but you can bet your ass that we plan to find out who did. Second of all, I want you as far away from this town as you can possibly go. Not Stanton, not even the other side of the state. You're gonna go home and pack all your shit, take your mom, and get the fuck out of here."

He sighs. "Did you miss the part where I said that we lost everything?"

"I'll give you enough money to get started somewhere else. Get a job, tell your mom to get a job, it's what people do. Make money on that fucking app. I don't care how you do it, but you will leave. If you don't go, your scholarships will wash down the drain. Coach will find out how you get all of your endurance, and you and Mommy Dearest will be welcoming Daddy home from prison on the side of the street."

"And what if I tell you that I'm not going, but you're giving me the money, anyways? You see, you might not have killed Josh, but you didn't report it either. You've tampered with evidence and you still need to be held accountable for your part in my dad's downfall. If you'd have went to the cops, Core Associates would have never been investigated."

Forcibly, I grip his chin in my fingers. "Listen you little shit, I won't kill you, but I have people who will. You won't leave this fucking cabin alive if you don't quit trying to be such a hard ass. Your dad fucked up and he's paying for it. You're just sorry he got caught. You've been withholding information, too. We go down, you go down."

Fear washes over his face and he swallows hard.

"Zed," I holler, "get back in here." There's something enlightening about calling the shots this time around. I sort of like bossing people around.

He comes back in and Wyatt follows.

I reach in my pocket and pull out my wallet. "Take Shane to his house." I hand him my credit card. "He's gonna pack up his things and then I need you to take him and his mom to the airport. Book them a flight to...I don't fucking know, Michigan. If he puts up a fight, take care of him." I don't have to say what I mean, Zed knows, and so does Shane.

Zed is on the verge of a complete and mental breakdown. I can see it in his eyes. He's giving up on everything. Those who have nothing to lose are willing to risk everything. Once this is done, I have every intention of pulling Zed back to reality. His life is worth fighting for, even if he doesn't believe it right now.

I look back at Shane. "I'll give you a check. Once it's cashed, our agreement is final and you'll never show your face around here again." I pull my knife out of my pocket and Shane's eyes pinch shut. In one swoop, I free his left hand, and then the other.

"I'm just gonna go," Wyatt says as he points a thumb over his shoulder.

Stepping behind Shane, I cut the rope that's wrapped around his waist and the chair. "No, you're not. We need to talk."

Shane stands up and I give him a shove. Zed grabs him by the arms and pulls him toward the door. Before they walk out, Zed stops himself. With his head hung low, he slowly lifts it and looks me in the eyes. "Take care of yourself, man."

"I'll be in touch," I tell Zed.

He doesn't say a word; he just walks out, dragging Shane with him.

Enveloped in silence, Wyatt and I stand there looking at each other. Unsure where to begin, I start with tonight. "Looks like we were both on the right track thinking it was Shane."

"I didn't think it was him until I was led to his house. After that, I was pretty certain."

"Sorry I doubted you. For a while, I thought you were behind this, maybe even in cahoots with him."

"You never told me about your part in Josh's disappearance, why?"

I retort, "You never told me about Anderson."

His head nods. "True. But, in my defense, what I did wasn't illegal."

"Also, true." With my hands in my pockets, my back steels. "Alright, let's get this out of the way. I need to know what I'm up against. Are you and Anderson over?"

"Anderson and I were over before we even began. It should have never happened."

"But it did, and—"

"Listen," he interrupts me, "it was stupid. I was stupid. What started as flirtation at his house, escalated into a crush on my part. Yes, we slept together. Yes, we went on a trip together. But, it ended as soon as I found out that he was dating someone else. I found out the night that Josh was hit. I took off in tears after walking in on him and another guy. I told him to choose and he chose the man in his bed."

"And he followed you?"

"I don't know. Maybe. I just kept driving to get as far away as I could. We were supposed to go on another trip that night and I haven't talked to him since I left his house. He sends me texts constantly, but only because he's worried that I'll tell Marni about us. He never cared about me, and even if I thought I loved him then, you proved to me that I never did."

"I have no right to be mad at you for that. I've done some things I regret. I screwed Shay right next to you while you were supposed to be passed out."

He smirks. "Why did you do that, anyways?"

"Trying to prove a point, I guess. To myself. To you. I thought that if you saw me with a woman, you'd assume women are what I'm interested in. I was also trying to convince myself the same thing."

"And, did it work?"

I take a couple steps toward him. "No. I'm not interested in Shay or anyone else."

He meets me halfway and takes my hand in his. "So, what now?"

"No fucking idea." I grab his other hand. "All I know for sure is that I can't stop thinking about you. I've never felt like this about anyone before and it scares the hell out of me."

"It's been scaring the hell out of me for months now.

Because, you're all I think about, too. Even when I was with Shane, I was never really with him."

My hands tremble with nervousness. "So, are we doing this?"

"I want to if you do."

"No more secrets, from either of us. I know I've had my share of them, too."

"No more secrets."

I pull him close. His chest meets mine and my arms tangle around him. His head rests on my shoulder and my heart feels so full that it could burst. "Eventually I'll tell my friends. I just need you to be patient with me."

He retreats, his eyes boring into mine. "Take all the time you need." Tilting his head, his lips graze mine before I wrap my hand around his head and pull him closer. Excitement swirls in my stomach, mixed with nervousness and arousal.

I feel so alive when I'm with Wyatt. A feeling I could get used to.

CHAPTER TWENTY-FOUR

WYATT

With the remnants of Tommy's torture on Shane laying at our feet, I pull him toward the room we were in last time we were here.

It's completely dark, so Tommy switches on the light when we step inside. The curtains are all open, so he pulls them shut.

He hums into the crease of my neck. "I've been wanting to get you alone ever since we left Briarwood."

"Oh yeah? What is that you wanted to do to me?"

"This." He grabs my dick through the fabric of my pants. "And this." He kisses my lips. His mouth parting and his tongue wrapping around mine.

Taking my face in his hands, he breaks our kiss. "Do you have any idea what you do to me?"

"I think I've got an idea."

"You drive me fucking wild." He pushes me back on the bed and this is a new side of Tommy that I've never seen. Not exactly true. I did see him with Shay and the way he took control made my balls ache. He was in charge and demanding and it was sexy as hell.

My timing has never been impeccable, and this time is no

different. I shift my body up so that I'm braced by my elbows. "This thing with Shane, was it planned all along? Ever since you brought me here last week?"

With his hands on either side of my body, ready to climb on top of me, he stops. "I had a bad feeling about the guy. Knew he was up to something." He comes closer, but I stop him again.

"Were you ever gonna tell me about what you guys did to Josh?"

He backtracks his steps until he's standing at the foot of the bed. His hand sweeps across his forehead. "Probably not. We never planned to tell anyone. Don't worry, though, we'll take care of everything."

I nod. "Yeah. Everything will be fine." At least I hope so. My secret is safe, because I know theirs, too. Shane is leaving town, and life is going to be different without him around, but I'm looking forward to this next chapter in my life.

Tommy pulls his shirt over his head in one fell swoop then climbs up my body on all fours. His gorgeous body takes my breath away. My fingers wrap around his firm biceps and his lower half drags against mine. Using his knee, he sweeps under my thigh and pushes it up so that he's between my legs. Sliding up and down, grinding his rock hard cock against mine. "I wanna suck your dick while you suck mine."

"Mmm, I like the way you think." I graze my teeth over his ear lobe. "Are you gonna let me come in your mouth?"

"I want us to come at the same time. I wanna taste you while you taste me."

"Fuck yes." I buck my hips up, gaining friction against him.

He gets on his knees and unbuttons my pants, then slides them down, taking my boxers with them. One by one, he takes off my socks. Then he stands up and strips down while I take off my shirt.

"You're so damn sexy," he growls, before parting my legs and diving down. His tongue sweeps up my balls and he sucks one into his mouth. I bite the corner of my lip and revel in the sensation of pleasure.

"Twist your body around," I tell him.

He turns around with his ass end facing me and he backs up slowly until his dick is lined up with my face. Using my thumb, I sweep up the bead of precum then pop my thumb in my mouth. "You taste as good as you look." Opening my mouth, I take the first half of him. Humming against his cock, causing a vibration that has him moaning in pleasure.

He licks a long stroke up my length. "You keep that up and I'm not lasting long."

"You better hold out, we're coming together, remember?"

Taking all of me in his mouth, I can feel his lips at the end of my dick. When I cup his balls in my hand, he does the same, giving them a gentle massage as we both suck each other off.

I'd never guess that he was new to this. The way his firm lips wrap around me, creating the perfect home for my dick in his warm mouth. I let out a raspy groan when his tongue flicks under the sensitive skin of my shaft.

Taking him out of my mouth, I spit on his ass and massage my fingers in a circular motion before sliding one inside of him. His body jolts, so I freeze. "You ok, baby?"

"I'm great," he mutters.

I wonder if it bothers him when I call him baby. I've never called anyone that before, but it just sort of comes out with no thought behind it.

Sliding another finger inside of him, I prod the pads of my fingers against his spot. "Do you like when I call you, baby?"

"I love it. Keep that shit up." He slops spit all around my cock, lubing it up really well as his head bobs up and down.

Watching as my fingers slide in and out of his tight ass, I line his cock up with my mouth and lift my head up. When he drops down slightly, all of him goes inside my mouth, hitting the back of my throat as his ass goes up and down in the same rhythm he uses to suck me. I push my fingers farther until they are both all the way inside of him then I twist and turn in a circular motion.

His slippery hand wraps around my cock and he strokes while his tongue teases my head. "Fuck baby, that feels so good."

When he picks up his speed, I do the same. Closing my lips tightly around him and sucking faster, while pushing my fingers deeper and harder.

Tiny shots of electricity course through me and my body fills with pressure. My cock throbbing and ready to blow. "I'm gonna come," I say around his dick on my tongue.

Kneading his prostate, I cause his body to flinch in reaction before he shoots down my throat. I release at the same time. He gags for a sliver of a second, but neither of us stop. I swallow then lick his head, cleaning up every last morsel while he does the same.

Pulling my fingers out, I smack my hand to his ass and tease, "Better than pussy?"

He spins around with his hands pressed to either side of me. "So much better." I pull his head down and press my lips to his then give him a taste of himself.

"Can we just stay here forever?" he asks.

I thought you hated this cabin."

"I did, until now."

His mouth meets mine again and we kiss for what feels like hours. Until our lips are swollen and the stubble from his chin leaves behind the sting of whisker burns on my face.

Dropping to his side, he lies down beside me. His finger trailing up and down my stomach. Drawing pictures, making art in his head. "What are you drawing?"

"Us."

I laugh. "And what do we look like?"

"We're happy—together. In a world where nothing seems to make sense, I've finally found something that does."

I turn to face him. Both of our heads propped up on our hands. I draw a heart over his heart then look him in the eyes. Cupping his cheek, I whisper, "I'm falling for you, Tommy."

His lips press to mine then he pulls back and smiles. "I feel the same way."

CHAPTER TWENTY-FIVE

TOMMY

After spending the night together, and half of the day, Wyatt and I figured it might be a good idea to face everything waiting for us back in Redwood—me, with the guys, and him with Marni. Lying in bed, we talked a little bit about who hit Josh, attempting to follow all leads to try and figure out who did it. I did a little google search last night, and I might have an idea.

After my search, Talon sent a group message and asked us to come out to Briarwood. He seems to think someone was out there vandalizing the place. I'm pretty sure he's talking about the broken window upstairs, but I'm not ready to tell them that I was there when it happened. Questions will be asked, and I'm not ready to answer them.

I do have answers, though. I know that Shane was the mastermind behind the threats to Willa and Wyatt. He also sent the death certificate to all of us. Yet, he isn't the one who hit Josh. I haven't shared any of this information with them yet.

Killing the engine of my truck, I jump out and take a deep breath of fresh air.

Talon and Lars are standing next to the building, while

Talon points up at the window and impersonates someone throwing a ball. His hands fly in the air like he's clueless as to how or why this happened.

I follow their gaze to the broken window. "What's up, boys?"

"You see this shit?" Talon waves his arm in the air. "Someone threw something through the window."

"Probably just some kids out here messing around. I wouldn't worry about it."

"Someone was out here. Found this on the floor inside." Talon holds up a bottle of lotion. Wyatt's lotion.

I bite back a smile. "Like I said, probably some kids." It's nothing new. Kids get their kicks out of coming to this place because they think it's haunted. Even though there are no trespassing signs posted all over the property, no one pays attention to them. "Let's go sit on the steps, I come bearing news."

"Yeah," Lars beams, "did you get what you wanted last night? I sure as hell did, and I'm paying for it with a hangover from hell."

"Oh yeah? Baby mama let you live a little last night?" I tease.

"Fuck off. She doesn't control me...much."

Talon and I share a look, but I call him out, too. "Don't act like you aren't whipped. Your leash is just as tight as his."

"You just wait. One day you'll be in the same boat. Doing anything to keep your girl happy. Never wanting to see her sad."

"There will be no girl for me." I don't elaborate on that.

I sit down on the cement slab steps in front of Briarwood. Me on the bottom step with my legs stretched out on the ground and my elbows pressed to the row above me. Lars is lying across the third step with his legs bent and his hands over his eyes. "Fucking sun. It's burning the inside of my head." He whines like a baby.

Talon is standing in front of us with his arms crossed. "Alright, let's hear it."

I hear the flick of a zippo and twist around to see Lars lighting up a smoke. "Thought you quit that shit."

"Did. Sort of." He takes a drag and lets the cigarette dangle between his fingertips.

Looking back and forth between the two of them, I start with the most important matter. "Shane sent the text with the death certificate."

"Shane Velmont? What the hell does that prick have to do with any of us?" Talon scoffs before reaching behind me and snatching the cigarette from Lars.

"Yeah, that Shane. He also sent Willa the messages, went to her house. All of it. It was him the whole time."

Talon takes a long draw and smoke rolls out of his mouth as he talks. "It was him then? He hit Josh?"

I shake my head. "No. He didn't hit him. In fact, he thought we killed him. Apparently his dad's undoing all happened when Josh died. Shane's dad is Josh's godfather. Their dads were best friends, worked together for years, and when Josh died, his parents were investigated. That investigation led to evidence of money being embezzled from the company. The blame was all put on Shane's dad, who is apparently in prison. Shane's acts were all out of hatred because he thought it was us."

"Wait a fucking minute." Lars growls as he gets to his feet and jumps off the steps, landing next to Talon. He grabs his cigarette back and flicks the ash. "Shane knows about our part? We have to silence him. We have no choice."

"He's gone," I deadpan.

"Gone? Like six feet under gone?" Talon asks.

"No. But he might as well be. He's out of Redwood and he's not coming back."

"Alright," Talon says, as he rubs the stubble on his chin, "so it wasn't Wyatt and it wasn't Shane. Who was your revenge or are we just sifting through people until you're satisfied?"

"A little of both. I got what I wanted from both of them. My act is complete. Shane's gone. I made sure that he'll never say a word. And Wyatt, let's just say my secrets are safe with him."

"Ok then," Lars throws his hands in the air, "four acts done. Game over."

"There's still one problem that hasn't been resolved?" I tell them. I'm sure they know exactly what I'm talking about.

That's confirmed when Talon nods his head and speaks, "Who killed Josh?"

Snapping my fingers, I point at him. "Exactly." I sweep away a cloud of smoke that's lingering around me. There is absolutely no air movement today and the sun is really burning down on us. Even for the end of February, it's pretty fucking hot out here. "I know that you all sort of put the WatchMeNow app to rest, but there is still one more person we haven't looked into and I think it's time we start."

Taking a step back, Talon digs the tip of his toe into the ground with his hands snug in his front pockets. "The mystery profile? We've got absolutely nothing to go on. No mutual contacts—nothing."

"This could be a long shot, but hear me out. What if we start up a conversation with him or her and then trace the IP address? It could work. I happen to know a guy who's pretty good at tracking shit."

They both immediately know who I'm talking about. Talon cocks a brow. "Until Marni sorts this shit out with Wyatt, I think it's best if we leave him out of this. He might not have killed Josh, but he knows he's dead. It's possible that Wyatt thinks it was us that killed him. Hell, it could be him on the app."

I haven't told them that Wyatt already knows everything. They have no idea what he walked in on last night. As far as they're concerned, he's still a suspect. "It's not him, and we can trust him."

"What makes you so sure?"

I raise my voice. "Because I trust him. Just leave it at that."

Lars holds his hands up in surrender. "Woah, dude. Calm down."

"I'm just saying, Wyatt isn't an issue, so I'd like you guys to lay off him. I know he messed up with Marni, but that's between them. He can help us."

Lars cranes his neck and scowls. "What? Are you two like friends now?"

"Maybe we are. So just leave him alone. He's not as bad as I thought. He's a good person. Got it?"

They both share a glance and nod. "Ok. I guess," Lars says.

Talon doesn't have to say much. Marni has already made it clear that if he messes with Wyatt, she'll chop off his balls and feed them to him. Ok, maybe not to that extent, but she'd be pissed.

"Now that that's settled. Who wants to start up a conversation with our mystery app user?"

"Not me." Lars takes a step back. "I'm swimming in baby shower stuff with Willa."

"Have Marni help her. She's a chick. They love that stuff," I tell him.

"She's been helping some. They're starting to bond a little more. Which is good for them both."

"Alright. It's on you then, Talon."

"Why me?"

"Because you're the master of that app. All you have to do is get them to respond. Wyatt can get back into Magna Tech and use the IP tracker to find the source. Once we have a hit, we can trace the location."

Lars snorts. "Damn, man. How do you know all this shit?"

"I've been thinking about that app for a while. Did a little research on it last night from my phone. Wyatt thinks he can get the location. We have nothing to lose by trying."

"Ok," Talon tosses his arms in defeat, "I guess we start now."

He pulls his phone out of his pocket and thumbs through it while we watch. A few minutes later, he sticks his phone back in his pocket. "Done."

"What'd you say to them?" I ask.

"Sup?" he responds with a smirk.

"Sup? You fucking said *sup*?" Lars scoffs. "Who even says that anymore?"

Talon throws his hands up. "Hey, you said all we need is a response."

I interrupt their conversation. "Alright, this is fun and all, but I've gotta get home. My parents return today and want me to have lunch with them. Shoot me a text when she responds and I'll come grab your phone from you."

"I need my phone, though," Talons says nonchalantly.

I huff. "Why the hell'd you send it from your phone then?" I wanna smack him upside the head, but I refrain.

"I've got another phone at home. I'll clear it out so you don't know all my business then add the app and send it again." His shoulders shrug.

"All your business?" I laugh. "As if you have anything to hide from us."

"It's a phone I had pre-Marni. Ya know, lots of nudie texts from the ladies who were begging for a piece of this." His hands slap to his chest as he smirks.

He's so full of himself. "Just send the message. I'm out."

"I'm out, too," Lars says.

"So no one is sticking around to help me take out this window? Thanks a lot, assholes." He flips us off and heads up the stairs to the door.

Neither Lars nor I give it a second thought before heading to our vehicles.

CHAPTER TWENTY-SIX

WYATT

"How was lunch with your parents?" I ask Tommy. Nuzzling my face into his neck, I draw in a deep breath of his skin, giddiness sweeping through me.

His eyes glance up and down my driveway, making sure no one sees us. "It was lunch. Nothing too exciting."

"It's just us here. No need to worry." I can tell he's nervous with the display of affection I'm giving. It's different at the cabin, no one can see us there. We're not exactly in public, but being this close in this town has him on edge.

"I know." He smiles, attempting to reassure me that he's not worried, though I know he is. "I'm just looking around."

"Uh huh. Sure."

"When my friends find out, I wanna be the one to tell them. Not because someone caught us and rumors spread." Pulling my mouth to his, he mutters, "Do I look worried now?"

"A little more convincing, please."

His tongue darts into my mouth, dancing around mine before he tugs my bottom lip between his teeth. "Mmm, how about now?"

A car turns at the end of the driveway and he pulls away from me before they get any closer. "Definitely worried." I chuckle.

His hands brush down his shirt then he wipes the corners of his mouth. "Who is that?" He nods toward the SUV. Leaning forward, he gets a better look. "Wait, that's Talon. What the fuck is he doing at your house?"

"Your guess is as good as mine."

A moment later, Talon is pulling up beside Tommy's truck and gets out, leaving the door open behind him. "What are you doing here?" he questions Tommy with dipped brows.

"Stopped to fill Wyatt in on the plan."

Plan? He never filled me in on any plan. I guess we hadn't made it that far yet.

"Here." He smacks a phone to my chest.

"What's this?" I grab it and look at the black screen.

"My phone." He looks at Tommy. "I thought you said you were filling him in?"

"I got here right before you pulled up. I thought you were gonna text me when they responded," Tommy tells him.

"Figured it was pointless to make you the middleman. He needed my phone, so I came to deliver."

"Any idea on who it might be?" Tommy asks.

"Not a clue. I said 'Sup' and they said, 'who is this?' When I didn't respond, they asked again and again. I was told to just get a response so I'm leaving it at that."

Tommy and I talked a little bit about this last night, so it makes sense now. They want me to track an IP address for them. This time around might be a little trickier since I've likely already raised some suspicion, but these devices are much like the transfer box I used for Marni to download the data from a phone last year. Dad usually has samples in his office, but somehow I need to get in there to get it.

I hold up the phone. "I'll try my best, but I have to wait until my dad leaves town again."

"No hurry. We've waited this long. What's a couple more days," Tommy says.

"Alright, I'm out. Call me later, man." Talon bumps his fist to Tommy's. Without giving me a second look, he heads back to his truck.

Once his brake lights come on at the end of the driveway and he turns out, I turn to face Tommy. "Do you think they'll ever accept me?"

"Are you kidding? They'll love you."

"I'm not so sure. They don't like me much."

"If I like you, they will, too." He presses his lips to mine.

When he steps back, I hold up the phone. "Hopefully this will give you guys some answers."

"Hope so. Listen," he runs his fingers through his hair, "I'm ready to tell them. Tell my parents. Everyone I guess."

My eyes light up. "Seriously?"

"Yeah, I mean, I'm not changing. I like you, a lot, and I know what I want. I'm tired of pretending."

I'm pretty surprised. Minutes ago he seemed nervous to be seen with me. He did say that it's because he wants to tell his friends and family himself. As much as we've been together lately, it's probably a good idea to do it before we do get caught and rumors spread. "I'm ready when you are. Do you want me there with you?"

"Come with me now." He pulls me by the hand as we walk to his truck.

I have no idea where we're going, but now that we are going somewhere, I'm not sure that *I* am ready.

"What are we doing?" I ask nervously.

"We're going to see my parents."

"Tommy!" I squeal, "we can't just drop this on them. Maybe you should do it alone."

"Nope. We're in this one together. I need your moral support right now."

Ok. Ok. We can do this. He needs my support. I remember that feeling when I came out to my parents and it was the most nerve wracking thing I'd ever done. I only wish I had someone there as support. Though, my parents said they already knew and didn't make a big deal out of it, it's hard to say how others will react.

It's a quick drive to his house, considering he lives within walking distance. We're parked in front of his house and his hand is on the door handle. He looks at me. "You ready?"

"Are you ready? Think about this long and hard. Are you sure you're ready?"

"That's the thing, I don't wanna think about it anymore. I'm tired of thinking about it. I know who I am and I know what I want. I'm doing this."

"Alright then. Let's do this."

We get out at the same time and our doors close simultaneously. As we approach the front door, Tommy takes my hand in his. I look down at our entwined fingers and squeeze tightly before he pushes open the door.

"Mom. Dad," he hollers.

"In here, Tommy," his mom yells from the kitchen.

My feet stay planted and Tommy has to practically drag me across the hardwood floor. I'm more nervous than he is, which seems a little bit backward.

His mom is standing at the center island with a mug in her hand and his dad is sitting on a bar stool in front of it.

Both pairs of eyes stare directly at our joined hands. Tommy wraps his fingers around mine tighter. "Mom, Dad, this is Wyatt. My boyfriend."

My heart sinks into my stomach when the words leave his mouth. *I'm his boyfriend.* I've never had a boyfriend before.

Shane and I were dating and hung out a lot, but we were never official. Tommy's my first, and I'm his. Having the title makes what we have feel so much more real and I feel like my heart could explode.

"It's nice to meet you, Wyatt," his mom says to me before sliding her eyes over to Tommy. "A word please, Tommy."

"No," he retorts.

His mom scoffs. "Excuse me?"

"I said no. If you have something to say, you can say it in front of Wyatt."

"I think your mother and I are just both very...surprised," his dad says with his eyebrows raised.

"Ok then. I'll give this some time to settle. We're gonna leave. I'll be home later." Tommy turns around and I'm about to follow his lead when his mom stops us.

"Wait," his mom says, pausing our movements. "Your dad is right. We're just surprised. I'd prefer this conversation take place in private, but I'm glad you told us. We love you, Tommy. Girlfriend or boyfriend. It doesn't matter."

Tommy spins back around. "Really?"

His dad chimes in, "What she said."

"Thanks. I love you both, too."

Tommy looks at me, smiles, then leads me back through the house. My knees are knocking and I feel like my jelly legs are going to give out at any moment.

Once we're back outside, he gasps for air. "Holy shit, that was intense and I'm mind blown right now. Who are those people in there and what have they done with my parents?"

"I'm not gonna lie. I'm pretty shocked, too. But, sometimes we don't give people enough credit. We're all just people trying to find happiness in a world where people try and tell us how to be happy." I give him a kiss on the cheek. "You never asked me to be your boyfriend, by the way, but I accept."

His blush colored cheekbones rise up to his eyes as he smiles, and it twists my stomach in knots of excitement. A year ago, I came out and I remember the feeling of that heavy weight being lifted off my shoulders. I was free to be me. Now, Tommy is free to be himself—we're free to be together.

CHAPTER TWENTY-SEVEN

WYATT

"Yes, I know, Dad." I huff into the phone. "I wanted to do some measurements on your desk to see if it'll fit inside my office. I'd like to get the exact same one you have."

"It's a big office, of course it'll fit."

Dad's smart, but he despises mundane conversation—he's too busy for it—so if I just argue it enough, he'll eventually give in.

"It might not with all the other stuff I plan to bring in."

"What the hell are you bringing in, a goddamn elephant?"

"I don't know, a bookshelf, maybe a loveseat. Just tell Glenda to let me in there. Come on, Dad, I really want to get a kickstart on things."

"Fine. I'll call her. Get the measurements and lock it up when you leave. I'll be back home in a few days and we'll start going over your contract."

"Thanks, Dad. Have a safe trip."

He ends the call and I pull my key out of the ignition. I've been sitting in the parking lot of Magna Tech, arguing with him over this for fifteen minutes. I knew he'd cave if I kept persisting. The measurement thing was a lie. In fact, I don't even plan on having an office at this place—at least not for a while.

Getting out of the car, I close the door behind me and walk up to the main doors. My fingers wrap around the silver u-shaped handles and I pull it open. I immediately spot the scorching scowl on Glenda's face when I step inside.

"Good evening, Glenda," I say with a smile.

She snubs me. "Hello, Mr. McCoy."

"Please, call me Wyatt."

"Your dad's office is open. Enjoy your evening."

Wow. He called her fast.

I give her a nod and walk past the reception desk and down the hall to Dad's office. I really should send Glenda some flowers or lunch or something nice to make up for threatening her job.

When I step inside, my eyes dart right to the closet, then straight to Dad's desk. I walk over with slow strides, knowing exactly what I have to do. Sweeping my finger across the desk, I look at it. Not a speck of dust. Dad's obsessive cleanliness wouldn't allow that. Wouldn't surprise me if he pays the janitorial company more than he pays his own employees.

Stepping behind the desk, I flip open a closed notebook that sits on top of a black leather desk pad. I rip a piece of paper out and strands of the binding drop freely on his desk. I sweep them away, knowing that it'll drive him mad when he sees them lying on the floor. Smiling inwardly at the notion, I snatch a pen out of the holder and begin.

Dad,

You've built yourself a business to be proud of. I don't doubt that you'll take Magna Tech to the next level and be one of the biggest software developers in the nation. Just like you always dreamed of. The thing is, that's your dream. It's not mine.

This letter serves as my one and only refusal of your offer to start employment directly following graduation. I will not be working for you as CEO of Magna Tech, at least not now. I'm going to college in the fall like I planned. I'm open to the possibility of stepping in after I've completed the four years I planned.

Therefore, for the next four years, you'll still just be my dad. Not my boss, not my co-worker, not my business partner. I hope that's enough for you.

Ps. Consider Marty. He's a good man and I think that he'd do a stellar job.

Love ya, Dad

-Wyatt

I put the pen back and lay the paper on top of the notebook. I knock my knuckles to it with a smile.

I'm taking back control over my future.

Now, I need to ensure that it's safe by getting what I came here for. My eyes zip back to the closet. That's where they'd be if he had any samples in here. I know he uses them during meetings and presentations with board members. I searched through a catalog he had in his study at home and I'm pretty sure I know what I'm looking for. Pulling out a couple boxes, I flip the top on one and close it when I see a bunch of papers. I try the other, but it's not the device I need.

Three boxes later, I've got it. It's about the size of a brick, but much lighter. I have no idea how I'm supposed to get this past Glenda. I stuff the other boxes back in the closet and close it, then search the room for something to hide it in. There's nothing too obvious.

A jacket. Dad always has extra jackets. I pull open the bathroom door, flip on the light, and sure enough, there's three hanging hooks on the back of the door and all three hold a jacket. I take one down, roll the device up in it and shut the light off.

When I go back out into the hall, I hold the jacket snug to my chest.

"I told him to stop wearing my clothes." I shake my head with a snort. "Have a good night, Glenda."

"You, too, Mr. McCoy." I cringe when she calls me that name again.

Definitely sending her flowers.

TOMMY

I'm hovering over Wyatt's shoulder as he connects his computer to the device. I have no idea how these things work, and I'm really surprised they even exist. I suppose technology really has come a long way.

He had to download the app to his computer so that he could open up the message between Talon and the mystery person on the screen.

"So you just wait for the software to download to your computer and then what?"

"I think I have to set up some sort of account," he says when a login screen pops up. "Damnit." He slaps the desk.

"What's that mean? Where do you get an account from?"

"Likely the company I *would have* bought the device from. I could try and set one up, but I might have an idea." He slides the chair back and gets up. "I'll be right back."

I press my palms to the back of the desk chair in his room and look at the screen. This is all too high tech for me. I'm paint splatters and photographs, not codes and numbers.

A few minutes later, he returns with a paper in his hand. "Got it."

"What's that?"

"My dad has an entire file cabinet with brochures, catalogues, and information on all of the devices. He also has an account." He sits back down and punches in the login information from the paper and we're in.

He opens up the app and logs Talon in before pulling up the conversation. A couple clicks and some other shit that I don't even catch and something starts loading on the screen.

"That's it?" I ask him.

He shrugs. "I think so."

Once the loading bar disappears, it gives some options. "Click that one." I point to the screen. "Geological Search."

He clicks on it and a couple seconds later, a map appears with a pinpoint of an address.

"What the fuck!" I gasp. "That doesn't make any sense."

"What? Do you recognize the address?"

"Yeah. But it's impossible. That's Josh's house. Josh is dead."

"Is there someone else who lives there that could have sent the message? I mean, there has to be."

"It wouldn't be his parents. It has to be her."

"Who?"

"His sister. Vi Moran."

CHAPTER TWENTY-EIGHT

TOMMY

It's been almost a week since I came out to my parents. I went home that night and they treated me like they normally do. They didn't poke at me with questions and we actually had a really nice dinner together. Wyatt and I are still keeping things on the down low since I haven't told my friends, but once I do, I won't care who knows that we're together.

It's also been a week since we found out that Vi is the mystery girl on the app. We have no idea what it means, but Willa invited her to the shower and we're hoping to find out.

"Shouldn't you be out there helping your girl get things ready?" I ask Lars, who's kicked back in a recliner in his bedroom. This place brings back a lot of memories. Ever since Talon got his house, it's the only place we hang out. There was a time that we'd shuffle back and forth from all of our houses, now we just all hang out at Talon's.

Locking his fingers behind his head, he closes his eyes. "Marni and Amy are helping her. She's good."

"Amy?"

"My dad's new girlfriend. Probably step-mommy number

three. Did I mention she's only six years older than us?" He shakes his head with his eyes still closed.

"Well, on the bright side, she won't be bringing in any psycho teenage daughters." Lars' former step-mom had a daughter who was a few crayons short of a full box. Once her true colors began to show, she was sent back to her estranged dad in Colorado, who stuck her in some juvenile delinquent academy.

Talon walks in the open door and shoots his thumb over his shoulder. "There's way too much pink out there for me. Our boy Lars is gonna be swimming in pink. I can barely handle one girl, let alone two." He chuckles.

Lars lifts his head and looks at Talon. "You just wait. One day Marni will want kids."

"Nope. We both agreed, we don't want kids. Besides, even if we did, it would be at least ten years from now." Talon laughs. "You'll practically have a teenager."

"Yeah. And you'll be old as shit when your kids are teenagers," Lars retorts with a scowl.

I'm chewing on the skin of my nail when they both look at me, realizing I've been more quiet than normal. I know I'm ready to do this, but it doesn't ease the worry that they'll look at me differently.

Lars tosses a blue squared pillow at me. "What's up with you?"

I catch it before it hits me and set it in my lap. I hesitate, looking at them both. Then I open my mouth to speak and close it again. I've rehearsed this in my head for days and now it's all scrambled and messy. *Just fucking say it.* I look down at the pillow and open my mouth again. "I'm gay," I spit out.

My eyes hold tight to the pillow as I wait for a reaction. *Someone say something.*

Another pillow flies at me from Talon and, this time, it hits me in the side of the head. "I already knew that."

My eyes shoot up to him. "What? Marni told you?"

"I didn't know anything," Lars says. "Why didn't anyone tell me?"

Talon continues, "Marni didn't tell me. Didn't even know she knew, but I guessed it a long time ago."

"Why didn't I know?" Lars says again.

"Because you're fucking oblivious," Talon teases him before looking back at me. "So, you got anyone you're interested in or just playing the field?"

I can feel my cheeks flush and my palms sweat, but I still smile when I think about him. "There is someone."

"Wait. How did everyone know about this and I didn't?" Lars asks, again.

I chuckle. "I'm telling you now. I fought myself a lot on this. I tried to deny it, pretend it wasn't real or it was just a phase, but I've accepted that this is me. I was so focused on how you guys would react. I didn't wanna be looked at differently, ya know?" I throw my hands up. "But, I'm done pretending."

"Dude, this doesn't change you," Talon says. His hands gesture from him to Lars, then to me. "We're your boys. Be with whoever the hell makes you happy. You know we don't care about that shit."

Relief washes over me. More than that, peace fills me. A sense of happiness. I finally feel like I fit inside of my body and my mind is working with my heart instead of fighting against it.

"Yeah. We're good. Like Talon said, nothing changes," Lars assures me, "but, we need to know who this guy in your life is, because he needs to be approved by us first."

My phone buzzes in my pocket and I lean back to stretch my hand inside to grab it. I look down at my phone, then back up to the guys. "As a matter of fact, he just got here."

Wyatt and Marni have been working on repairing their friendship. It's going to take a little bit of time, but they're headed in the right direction. With Marni and Willa's approval, I was able to convince Wyatt to come here today—as my date.

"So, Wyatt, huh?" Talons asks.

It's not like it's hard to guess this one. There is only one guy that I've been spending a lot of time with and have become slightly protective over. And not to mention, I'm sure that Talon caught us kissing in Wyatt's driveway last week. Even if he didn't say anything.

"Oh for sure. It's definitely Wyatt," Lars says before getting to his feet.

"Yeah, it's Wyatt." I bite back a smile and feel my cheeks flush again.

"Look at you blushing," Talon squeals as he rubs his hand over my head, messing up my hair.

"I'm not fucking blushing. It's hot in here." I stand up and follow them out of the room.

Wyatt's talking with Marni in front of the gift table with a clear cup of red punch in his hand. It's like he immediately senses my presence when I walk into the room. His eyes find mine and my heart rate picks up.

I walk over to him slowly, my smile growing with each step. I can feel people watching—whether they actually are or not, I don't care.

"Happy to see you two talking," I say to him and Marni. "Mind if I steal him for a minute." I nod toward Wyatt.

"Sure can. I have to help Amy with the food. We're starting soon." She walks away, leaving us alone in a room full of people.

"I've missed you," Wyatt says with his hands held tight in his pockets.

"Missed you, too. In fact, I missed you a lot. There's actually something that I want to say to you."

His eyes perk up. "There is?"

"Mmhmm." I nod. "Thank you."

"For?" He drags out the word.

"Accepting me. Trusting me. Showing me that it's ok to love who I want to love."

His expression drops, right along with his jaw. "Love?"

I nod again. "Yeah. I think I love you." That sounded so fucking awful and not how I planned it at all. "Not think. I do."

He smiles from ear to ear. "Well, it just so happens that I *know* that I love you."

I return his gleeful expression. Hearing him say that warms every part of my body and squeezes my heart. "I told them," I say.

His eyes widen in surprise. "You did? When?"

"Just now."

He bites the corner of his lip and it does wild things to my insides. "How did they react?"

"You were right when you said that I need to give people more credit. All this time I was so worried what everyone would think of me, and now, at a point where I wouldn't even care, they're all happy for me." He goes to take my hand in his but shies away, thinking I might disapprove. But I grab it back and lock my fingers with his. "I'm sure I'll deal with a lot of harsh words in the future, but we've got each other and together, we're untouchable."

His eyes bore into mine. "Unbreakable."

For the first time in my life, I feel seen. "Unstoppable."

THE SHOWER IS HALF OVER, all the guests have arrived and some have already left. All but one showed up. Wyatt and I skipped out as Willa was opening presents and we're headed over to the Moran house to talk to Vi. The plan is to offer her our condolences as Josh's birthday is approaching. At which point, we'll dig for whatever answers we can get without being suspicious.

We waited all this time because the plan was to talk to her at the shower, but she never showed.

Pulling up to the Moran house, it feels like a cloud of doom rests over it. This family has been through so much and I can't imagine what goes on between those walls. So much hurt, anger, despair. They assume that their son was a victim of Pastor Jeffries. They have no idea that he wasn't a victim of his at all.

Wyatt gets out with me and we walk up to the house. I knock my knuckles to the door and it immediately opens.

Mrs. Moran is standing there, looking as sophisticated as always. A fake smile plastered on her face and three inch heels on her feet. "May I help you?" she asks.

"Hi, Mrs. Moran. We were wondering if we could talk to Vi for a minute."

Her smile drops, her shoulders slouch and her hands clap over her chest. "I'm sorry, Vi is not here and we're not sure when she's coming back."

Wyatt and I share a look before I turn back to Mrs. Moran. "Did she say where she was going?"

Her head shakes in small turns. "No. She left a note that said she had to get away, but she was safe. The loss of her brother has been hard on all of us, and poor Vi has been hit the hardest. I truly think she just needed some time to be alone in her thoughts."

I nod. "Of course. Well, if she comes home. Please tell her that Tommy stopped by."

"I sure will. Take care now."

Wyatt and I walk away without saying a word. As soon as we get back in the truck and the doors close, we look at each other. "She must be on to us," he says to me.

"No," I shake my head. "We're onto her. And now it's time to find her."

The End.

EPILOGUE

Nothing. Silence. Finally.

They've stopped.

The voices, the screams, the horror inside my head. Could it all be over?

Warm hands wrap around my arms and I swat them away. Only they're not real. It's not over.

It will never be over.

Mom is still dead. And that sick man still lives inside my head—touches my body and steals my thoughts.

I have no choice. I have to do this.

My toes titter on the edge; I wiggle them inside my boots. My eyes close. Tilting my head back, I take in a deep breath right before I lean forward, ready to fall. Ready to escape the nightmare that never ends.

Almost there.

It's almost over.

My body drops, but I don't fall forward. My eyes open as my back hits the ground. "What the fuck!" I hiss. I push myself up and bend my legs. Twisting around to get a look at the person who has a death wish. My chin drops to my chest when I see her. Releasing a pent up breath, I huff, "What the hell are you doing here?"

"I need your help. They're coming for me."

I shake my head, picking up the twists and turns of my movements rapidly before I scream, "No! I'm done helping you." I point a finger behind her. "Now get the hell out of here or I'll take you over that cliff with me."

"Oh no you don't. If I don't get to quit, neither do you."

"Go!" I scream even louder. My wrists go weak. My arms drop into the dirty sand, taking my body with it. I'm lying there curled up in the fetal position while someone stands there holding witness to my demise. I can't do this anymore. I just can't.

Her arm sweeps under my head, hoisting it up. Her face hovering over mine. "If I have to live in this hell and burn because of my sins, so do you. Now suck it up. Pull yourself together and get your ass off this ground."

"You should have just let me jump."

"I won't let you do it. And if you try, I'll hold your hand and fly with you. Because if anyone deserves an easy out, it's me."

Looking up at her, while she cradles my head, I search for something. I'm not sure what it is but she offered a brief moment of calm and I want more of it. "Why are you here? I told you to never come near me again."

"I followed you. And now I'm staying with you, whether you like it or not."

Crawling onto my knees, I force myself off the ground and to my feet. "You ruined everything, you know that right?"

"It's called survival. Are you ready to take your life back, Zed? Or do you plan on letting the monsters in your head win?"

I smirk. "You want me to live in this hell? Well, prepare yourself little lamb, because nothing is more terrifying than a man who has no will to live."

Her arms cross over her chest as she tries to act all tough. "I'm not scared of you, Zed."

"That would be your second mistake. Your first was not letting me jump."

She'll soon learn that every choice has a consequence. If I'm being forced to face mine, it's time she faces hers, too.

Zed's story, Reaper, is coming May 27th.
Preorder now!

ALSO BY RACHEL LEIGH

Redwood Rebels Series:

Striker, Book One

Heathen, Book Two

Vandal, Book Three

Reaper, Book Four

Redwood High Series:

Like Gravity, Redwood High Book 1

Like You, Redwood High Book 2

Like Hate, Redwood High Book 3

Standalones:

Guarded

Four

Duet:

Chasing You

Catching You

FROM THE AUTHOR

Thank you so much for reading Vandal. I hope you enjoyed Tommy and Wyatt's story.

Thank you to Greys Promo for helping me spread the word and for being so wonderful to work with.

Carolina, thank you for all that you do for me. You're the best!

Thank you to my wonderful beta readers: Sara, Amanda, Rachel, & Christine. You helped me more than you know.

Also, thank you to Amanda, Sara, and Chelsea for holding my hand through this. Your "knowledge" and advice was so helpful!

A HUGE thank you to the bloggers who share and support my books. You are all such a blessing and I appreciate you all very much.

Thank you to my Rambling Street Team for your daily support and kindness. Much love to you, all!

Rebecca, at Fairest Reviews and Editing, thank you for another beautiful edit!

Kate, at Ya'll. That Graphic, thank you for another gorgeous cover!

Readers, thank you for giving me a chance. I'd love to hear what you thought about Vandal. If you could leave an Amazon review, I'd greatly appreciate it.

I'd also like to invite you to my readers group, Rachel's Ramblers.

xoxo-Rachel

ABOUT THE AUTHOR

Rachel Leigh writes Contemporary and New Adult Romance with twists and turns, suspense and steam. She resides in West Michigan with her husband, three kids, and a couple fur babies.

Rachel lives in leggings, overuses emojis, and survives on books and coffee. Writing is her passion. Her goal is to take readers on an adventure with her words, while showing them that even on the darkest days, love conquers all.

facebook.com/rachelleighauthor
twitter.com/rachelleigh_1
instagram.com/rachelleighauthor
amazon.com/author/rachelleighauthor
bookbub.com/profile/rachel-leigh

www.ingramcontent.com/pod-product-compliance
Lightning Source LLC
Chambersburg PA
CBHW030608310726
48979CB00003B/615